MOONSHINE

MOONSHINE

R. J. King

authorHOUSE®

AuthorHouse™
1663 Liberty Drive
Bloomington, IN 47403
www.authorhouse.com
Phone: 1-800-839-8640

Published by AuthorHouse   10/01/2012

ISBN: 978-1-4685-7742-6 (sc)
ISBN: 978-1-4685-7741-9 (hc)
ISBN: 978-1-4685-7740-2 (e)

Library of Congress Control Number: 2012906607

Any people depicted in stock imagery provided by Thinkstock are models, and such images are being used for illustrative purposes only.
Certain stock imagery © Thinkstock.

This book is printed on acid-free paper.

Because of the dynamic nature of the Internet, any web addresses or links contained in this book may have changed since publication and may no longer be valid. The views expressed in this work are solely those of the author and do not necessarily reflect the views of the publisher, and the publisher hereby disclaims any responsibility for them.

Acknowledgements

To my wonderful daughter Charmin, who encouraged me to take my first formal writing class and who gave me as a gift, my first introduction to a writing workshop (she knew I needed that little push).

To my Mom, who pushed me out of bed every morning from the day I turned three, come rain or shine saying, "If I have to get up and go to work, you have to get up and go to school."

To Joan, my other mother, my mentor, my teacher, my friend and the first person who told me "Words mean a lot to you."

To my best friend Debbie, I don't know what to say because words don't seem to fit what you have meant to me over the years, your laughter, how you make me crazy, and how crazy you are.

To my three compasses, Darlene, Piper, and Maura, you came into my life by fate without you my journey would be dimmer. You have given me more than you know. You gave me the courage to share my voice. You gave me your light. You saw what others did not, the inside me.

To Lori your paintings gave me emotions I never thought I could see. To Leslie what can I say? Editing my manuscript must have been painful. And to all the other people in my life, thank you for being you.

a midwife's hands

when my body pushed through
the womb, I felt them.

hands tempered in love, polished in
sacrifice.

hands that have t
ouched a thousand firsts.
my sisters, my brothers
before me.

hands cradling fragile souls
as they whispered and caressed

hands bringing creation from darkness
to illumination.

Prologue

Teresa stared into the moonlight that blanketed the ruins. She felt warmth from the woman's hands as she spoke. They seemed to caress the night.

"By passing the world through others, you have kept the secret. This was and is your destiny, your fate," the woman whispered. "We gave you the power to touch life, the very essence of the universe. It will soon be time for you to pass through your hands what we have given you."

"I am old," Teresa said. "What can I do now?" she shivered. She didn't know what to do, but she knew she would do whatever was asked of her.

"For now you will continue until time shifts and expands. One day, you will no longer be able to touch new life. It will slip from your memories, your moments, folding into your consciousness until you are ready to tell our story. When you do, you must choose, one who is of your blood to find the heir to the gift. She will not accept this journey willingly, at first. She will hesitate but her love for you will prevail.

She must find the two heartbeats, one heartbeat creating the other, but they beat as one, the last of the first, the first of the last.

Although the gift of firsts will not pass to your daughter or your daughter's daughters, it is through them the hearts will survive. You must send them to find her, to find the beginning, of the beginning, the one who holds the future."

Eyes closed, Teresa trembled as the woman continued.

"This journey will begin in the winter of your life, ten years into the new millennium. In that moment of uncertainty, you must find peace with this knowledge. You must be strong. You must have faith. You must remember."

When Teresa opened her eyes again, the woman was gone.

Chapter One

Matlin, Mississippi 2010

Up highway eighteen, then turn right on Sugar Hill. The area hadn't changed much. Magnolia trees with huge white flowers lined the road. Even the burned out juke joint—called by the same name—was still there. At the beginning of a long driveway, a sign read: Claremont Community Center. To the right of the sign behind two small white columns stood a one story building made of deep red brick with green shutters bordering all the windows—a wrought iron fence circling the entire place making the place look warm and inviting.

Inside down the hall on the left pass the nurses' station, was room 22 the numbers on the door were made of brass, bronze nails held them there like two tiny eyes peering into the hallway. Like the numbers, everything on the other side of the door was in pairs; two beds, two bureaus, two nightstands,—both made out of fabricated wood, two wheel chairs and two call buttons, but only one occupant, occupied the eight by ten room.

Teresa Monroe sighed, she felt like a prisoner as she sat in her wheelchair staring at the sterile walls. There were no pictures on the walls because she had hoped that one day she would be able to leave but her knees frozen from the rheumatism invading her body like a parasite told her different. She shifted as the pain came. Sighing again, her gaze taking in the room she had come to know well, living in such a small space suddenly made her think of a quote she had heard a long time ago. "I am the master of my fate I am the captain of my soul." Teresa smiled. "Whoever said that didn't have to live here."

It was 2010, ten years into the new millennium, ten years, and Teresa was still alive. Born in 1915, Teresa was the oldest and the last of twelve, all girls. Rubbing her knees as she leaned forward trying to get comfortable she tilted her head as if listening to the past. She could almost hear the growing frustration of her papa as he watched yet another girl scream into the world. She felt sorry for him back then because she saw both joy and disappointment knit his brow. She chuckled to herself remembering all the trouble the twelve of them got into when they were together. All born two years apart; how her mother timed it she would never know. When Teresa and her sisters walked down the street on Friday nights, people would stare and whisper, "Here come those Monroe girls." Their faces, high yellow, caramel, deep chocolate—a rainbow of a different color; earth tones against a cloudless sky. They were close, a closeness which gave them strength. After all it was the early 1900's. A time when being colored and being raised in the South meant you were disposable.

Falling like leaves in autumn, one by one Teresa watched those same sisters pass this life. In 1986 when her youngest sister Sarah died at fifty two from acute asthma she was devastated but she barely had time to grieve because two other sisters died the following year, one of a heart attack and the other from ovarian cancer. There was something to be said about everything happing in threes. And just this past Thanksgiving, her sister Belinda left this world leaving Teresa alone. Teresa had outlived them all. As she sat there, waiting for her chance at heaven, because all she could do was to wait, she pictured all eleven sisters perched on the fence of the pearly gates wondering why heaven didn't have a juke joint that sold moonshine. She laughed despite the tears that fell down her cheeks. She missed them so much. Teresa shook her head. She should be the one turning in her grave, many times over.

By the time Teresa's sister Sarah was born, Teresa had become a fully-fledged midwife at the age of fifteen. Back then 15 was not considered young most people were married and some even had children. You didn't need some kind of fancy license to practice like women need today. You just needed the skills and the love to do what Teresa had done for almost seventy years in Matlin, a rural community along the Mississippi River where Teresa had lived all her life. Also back then there were no doctors for colored folks. A midwife was all they had.

Being a midwife ensured Teresa that she would always be busy. Colored folks knew how to have babies and babies they had as her mother could attest to. Teresa had only stopped long enough to get married and soon after to become a mother. Surprisingly Teresa had only one child, Michaela. When Michaela came Teresa thought she had everything, a job she loved and a daughter she loved beyond measure. That is until her only child had two girls of her own. When her granddaughters came into the world, Teresa knew she had been blessed.

Teresa looked down at her hands, calloused now, and rubbed them as the memories kept coming. She had begun as a midwife's assistant traveling around the countryside along with two other midwives, Meira and Melana. Teresa had spent most of her life with those two old ladies. Both women had been in Matlin Mississippi for as long as Teresa could remember.

She hadn't thought about them in forever until several days ago. Teresa had begun to dream of yesterdays; memories once trapped now came unbidden, reminding her of what she was told all those years, what she needed to do. She was afraid at first which was a first for her, thinking it was all just a dream, but she knew better.

No one in Matlin knew what really transpired as she, Melana, and Meira did what was ordained. No one knew what the three midwives held. Something that had been locked in Teresa's subconscious until recently. Why had God spared her? It wasn't a question, not really, she knew the reason. Could she do it? Time was not her friend. Unconsciously touching her heart as if trying to erase something only visible to her, Teresa straightened her shoulders when she heard the knock at the door *it begins.* "Come in," she said.

Peeking around the door was her youngest granddaughter, Kayamia. Teresa shook her head. She still couldn't get over the names people gave their children these days. Everybody called her granddaughter Kay. At least it came off her tongue without causing Teresa to twist herself in a knot trying to remember the pronunciation.

* * *

As always Kay was astonished as she walked through the door. Her grandmother was beautiful. You had to look hard to find wrinkles in her face. Even after 95 years, time had not stamped those lines on Teresa. The long gray hair cascaded down her shoulders like a waterfall shadowed in moonlight with its brilliance. Kay was sure Miss Clairol had something to do with the way it looked, but to her knowledge she had never seen her grandmother's hair any different. Kay's mother told her once, "Mother would go to her grave with the secret." Although her grandmother could no longer get around without her wheelchair, she was very healthy. Kay hesitated when she saw the familiar melancholy look on her grandmother's face. The look told Kay that her grandmother had been thinking about her great aunts. But when she stepped all the way into the room, Kay was startled the look she saw now was one of urgency. "Hi, Granny," Kay said as she bent down to kiss the cheeks of her beloved. When she raised her head the look of urgency was still there. "Granny, what is it?"

When her grandmother didn't answer right away Kay got worried and started to say something but before she could she watched as Teresa reached into the drawer by her bed and to Kay's astonishment, pulled out a tape recorder. What was her grandmother up to now? Where could she have gotten a tape recorder? And from the looks of it, she knew exactly how to use it. Kay had never seen her grandmother with anything like that. Teresa didn't even like using the phone. She once told Kay that she was allergic to the stuff the world made. She never said manmade. She always said "world made" so how and why . . ., as the question was beginning to form Teresa said, "I made this recording so I won't forget anything. I need you to listen closely." Teresa looked at Kay to make sure she was listening. Too shocked to say anything Kay nodded as she sat down in the chair facing her grandmother's wheel chair as Teresa played the tape.

The click that sounded the end of the tape was loud in the silence that had engulfed Kay as she listened. She was speechless. Her grandmother turned off the recorder, took out the tape and gave it to Kay to put in her jacket pocket. Kay realized the whole time she was listening; she hadn't bothered to take her jacket off. She started. "How am I supposed to understand what just happened?" Kay asked. She jumped up and started pacing she couldn't get very far in the small space. She stopped and looked at her grandmother as if seeing a stranger. "And all this time you kept this? What am I supposed to do with it?"

Unperturbed by her granddaughter's outburst, Teresa said "You'll know what to do. Why do you think I chose you? You're the strongest of my children. Now it's up to you." She didn't tell Kay that she herself had forgotten only to remember it recently in her dreams.

"And what is it you expect me to do?" Kay shook her head trying to understand. What she had heard was . . . her grandmother was 96, maybe Teresa's mind was playing tricks . . . no . . . Kay knew better. "I can't promise . . ." Her grandmother started to say something when Kay interrupted her, "Granny, you have to give me some time to absorb all of this." The anxious look Teresa gave Kay almost made her promise anything. Her grandmother was always there for everyone.

Teresa was the matriarch of the Monroe family and Kay didn't want to let her down but this was way too big. Right now all Kay wanted was to be as far away from the Community Center as she could get. "I have to go granny. I have to run another errand. Please I have to think about this before I can give you an answer." Kay bent over and kissed her grandmother again. Kay turned, opened the door leaving her grandmother staring at her back.

Teresa watched Kay leave. She wasn't surprised at all by Kay's reaction. If someone had told her these things, she would have reacted the same way. She was glad; however that Kay hadn't dismissed what she heard outright. Alone again in her room, Teresa buzzed the nurse so she could lie down. She was suddenly tried. Judging by Kay's response Teresa wondered if she had done the right thing but it was too late. Only fate could intercede. She only hoped what she told Kay would be enough to find them. As Teresa lay in her bed, she stared at the walls once more. *It was time.* As she drifted off to sleep the visions came, transporting her back to the time when her life changed forever.

Chapter Two

Matlin Mississippi 1931

Teresa held firm to the squirming baby as she washed the tiny body. After she wrapped the baby in a blanket she turned watching Melana and Meira. Teresa watched the two midwives closely, as she had done for the past year. She was always awed at how close the two women seemed, almost as if they were extensions of each other. When Melana started a sentence, Meira often finished. But how could that be? Melana and Meira were different not because they were midwives who practiced together. Midwives sometimes practiced together. What was unusual, in fact unheard of, was Melana was Negro and Meira was White and by the sound of Meira's voice she was not from Matlin or anywhere else in this country. How both of them ended up in Matlin Mississippi together was still a mystery.

Matlin rested along the shores of the Mississippi, population two thousand, if you counted the people who lived beyond the incorporated area. General Ulysses S. Grant was rumored to have called Matlin, "The town too beautiful to burn." Antebellum homes, once plantations, stood out as stark reminders of what Teresa's ancestors had endured. It was 1931 and Lincoln had long since signed the Emancipation Proclamation, almost seventy years ago. But here in the south it might as well have been 1831. Jim Crow was in its heyday and the Klan, or Night Riders as they were sometimes called, was terrorizing the countryside in Matlin as well as all over the south.

Because of this, Teresa was sure every person in town, including her, was wondering how it came to pass that no one tried to stop Meira and Melana, not even the Klan. She called Melana and Meira old, because they had been a part of the town for a long time, but in reality, she didn't think they were that old. They looked so young. Teresa believed they were both in their early forties. The two of them had delivered almost every Negro as far back as Teresa could remember. And Meira delivered both Negro and White, the poor ones that were isolated miles into the woods.

When Teresa decided she wanted to become a midwife, her mother had balked. "I don't know why with all the children I have. Besides I need you here."

Then twelve, Teresa stood in the door of their small house. "Mama, I want to be a midwife so I can help other people." Teresa's parents were sharecroppers so they didn't really own anything. Sharecropping was just one step up from slavery. Teresa wanted to do something besides picking cotton and cucumbers especially since it seemed like her parents would never be able to pay their debt. If she became a midwife maybe she could help them.

By Teresa's fifteenth birthday, she felt she was ready. She went to Melana and Meira. She knew they would teach her everything there was to know about being a midwife. Teresa remembered the day she asked permission to study with them. They had looked at her for what seemed like forever—to a fifteen year old at least, and then by some silent consent they told Teresa they would train her. She had prayed for this but she was still surprised how quickly they agreed. She remembered how they looked at her that day, like a puzzle piece was falling into place, the last piece that completed a picture. At the time, Teresa didn't know how foretelling her thoughts were.

Drawn from her thoughts, Teresa looked down at her "first catch." The little girl felt wonderful in her hands. She could feel the tiny heart beating, pumping life's blood to the heart. Every beat, every tiny breath washed over Teresa. The small face looked up at her. The wide smile, the eyes that looked like brown cinnamon were shining like topaz. She caught her breath when the baby blew tiny bubbles. It was this beauty of creation that Teresa wanted to always be a part of. She knew in that moment, this was what she was meant to do. She gave the baby to its mother and gathered her things.

Melana and Meira instructed the young mother on things she would need to do like how to put a small amount of camphor in a jar with warm water for colic, to also take a straw from a broom, breaking it in half, burning the tips and placing in the baby's head to make the hole in the top of the head close up. When they finished, they turned to Teresa and smiled. "You did well." Teresa was over the moon.

Curiously, Teresa had noticed as she watched the two women, not unlike tonight that every time a girl baby was born, Meira and Melana touched the babies and whispered some kind of strange words. Teresa didn't understand or know what the words meant, but she heard them. But like always she had put her curiosity in the back of mind to think about later. And tonight was a special night Teresa had gone from apprentice to midwife. Teresa would remember this moment for the rest of her life.

*   *   *

As the months past, Teresa didn't have time to think about what she saw or thought she heard because little by little Meira and Melana allowed Teresa to make decisions. Being a midwife was indeed a craft. Teresa couldn't be happier.

Later that year, however Teresa found herself in a situation that all midwives dreaded, a breeched birth. In that instant, Teresa understood being a midwife was more, so much more.

Chapter Three

Teresa trembled as she reached inside the mother's womb to turn the infant around. She was so scared she wouldn't be able to do it. Melana and Meira watched her carefully ready to jump in at any time. They had to let Teresa attempt this. It was hard. If this situation came up again Teresa might be alone, so they needed to know if she could do it. Both looked on as if this was Teresa's biggest test. It was.

Sweating, hand deep inside the mother's womb, Teresa slowly turned the baby. She was mindful of the umbilical cord; she could feel it. She prayed that it was not wrapped around the baby's neck. If it was, she was in more trouble. As sweat poured down her forehead almost reaching her eyes Teresa gently turned the small body until the baby's head was pointing south. She asked the mother to push as she guided the baby into the light. Teresa looked into those beautiful eyes staring back at her. She could have sworn the little girl acted as if she knew her.

As usual Melana and Meira put away everything while talking to the mother. Teresa cleaned the infant and placed little girl on the mother's stomach. This was the best part. Being able to hand a mother her child, after all the hard work that both mother and midwife had to do, was worth it in the end. "You have the gift," said Meira as she touched the infant, "and I must say it was a bit of a miracle."

Joy was the only word Teresa could think of as she looked at mother and child. She had been following Melana and Meira around the country side for over a year and this was the first time they let her take the lead in this situation. When she saw them whispering to each other again she tried to listen but like always Teresa couldn't understand them. When they got like this it was like they were alone. Teresa was so happy that everything had turned out right, that she didn't notice the faint light in the baby's eyes.

Teresa's smile fell a little. She didn't know at the time she started her training that most people didn't have money. They would pay in whatever they had. Chickens, cows, one patient gave Melana a beautiful quilt. Teresa's mother told her that sometimes quilts had hidden meanings. Some told a family's history and sometimes people hung them on the fence to show slaves the way north. Some of the things the people gave Teresa, neither she nor her family really needed but it would be disrespectful she gave anything back and her mother would be very upset. So when she brought yet another piece of livestock home, her mother just accepted them.

When they finished they said goodbye to the family and told them they would be back to see them. With such a difficult birth they knew they needed to keep a closer watch on mother and child.

Teresa and the women climbed in the carriage and headed home. When they dropped Teresa off, she realized she was tired and hungry. Even after everything that had transpired, Teresa still felt like she had a lot of growing and a lot of learning to do. She could name most healing plants and could pick out herbs that helped young mothers recover from the various elements that could come up during pregnancy. Yet still, she didn't think she had learned nearly enough. One thing for sure, she was proud of herself this night.

By the time Teresa removed her clothes, she was too tired to eat. She said her prayers and tucked herself into bed. Pulling the covers up to her neck she folded her hands behind her head on the pillow and stared at the ceiling. She kept thinking about Meira and Melana, what she saw and heard and this time she couldn't put it out of her mind. She wanted to ask what they said each time but, for some reason she didn't think they would give her an answer. Before she fell asleep, however, she decided that tomorrow she would at least get up the courage to ask Meira and Melana how they met.

*   *   *

The next day Teresa climbed in the carriage. Settling into her seat behind them as Melana coached the horses in to an easy gait. As the countryside past slowly, Teresa leaned forward in her seat head peeking out between Melana and Meira. Almost shyly she said. "Can I ask you something?" When the women nodded, Teresa asked. "How did the two of you come to practice together?"

They both smiled. "We were wondering when you were going to ask," Melana said. "We were surprised by your patience. I don't think I would have been so patient." She looked at Meira. "She's been with us awhile now. Don't you think it is about time we did?"

Meira nodded, "And the rest?"

"Shush, I don't think she's quite ready for that," said Melana. She pulled on the reigns and stopped the carriage. Melana looked out at the field of lilacs. Lilacs grew wild in Matlin. *God sure loves the color purple.* "Let's stop here," she announced." We can sit under that tree." She point to the oak tree that stood in the middle of the field. The sun was shining brightly overhead already warming their skin. The shade from the tree would keep them cool. "There are no real emergencies right now." She hadn't forgotten the baby Teresa delivered but knew it would be okay. What she and Meira had to say would take a while.

They got down from the carriage and walked through the field. The fragrance from the lilacs settled around them. Under the tree, Meira spread the quilt she had removed from under the seat of the carriage. They used the quilt to cover them on cold nights. Meira sat down close to Melana, shoulders almost touching, and Teresa sat cross legged facing them.

As they all got comfortable, Melana looked pass Teresa as if she was watching time moving back slowly. Melana chuckled. "I have to confess when Meira came crashing, I mean that literally, into my life, I didn't know what would happen on that fateful day and I can tell you, I sure wasn't ready for what it all meant."

"We both weren't," Meira agreed as she met Melana's eyes in silent understanding. Teresa sat quietly and listened to Melana and Meira relive the day they met.

Chapter Four

Matlin Mississippi, 1916

The dust swirled around Melana's feet as she walked down the road making her way home. There were no sidewalks, just dirt paths leading to the small shops that lined Main Street. Eyes always forward, Teresa never paid much attention to the people around her. The people in Matlin thought Melana was strange anyway. Mostly because she was always alone and didn't have much conversation for anyone but the parents of the children she delivered. She was part Negro part Cherokee but you wouldn't know it to look at her. It didn't matter anyway; to the world she was just a Negro, skin dark like coffee with a touch of crème. Her hazel eyes made her look intense and this intensity usually got her where she was going. She didn't mind people staring. She carried herself like a queen. She would never say anything like that out loud, even to her own people. They had their own words for her, said behind her back, of course. Mostly it was, 'Uppity.' They said these things because Melana was considered educated. She read books when she could find them. Her parents had taught her to read. And the people who owned her grandparents taught them to read, which was really rare.

Melana could hear the clang of the hammer echoing from the blacksmith shop as she passed. The smell of sweat and iron mingled in the air. She liked watching the sparks fly as hammer met anvil. The blacksmith, like Melana, used his hands to create. It had been a long day and she was concentrating solely on the path that would take her home. Moving hurriedly, Melana was startled when someone almost ran her down in front of the Piggly Wiggly, the only dry good store in town. Frowning, as she stumbled a little. "What . . . ?" She righted herself and turned to confront the person.

Their eyes met. It was a woman, a woman with long red hair that fell to the curve of her back. Melana noticed the woman's olive skin was not like the pale skin of the white people that lived in Matlin. She didn't look much older than Melana. The way she dressed also didn't match that of the white women in town. She looked like she was born of finery. The silk shawl she wore around her shoulders was purple and yellow, the color of buttercups like the ones Melana picked as a child. The woman was tall even taller than the men who were standing around in front of the store. Melana was tall, too so she didn't have to look up to see the woman's eyes. The color reminded Melana of the lily pads on the muddy Mississippi. Melana had seen those eyes in her dreams, eyes not quite gray and not quite green. Melana's mother had often told her when you see eyes like that it meant bad luck. She never placed much stock in superstitions. Melana believed you made your own luck. Hers though, it seemed, might be running out, not only that her dreams had manifest itself into the woman staring back at her.

Melana gave nothing away, she couldn't believe it. *It's her.* They both stood there neither one said anything. Without looking around Melana knew people were watching and this was Mississippi, the hot bed of the south. Mississippi's cruelty to Negros was commonplace. She hated it, but Matlin was her home. She was born here and here she would die. Her people needed her and to be honest Melana needed them. She didn't like the way things were but she had a gift. She touched new life. It didn't matter to most white folks in Matlin who Melana was or what she did. She was a Negro, a Negro in the south. Often times, whenever she was in a situation, not unlike the one she was in now, something or someone would always intervene. Someone she couldn't name, seem to watch over her. Besides, being carted off to jail for confronting a white woman wouldn't help her people. When the woman bumped into her, Melana thought maybe her time had come.

Melana started moving. Now was really not the time to think, just to escape unscathed. Even if this woman had appeared in her dreams, the situation was unsettling. What was she going to do if the women said something? Melana was hoping she could just hurry off before other people realized what had happened. Melana froze when the woman spoke. "Excuse me. Are you alright?"

Melana was speechless. So it seemed were two men who stood close by because they had both stopped talking. Before Melana could recover, she

13

heard one of them say to the woman. "Hi Miss is she bothering you. I saw her almost knock you down." Melana almost fainted when the woman answered. "No, it was I who almost knocked her down. I was trying to apologize." Melana didn't know what to make of it.

Again Melana tried to move along but, the woman said it again. Head down Melana murmured, "It's okay." As she hurried away, she heard the woman calling to her. *She knows.* Melana pretended she couldn't hear and kept moving.

*   *   *

Meira watched as the woman hurried off. *I have found her. I have found Melana.* When she said the name, Meira felt the push vibrating from deep within her being. She needed to be patient, but the humming continued as she looked at Melana's retreating back.

Meira knew somehow the other woman felt it, too. Although fleeting, Meira glimpsed the recognition in Melana's eyes. Their feet had been set on the same path. Meira was the soul twin and Melana was the spirit twin. They were standing on the precipice—twin souls, both needing the other. Would Melana understand or would she send her away? Meira had no choice. It was not her decision. She had not started this journey without trepidation. How could she convince Melana, a Negro woman, in Mississippi mind you, to trust her, a white woman? "Could she . . . would I trust someone who just almost knocked me down?" To give her strength Meira read the inscription on the silver bracelet she wore, "The impossible can always be broken down into possibilities."

Meira turned to follow Melana but the man, who had spoken to her, was still standing there, looking confused. She held out her hand. "Excuse my manners. My name is Meira McDonald. Could you tell me where I might find lodging?"

Still perplexed, the man took Meira's hand and shook it firmly. "I knew you weren't from around here," the man said. "You don't have to be apologizing to the likes of her."

Meira didn't want to get into a conversation with this man. She needed go after Melana so she said, "I will remember the next time, about the lodging?"

"Yes, there is a rooming house on the next street. If you turn here," he pointed down the street, "you can't miss it."

"Thank you." Meira headed in that direction.

Meira had already checked into the rooming house the man mentioned. She just didn't want the man to know where she was really headed. Right now she was going to find Melana.

Chapter Five

Melana only dared to look back when she made it home. Her house was located at the bend of a dirt road about a mile out of town. The outside of the house was welcoming. Melana planted all kinds of flowers in the small yard. She loved the scent, especially in the summer when the honey suckles vines grew along the fence surrounding the house. She had built the fence herself. The fragrance always called her home. It seemed to linger in her clothes. She couldn't help but smile when she saw children pass by and stop to pull the flowers from the vines, white petals shaped like the head of a Graphophone. She would watch as they took the delicate flowers in their hands, pinching the bottom and pulling the tiny stigma to reveal the drop of honey on its stem catching it with their tongues. It was something she had done many times as a child.

Taking off her coat she hung it on the hook behind the door. The house only had two rooms, one that was a combination sitting room and bedroom, the other a small kitchen in the corner. There was a fireplace which kept the house cozy and warm. Melana had lots of plants inside her house too, mostly herbs and other plants she used in her job. She had them in small pots along the window sill in the kitchen. She also had all sorts of knick knacks. The people she cared for didn't have much money, so they gave her whatever they could. This didn't bother Melana because she was doing what she loved and quite frankly she wouldn't have it any other way. She was an only child and had no children of her own. This was fine with Melana, because she had hundreds all whom she loved as if they were her own. Catching colored babies was wonderful as well as gratifying.

She leaned against the door. "It's her," Melana repeated to herself. "What was her name?" She searched her mind recalling the dream, *Meira*. Pushing away from the door, Melana lit the kerosene lamp by her bed. When she heard the knocking, she knew it was Meira on the other side. Sighing deeply, she opened the door a crack.

*   *   *

When the door opened, Meira stood there staring into the depths of eyes that were like flint, the color of onyx. Those eyes, piercing and intense, were narrowing until they were lines. They made her trembled, but she couldn't stop now because time was pushing her. At first she thought Melana would slam the door in her face. But to her surprise, Melana motioned her inside, closing the door, quickly. Meira looked at Melana's hands and whispered, "You are Melana the midwife, aren't you?"

Melana's eyes showed nothing. She hid her emotions very well. She had to for the work she did. She learned a long time ago she had to separate herself from the emotional roller coaster that can happen in child birth. Right now she was glad she was able to control her emotions. "What if I am?"

Meira smiled, "So am I." She couldn't read anything in the eyes of the woman who was looking back at her.

"Well I guess you know more than me because I don't have the slightest idea who you are," Melana lied as she stood waiting for the Meira to answer.

"I am Meira." She reached out as if to shake Melana's but she thought better of it she knew Melana did not trust her, so she started to explain when . . .

When Meira hesitated for a second Melana said, "and?" She waited for Meira to continue. The day had been long and she wanted, no needed to understand how the woman found her. She didn't say anything.

"Well," Meira said, "I came to you because I want to practice here. I mean I want to practice with you here in Matlin." She knew she was beginning to babble but she continued determine to make Melana understand. "Besides, who would know better about a town than a fellow midwife?"

Melana wanted to rewind this day and start over. The woman in her dreams was standing there; *a white woman*, standing there like she was at home and they were having a cup of tea. Right now Melana could use a glass of moonshine. Although she knew better, she tried to scare her away.

"Meira or whatever your name is, I think you ought to leave before people see you here. I can imagine what they might do to me if they knew you were here in the "Quarters." In most towns there was a quarters, a place where only Negros were. It had many names "nigger town," "cross the tracks," in the bottoms," or the quarters and in the South there was always one. "Can't you see? I am a Negro."

Meira was confused. She could plainly see who Melana was. "I know you are a Negro. I am Irish."

"Well if you know that then you should know that you shouldn't be here." It didn't matter where you were in the world, people didn't like Negros, at least as far as she knew, although she hadn't been anywhere but Mississippi all her life. She had been told the North was a lot friendlier than the South. Melana closed her eyes, wishing Meira would be gone when she opened them again, but she knew that wasn't going to happen. Melana was beginning to understand what the dreams she'd been having for months now, meant. Not wanting to believe, Melana asked again. "What do you want from me?"

"May I sit down?" Meira had grown weary her journey had been long. The two of them had been standing there for a while. Her feet hurt and she needed to rest them.

Relenting but still cautious, Melana nodded and pointed to a chair by the fire place. When Meira sat down, Melana asked, "Okay, now why are you really here?" Melana stood with her arms crossed below her breast, waiting.

Meira sat down in a rocking chair that looked like it was very old. There were markings on the curve of the arms. She pretended not to notice the familiar swirls. She had seen them before but she couldn't quite remember and right now she had more important things to do. She looked up at the woman standing and held Melana's gaze but it was difficult. "Like I told you, I want to practice here . . . with you"

"Why do you need me?" Why doesn't she just come out and say why she had come. Melana wanted Meira to admit the truth; even though she was just as guilty for hiding her own version. She pushed. "A white woman can practice anywhere she wants."

Of course Meira knew this was true. She pressed on. "But I don't want to just practice anywhere. I want to practice with you," Meira repeated for the third time wondering if Melana would believe the real reason. Somehow she knew she would. She just had to be patient and hope Melana would not throw her out before she explained. Then she thought what's wrong with me, I should have thought of this before.

Melana interrupted. "I work alone, always." Before Melana could say anything else, Meira grabbed her hand. Melana wanted to snatch her hand back, but she didn't move. She felt heat. It was as if something had passed between them. Finally, Melana pulled her hand back. "You need to tell me this minute. Why are you really here?"

"Okay. I want . . .," she hesitated. She suspected Melana felt something when their hands touched, but Melana hadn't reacted at all. Meira thought *maybe it's just me. I'm the crazy one.* And by the look on Melana's face Meira was fast running out of time. She hoped when she explained, when she told Melana, she would understand, gain her trust. *Why should Melana trust a stranger, not just a stranger,* but *a woman from a foreign land?* She had to try so Melana started again.

"There was a time when I was younger that I dreamed of this place." Meira hesitated as if gathering strength from the words . . ."In the dream you were there. I can't explain it but somehow I knew you. I shook it off at first and didn't think of it again for a long time. But when I had been practicing midwifery for about five years, I had the dream again. The dream told me to come to Mississippi. The dream also told me you were a midwife. Again I tried to ignore the dreams but they kept coming, invading my thoughts.

Then every time a baby girl was born your face was there. You were watching me and smiling. When the dreams became too hard to ignore, I started searching. I know it sounds crazy. My parents thought I had lost my mind when one day I told them I was leaving for America. They tried to persuade me not to come but against their wishes I came anyway."

When she looked into Melana's eyes, she could see behind all of the distrust, what she hoped to see. She knew with certainty Melana was who she needed so she kept talking. "When I started searching, something guided me here, to Matlin. I didn't think it was possible to find you but I had to try. When I finally made it to Matlin, I realized what it would mean if I started asking about you. I am not so naïve. I read and have seen what's happening here in the South. So, I made up a story. I told the people at the hotel that I was a historian and wanted to study the southern gentry. They seemed to believe me, so here I am." Melana still acted as if she wanted to throw Meira out any minute.

When Meira finished, Melana knew she had to also admit the truth. Melana had recognized Meira's when she bumped into her in front of the store. And when she felt Meira's hands, she knew. Like Melana's they brought fragile lives into being, soothing with gentleness as they placed each new life on the mother's breast. She had been told this day would come. Like Meira she didn't think anyone would believe. Melana always believed all midwives were connected somehow but what she didn't know was how much. She looked at Meira and nodded her head. "It's not the same here in Matlin as it is in . . . where did you say you were from?"

"Ireland, Dublin to be exact." Meira was about to say something else when Melana put her hands up.

"Okay, say I believe you, but right now I can't talk about it. Maybe we can talk later, and then we can discuss whatever this is. Now if you will excuse me." Melana tried to rush Meira out the door while grabbing her medicine bag. "I have to go see someone."

Meira was not to be swayed. She knew if she let Melana leave she might never convince her. "Is it a patient? Maybe I can go with you. Maybe I can help," said Meira.

Melana steered Meira out the door and headed for the carriage she used when she had to travel far from town. "Sorry but I must go." *You must bring her. No.* Ignoring the voice in her head Melana hurried toward the carriage.

Seeing Melana hurry, Meira ran as fast as she could. When she reached the carriage, Meira looked up at Melana as she started to snap the reins. She pleaded, "Let me come okay? I will be silent I just need . . ."

You must bring her. "Okay, okay," Melana whispered. Although she wanted to ride off and never see this woman again, she knew she couldn't. She looked down at the woman defeated and accepted her fate. Melana braced herself as she reached down to take Meira's hand to help her into the carriage knowing what would happen when their hands touched. When their eyes met, she noticed that Meira was bracing herself, too. "I have to go deep into the woods."

Meira got into the carriage and sat down. Not frightened at all, she nodded, "Okay." and fell silent as Melana snapped the reigns and the horses carried the women towards their destiny.

Chapter Six

The house in the woods

The sun had long since faded in the sky when Melana and Meira reached the house, if you could call it that, in the woods. To Meira, it looked more like a mud hut; like it grew out of the woods that surrounded it, the light emanating from the window glowed like it was shining from the bottom of a murky pool.

The two women hadn't spoken since they left Melana's so when the carriage stopped, Meira jumped when she heard Melana say, "You stay here."

Meira stared at Melana as if she had just awakened from a dream. "What? I thought . . ." She shook her head. It was hard to concentrate. The silence that she found herself in had lulled Meira into something that felt like sleep but, she knew she hadn't been asleep. Melana did not respond instead she said, "I have to go inside by myself." When Meira started to protest, Melana said, "I need to ask permission."

Everything Melana knew and everything she felt told her it would be okay, but she wanted to make sure. It was still hard for her to believe that after all this time; tonight the dreams would become a reality. For the first time Melana felt fear.

"Okay, I'll stay here." Meira only agreed because she had almost knocked Melana down, had followed her and then barged into her home telling her an unbelievable story. She hadn't given Melana a chance to say whether or not she knew what was happening.

Melana was surprised that Meira readily agreed. "I'll be back." She looked back to make sure Meira was okay, and then she headed towards the front of the house.

Meira watched as Melana approached the house, reaching the opening, turn back for a moment, and then get swallowed up in the light. This sent a chill through Meira. She was desperate to know what it was like inside, she had only seen fragments in her dreams, but she would wait until Melana returned.

Melana stepped silently into the entrance of the house. Melana knew *She* had seen her approach and would be waiting. Melana never spoke a word. The light would draw her in. It always happened this way. The first time it happened, Melana was scared and almost didn't go in. There was nothing to fear but the hairs on the back of her neck always stood out like some energy was surrounding her. It never got dark no matter what time it was. Even the temperature remained constant. She shook her head and went inside.

* * *

Meira hugged herself as she waited in the carriage. Looking around she saw the moonlight shining on the trees making them looked like giant sentries, limbs, sinewy and strong, reaching toward the sky. She heard a sound way off in the distance, could hear it clearly. She didn't know what to make of all the strange sounds in the silence. Funny, she thought, silence is never silent. There was always sounds, the heartbeat, the pulse beating through veins and arteries, rushing to and from the heart. The way a breath came and went. These things were a constant part of silence.

Swinging her feet back a forth, Meira hadn't been this nervous in a long time. She wanted badly to be right about what she had seen in her dreams. She had felt the pull for a long time, pulling her to this part of the world, pulling her to Melana. She also knew Melana was not really shocked to see her. She didn't know what was going to happen now. Instinctively Meira knew the house was a part it. But what she didn't know was how. Her dreams had only brought her so far. Whatever it was, Melana was the one she needed to be with. Meira kept waiting as the curtain of night slowly descended.

* * *

Inside the house, the fear Melana felt earlier melted away as eyes filled with wisdom held her gaze. Melana had been to the house in the woods more times than she could remember, first as a child then as a woman. The woman, only known to Melana as guardian, eyes never wavered from

Melana. The flowing gowns she wore always seem to float as the woman moved about the house. She was like a golden apparition. Melana had no real description for the guardian because she always looked different. It was if Melana was meeting her for the first time every time. Melana knew she was special, knew when she discovered the woman in the woods that she wouldn't tell anyone. Yes, somehow she knew and as she got older and started to practice midwifery she finally understood why.

"You brought Meira with you." The guardian was not asking Melana, so Melana didn't answer. She just looked back into the darkness where Meira waited. "Tell her to come inside."

"Are you sure?" Melana was still fighting with herself, but she knew she would not win this battle. "Why do you ask me questions that you already know the answers to?" The *guardian* asked. Melana bowed her head. "I'm sorry. I just wish I had known she would be . . ."

The woman caressed Melana's cheek and then with hands softer than anything Melana had ever felt, not even the babies she caught felt this way lifted Melana's chin. "You must not question your destiny child; you have known for a long time that this day would come. Now go and bring her here."

When the guardian let go of Melana's face, Melana turned and walked back to the carriage. She looked up at Meira. "Come on, it's okay. I'll take care of the carriage." She reached for the reins in Meira's hand and tied them to a tree.

Meira hopped down from the carriage and followed Melana into the house. From the outside the house looked old and worn almost like it was ready to fall down. As she walked through the entrance, Meira saw all kinds of objects inside. Paintings, some Meira couldn't begin to describe. Then she saw something that she did recognize. It was a painting of her and Melana but it wasn't quite them, more like their twins. Shocked she wanted to touch the painting, but decided not to.

"Sit," the woman told them. Both Meira and Melana sat down in chairs that felt as fragile as they looked. Careful not to break anything, that sat across from the woman. Smiling the guardian asked. "How are you Meira?" Startled again, Meira didn't know what to say. She knew she should say something. Answer her. "I . . ." was all Meira could get out. She tried again. "I . . ."

"I know it is a lot for you, child, even if in your heart you know what's happening." All Meira could do was nod her head. "Your reaction is not unlike Melana's when she first came here. She didn't believe and even now she tries to close herself to it. You both must understand it is important because there will be a time when another one will come to you and Melana, but for now the two of you will be enough."

Melana thought, *I wonder what she will look like.* The guardian eyes narrowed. "Melana, what have I told you about your thoughts?"

"I'm sorry," Melana cringed. She had forgotten that here in this house her thoughts were not alone.

Meira watched the exchange between Melana and the woman realizing for the first time that she and Melana would be forever a part of each other. She had no doubt that Melana was having a hard time accepting their fate because she was struggling with it too so she didn't blame Melana for her hesitation.

"Everything will become clear Meira, you both must be patient."

"What . . ." had she voiced her thoughts? Meira stammered. "I have seen you, this place in my dreams for a long time." Meira's green eyes glowed like emeralds as she tried to explain her feelings.

"I know how you must feel. When Meira started to speak again, the woman held up her hand, "Enough," the woman silenced them.

"Both of you have been given the gift to bring life and you have not disappointed. I have followed you in my mind. I have seen how special you two have become and for that I am proud." The woman hesitated. She seemed to be listening to something but then she looked at both of them and smiled. "Now however, you will not only bring life with your hands, you will also be able to pass souls to those who will become more than mere humans." The look on Meira and Melana's face was one of fear and doubt.

Again the guardian acted as if she could hear their thoughts, feel their fear. "Do not be afraid" The guardian spread her arms as she looked around the room. "You need to know this place is where you will find your strength. Melana discovered me long ago when she came here as a child. No, she didn't know then about her future, she was just a curious child. I was just the lady in the woods. When she became a midwife she still came. I didn't reveal my true self to her until then. The rest was not Melana to receive until both of you were together."

The woman stood and went to another part of the house. When she returned, she told Meira and Melana to hold out there hands. The woman had two hearts one made of wood and one made of glass. She placed one in each of their hands. "These hearts are the keys."

"The keys to what," Melana asked as her hand clutched the wooden heart in her hand. It felt warm. Meira didn't say anything but clutched the glass heart like she was holding a fragile soul. To answer them, the guardian began to speak of the hearts.

"The wooden heart is strong, a strength that endures throughout a lifetime. It finds itself protecting us from the rage of words, the sorrow of death, achingly, possessively without fear. It is the protector of our secrets, the guardian of our hopes and dreams. The wooden heart holds the journeys, swaying and bending when sometime paths collide. With each passing season the wooden heart sustains us, through the spring of our budding beginnings, through the summer heat of the one great love, through the fall of our failures, and through the winter of our darkest moments. This is the promise kept by the wooden heart forever and ever.

The glass heart is fragile, a delicate balance between now and forever. It holds the tears we shed when the memory of loss invades us. The glass heart sees the soul and the spirit—fills it with wanting. It laughs out loud, unwavering in its quest to love and be loved. The glass heart bleeds and cries in silence when there is no answer to the hurt—when friendships fail, when love dies. The glass heart shines its light on the world, magnifying its beauty. The glass heart remembers the first moments. It allows others to see inside where truth lies. The glass heart wears it's emotions outside without caution. This is the promise kept by the glass heart forever and ever.

Two Hearts—breathing, beating, expanding, two hearts residing in one soul."

Clutching the hearts Melana and Meira both started to speak. The guardian rose to her feet hugging them, she pointed. "Go now," the guardian commanded, "you will find the key in the ruins. You must go there to hear the rest."

"What ruins?" Meira whispered to Melana. Melana thought she knew want ruins the guardian was talking about but didn't respond to Meira's question.

"Melana will show you. You must go now. It is late." She had dismissed them.

Meira was shocked by the abrupt dismissal. "What just happened," said Meira as she and Melana headed for the door.

"I am as surprised as you are," said Melana, "but I know that we must go."

"Why didn't you say anything?"

"I have learned that patience is a virtue here and even if I don't always practice it, I know when *She* says to leave, then, I know to leave. Come on, let's go."

When they got back in the carriage, Meira held up the glass heart. It was no bigger than a walnut. The heart was brown almost like topaz. There was a small hole at the top as if it had been worn around the neck. She could see inside. In the center of the heart was a small pearl like object. The heart was warm to the touch.

Melana held up the wooden heart. It too was brown, brown like the banks of the Mississippi river. There were black swirls flowing toward the center as if it had been poured from a cup. It too was warm to the touch.

Chapter Seven

After Meira and Melana left the house, they returned to town without speaking. They stopped in front of the store where Meira had run into Melana. When can we go to the ruins," asked Melana. Melana was excited.

Instead of answering, Melana finally confessed. "I knew who you were even when you bumped into me. I had the dreams too. It's just that . . ."

"I know. I'm white."

When Meira said it out loud, Melana felt a little ashamed. She wanted to apologize for her thoughts, not about the south, but about Meira. Melana knew she had been missing something important in her life as a midwife. When she felt this way, the face she had always seen was Meira. She never knew the color because that part always seemed to be hidden. Melana always believed since she was a colored woman that Meira had to be colored, too. She was wrong. When their eyes held, they seemed to search each other, searching for each other. But Melana didn't say any of those things she simply nodded her head. "Yeah, that just about sums it up. Where are you staying, exactly?"

"There is a rooming house at . . ." She had been so busy trying to find Melana and after their encounter in the house she couldn't think. Now she wondered if she knew where the place was.

"You must be talking about the old Ross place," said Melana. It had to be the one because it was the only rooming house in town. It was really just a big old house like most of the white folk's houses in town. Big white picket fences, green shutters around every window and huge columns in the front. It was only a half a mile down the road.

"Yes! That's it!" She turned to Melana. "Well, I should be going."

She started to get out of the carriage when Melana stopped her. "At least let me drop you off." They started down the road. When Melana stopped in front the boarding house she said. "Have a good rest of the night."

"I will see you tomorrow?" Meira asked.

"Yes." Melana watched as Meira walked into the boarding house. Melana lifted her face to the sky before she tapped the reins. *The time has come Melana.*

*   *   *

Meira entered the boarding house. They had given her a key. So as quiet as she could, she crept inside. Before she could reach the stairs that lead to her room, a voice out of the dark asked, "Hi Miss, you sure have been gone for a long time?" Melana almost screamed. "Who is it?"

"It's me the owner of this establishment. I'm sorry I scared you. I hadn't seen you come back since you left to go to the store, so I was worried."

"Oh, I came back," said Meira, "but I went out again, you know to get familiar with the place for my research and all. I must have lost track of time."

"Well, you shouldn't be out at night. You are a foreigner in Matlin. All kinds of things can happen."

Meira just wanted to go to her room. She didn't want to have to explain herself especially to someone who was practically a stranger. And she was a grown woman. So she yawned and stretched." I guess I'd better get to bed then. I am sorry if I worried you." This seemed to satisfy the owner.

"Okay," the owner replied. "Breakfast is at seven. I'll see you then."

"Yes, well good night." Melana hurried up the stairs.

*   *   *

Melana watched from a distance as Meira walked into the boarding house. When the door closed, she snapped the reins for the horses to start. When she made it home she slowly got out the carriage. All she wanted to do was sleep. Maybe then, she could finally accept that she would no longer be alone. Melana was used to being alone. She had thought it suited her and because of this solitude, she could do her job without interference. Now that would be impossible. It was clear she Meira was here to stay. Deep down, she knew this day would come. She had been granted the power to help bring life into being with her hands. She had never taken it for granted. Melana knew what it meant when someone said "Our deepest fear is not that we are inadequate, our deepest fear is that we are powerful beyond measure."

Meira had the same power, of life and light. Together they would pass that gift on and then return from which that power came, two souls residing, two heartbeats echoing each other.

*   *   *

Back in the Lilac Field

Teresa legs started to cramp as she tried to stretch them. They had been crossed for a long time. She tried to grasp what Meira and Melana were telling her. She began to understand that these women were remarkable, not mere midwives but much more. Her eyes getting wider and wider as she listened to the soothing sound of their voices, she didn't say a word when they stopped talking.

When Melana looked at Teresa, she could see all the questions that were running through Teresa's mind as her face changed from curiosity to wonder and fear. "Maybe she isn't ready," said Melana. Meira nodded. Maybe they hadn't thought about it enough, but now it was too late.

"Let's give her a minute," said Meira. They had sensed Teresa's strength when she asked to become a midwife. Now they hoped what they saw in her was enough to carry on what had been started long ago. Their time was short. They were older than they appeared. When one received the gift, the aging process slowed. They both knew Teresa would live a long time. They waited while Teresa gathered herself.

Teresa took a deep breath. Hesitantly she asked. "Me, I am a part of this?"

"Yes," they both answered as one.

Then without speaking, Melana and Meira tenderly reached for Teresa's hands and stood. "Your hands," they said, "Our hands, midwife hands, hands that touch first always." Teresa looked at her hands. At first, she saw nothing, then, a light glowed from their hands as they stood in a circle. Now, Teresa understood when Meira or Melana touched a child, and whispered words she couldn't understand, something passed between them and the infant. It came from their hands.

Slowly, the light grew dim when the women released Teresa's hand. There was more to tell.

* * *

Back at the Community Center 2010

Teresa woke up at the center with a start. At first she thought she was back in the lilac field with Meira and Melana. She could almost smell the flowers. She was not in the field she was at the Center. The dream, the dream seemed so vivid. It felt like she had been asleep for a long time but, when she looked at the clock, Teresa had only been asleep for few minutes.

Shaking her head to clear the dream, Teresa sat up. She reached for the picture of her daughter Michaela together with her granddaughters that sat on the bedside table. The picture was taken at Teresa's house, all three sitting on the porch swing. Heads together more like sisters than mother and daughters. Out of all the pictures she had, this was the only one Teresa had taken to the center with her. This one always made her feel close to them. Michaela was the spitting image of her sister Sarah. Teresa wiped away the tears from her eyes, "*enough of that,*" she admonished. In the picture Kay was smiling as usual and Kris was smiling too although Teresa could tell that beneath that smile Kris also looked like she wanted to be somewhere else. As she touched Kay's face, she whispered, "You are my only hope."

Chapter Eight

Kay drove from the Community Center in a daze. She had left her grandmother staring at her back. Right now, she needed to think. She clutched the tape in her pocket as if her life depended on it. She knew Teresa was as tough as they came but this, this was . . . She couldn't even contemplate the strength it must have taken her grandmother to hold on to this information for eighty years. Kay laughed. She couldn't keep a secret for more than a minute.

Kay knew about the midwives, Melana and Meira. Her grandmother had told her long ago, but Teresa had never revealed anything other than the fact that she had practiced with them. What she had heard on the tape was amazing and scary at the same time.

Kay kept touching the tape. She was stunned. "Shit," she said as she threw on the brakes. She almost ran into the car in front of her. "How was she going to . . . ?" She shook her head. This was not the time to be musing. She needed help. What was she going to do? Again Kay wondered if she could do what her grandmother asked. Did she have the courage to act?

In the last few years, except for work, Kay hardly ever thought about anything else. Kay was a free-lance news reporter; words were her life and her friend. She loved the solitude it gave her. Lately, when it came to relationships she was introverted. She wasn't always this way, but something happened to her. She couldn't quite figure how and why she was. All she knew was at one time she had plenty of friends, from college mostly, but she had somehow lost contact with them.

When Kay got home, she sat down at the desk and opened her laptop. She needed to finish the story she was writing for the Matlin Reveille by six to meet the deadline. Right now her heart wasn't in it but she had a job to do. Going back to the tape Kay chuckle, more like a tiny gasp, maybe one day she could write about what she heard. It was a fantastic story but who would believe it? She didn't want to believe it herself. Sobering, she bent her head over her computer. When Kay finished she looked at the clock on the computer, it was almost 5:30, plenty of time. She emailed her story to the editor.

Afterwards she picked up the phone to call her cousin Kyla. She knew then that the answer to her grandmother's question was yes.

*   *   *

Kyla Thomas sat at her desk so bored she couldn't finish the reports that were begging her to do so. Good thing she only had thirty more minutes until she was off work. Looking around, she wondered, what else she could get into. Kyla was cocoa brown with a little milk thrown in. Her eyes were wide, some said sinuous. She just thought they were too big, like her mother's. Kyla worked at the university where she had received her undergraduate degree in accounting. It was a HBCU; Historical Black College & University, some, like the one where she worked, were called land grant colleges, which meant the land the colleges were built on was given to the descendants of slaves by their slave masters. She loved her work, but right now she wanted to be on a beach somewhere. Maybe she would go to the coast this weekend. Kyla jumped when the phone rang. Grabbing it before it could ring again she said,

"Hello, ASU this is Kyla."

"Hi Ky, it's me Kay"

Grinning Kyla said, "Hi *"me Kay"* what's up?" Thank God Kyla thought something to use up the next minutes.

Hesitating, Kay started to say "nothing" but that'd be ridiculous because she was the one calling. Besides, if she didn't say something, her cousin would know something indeed was up. So she said. "If you're free later, can you meet me at Granny's house? I need to talk to you about something."

Kyla had heard the hesitation in her cousin's voice so she said. "What's going on Kay? And why we have to talk at Aunt Teresa's?"

"Nothing is going on, really," *at least not now.* "Like I said, I need you to meet me at Granny's house." Kay knew Kyla was going to give her a hard time but she went on anyway. "Do you always have to ask why can't you just be happy that I want to see you?"

Again Kyla asked, "Why?" Her cousin sounded strange. "I just saw you yesterday at moms." Kyla was starting to worry; it had been a long time since Kay had asked her for anything.

Kay waited for her answer after a beat she said, "I know but I need you to come to Granny's. It's important."

Still puzzled by the request Kyla relented. "Okay, I'll meet you at Aunt Teresa's after I get off work. This had better be really important."

"I'll see you at Granny's then," said Kay.

"Okay." As Kyla hung up the phone she wondered, why was Kay being so cryptic?

*　*　*

When Kyla arrived at Teresa's house, she was surprised when Kay asked her to help clean up her aunt's house. Her aunt hadn't lived the house for years. What was Kay up to she wondered.

When Kyla asked, Kay told her she was inviting some of her friends from college to Mississippi and that her house was too small to accommodate all of them. Since her Aunt Teresa's was empty, Kay had decided Teresa's house would be the perfect place.

Her cousin had once been outgoing, especially when she was in college but lately Kay had stopped. She just went about her business writing for the paper. Kay hadn't talked about her friends in years. Kyla had wondered on occasion, why. Now she was inviting them to Mississippi. Kyla was floored. Why now and why at Aunt Teresa's. She would keep quiet, for now. Kay's expression told Kyla there was more to it than just inviting friends, but she hadn't pushed she just said okay. So they spent the next couple of days cleaning and airing out Teresa's house.

Chapter Nine

After Kay and Kyla finished cleaning, Kay dropped Kyla off at her apartment and headed home. Walking in the house, she headed straight to the library, her favorite place in the house. Kay settled in the chair behind her desk. She had been adamant about having a library when she had the house built. She had seen a house plan that included a library in one of the Home and Garden magazines and fell in love. She loved books and having them surrounding her when she wrote her news stories, made her think she was "Dear Abby" or something.

Sitting there thinking she mused, Kyla hadn't said anything nor had she asked anymore questions. And if anyone knew when she was being evasive it was Kyla. When Kay moved back after school Kyla was there. In fact Kyla never left. Of this she was grateful. Kay knew she would eventually have to tell Kyla the truth never doubting that Ky would simply ask "what do you need me to do." Like Kyla, Kay knew her cousin. But would the others?

A little scared, no she was a lot, if she was honest with herself. Years ago, she would have not hesitated, okay she would have thought her grandmother had gone around the bend, but she would still have jumped in with both feet. Sometime in all those years had she somehow lost her compass? What Kay had heard on the tape was so unbelievable. One thing was certain there was no way she could pull this off alone.

She frowned as she looked through the rolodex on her desk. She hadn't seen or talked to most of them in a long time. *When did they become just names she had written in the rolodex?* How would they react when she called them out of the blue? She was really nervous but, she had to try. She needed them. When her hands started to tremble; she intertwined her fingers as if praying. Muscling up bravery she dialed Katie's number.

* * *

Katie Mitchell shook her head. "How did she ever think she would be able to handle these small grownups?" She called her students small grownups because she taught at a gifted school in Atlanta, Georgia. She taught five and six year olds. Most of the kids were advanced beyond their years, but their small bodies hadn't caught up to those advanced brains. They were always trying to outsmart her. What they hadn't realized was that she was once their age, too. Like them she was also gifted. She knew all the tricks they constantly tried to play on her.

Katie watched them as they slowly came into their tiny bodies. It was amazing that such big brains could look so innocence in repose. This was the part that made Katie realize she had made the right choice. But right now, she just wanted to go home. It was Friday and a two week summer break started next week. She was ready. She taught at a year round school. Every three months they had two weeks off. It was the June quarter break. She looked at the clock. She had three hours to go before the bell rang, *none too soon.*

"Chanel! Will you please stop pulling on Tai's dread locks? They're real; they're real." Katie had said the same thing to the little girl over and over. Luckily, Tai didn't seem to mind. He was shy and quiet, but when he did say what was on his mind, he really said it. She knew whatever Tai said; he had thought about it for a while. Chewed on it, stuck it behind his ear like gum.

Before she could say anything else to the precocious little girl, she felt her cell vibrate in her pocket. "Who could be calling her?" Katie was adamant about people not calling her at work. She knew it couldn't be one of the parents because they always called the school office if they needed to speak to her. Katie didn't particularly like cell phones, but she knew they were a necessary evil and today when she was almost headed for some down time she had the urge to throw it out the window. Instead she reached in her pocket and snapped the phone open, "Hello."

As soon as Katie answered the phone Kay realized she shouldn't have called. She knew Katie's rule. "Sorry Katie. I forgot," said Kay.

Katie started laughing. "It would be you. You are the only one who would dare call me, only you. And although I am happy to hear your voice, tell me dear cousin what is it that is so important that you have broken my rule?"

Kay hesitated. "I'll call you back when you get home."

"Oh, no you don't, the little grownups are just beginning to rise from their naps. You have about two minutes to tell me what's going on."

Kay sighed. Katie was right she couldn't break her cousin's rule without explaining why she called. "Next week is your two week summer break, right?"

"Riiight," Katie said.

"Well," Kay rushed on. "I need you to come home. I'll have a ticket waiting for you at the airport. I'll even send a car to pick you up at the airport."

"What? Wait just a minute Kay." Katie blinked. Had she heard her cousin? Being gifted did not mean that her cousin was making sense. "Are you kidding? Kay, I have no intention of coming home. I plan on spending my vacation with a good book, some wine and a filthy movie."

"Okay," Kay said. "I know this sounds crazy and it's short notice, but I really need you to come home. I fixed up Granny's house so you can stay there."

"I can't come home," Katie repeated. "I have important things to do. And why would I be staying at Aunt Teresa's when as you know my mother, your aunt lives there." Her cousin wasn't making any sense, again she wondered.

Although Kay knew this was serious she couldn't help but laugh at what her cousin was calling important. "You just said," Kay reminded her, "you were going to read, get drunk and watch dirty movies. You can do that at Granny's. I will tell you why when you get there." Seriously she said. "I need to see you Katie okay?"

Katie was beginning to worry. Kay had never asked her to come home and to stay at her aunt's house? Katie didn't know how serious it was. "Please Katie," said Kay. "It'll be my treat. I'll pay for everything."

"Kay?" The long silence on the other end of the phone made Katie change her mind. "I'll see what I can do, but I can't promise you anything. Look, Kay I got to go. Chanel! Stop pulling his hair, I told you they were real. I'll call you tonight and let you know for sure. My grownups are up."

Kay shook her head as she listen. "It wouldn't be me." She wasn't positive but she felt like she had persuaded Katie to come. Katie needed to be around some real grownups.

* * *

Kay was still smiling when she hung up with Katie. She could clearly imagine Katie running behind the little girl as she tried to keep her from pulling the little boy's hair. Her cousin was a big kid herself. Katie was always ready for something new. And Katie's knowledge of languages would come in handy.

Looking at her rolodex again, Kay couldn't help but feel like her solitude was about to take a turn. It was one thing to ask this of family but another to ask people who were practically strangers to her now. Everything she had surrounded herself with spoke of her solitude. She stayed further out of town. Other than her family, she rarely invited people over.

When her eyes fell on the card that said Kaila Norwood, Kay thought, "This is a real long shot." From what she had been reading about her friend and former classmate, Kaila had become a great scientist. Kaila had said she would be when the two of them met at Vassar. California was two hours behind. She only hoped Kaila wouldn't hang up on her when she realized it was her.

Chapter Ten

Kaila had been looking in the electron microscope forever. Hubble had sent pictures from the international space station that hovered in lower earth orbit. Kaila knew they were on the brink of discovery but so far it was less than she had hoped for. But hope was the word. Kaila was a nanotechnologist, controlling matter at the atomic and molecular scale. She had been offered a job at NASA eight years ago. Kaila was doing what she loved and at the same time was able to do her part for science.

The research was going okay. NASA crashed LCROSS into the moon looking for signs of water and so far all Kaila saw was dust. "Moisture, she begged, "any kind of moisture would do." Kaila pushed her dark red hair from her face. She had small freckles that looked like tiny stars when she smiled. Her fair skin kept her out of the sun. This wasn't a problem because she was in the lab most of the time. She was of average height, about five four. Her German ancestry accounted for her aqua blue eyes.

Well known, Kaila had written dozens of scientific journals and was the recipient of numerous awards. She once dreamed of being an astronaut but didn't think she had the discipline for it. You had to go through so much and Kaila didn't think she wanted her body fluids to be plastered to her feet from the G force when the shuttle launched into space. She was however a big Trekkie fan. It was just a TV show, but it mirrored what NASA was trying to accomplish, sustainability in space. She rubbed the back of her neck trying to get the kinks out.

Kaila was happy every day she drove through the NASA gate except that one time when her badge was down in the bottom of her purse. Kaila's purse was where things went to die sometimes never to be seen again. As she dug in her purse, a line of cars had formed behind her stretching all the way out to the 101 Moffett Field exit. She was so embarrassed when the security guard told her she had to turn around and go to the parking lot until she found her badge. She thought about getting a temporary badge at the security office. *What good would that do?* She was the first one in her department, coming in at 6:00 am. Most of her colleagues started at seven. She would still need her badge to get in the door. She could laugh about it now, but it wasn't funny at the time. She could still hear angry horns blasting.

She looked up when the phone rang, picking it up. "NASA, Ames this is Kaila."

"Hi Kaila."

"Kay?" She was so surprised to hear Kay's voice that she nearly dropped the phone in the sink where they washed the Petri dishes. Kaila hadn't heard from Kay since their graduate school days. "Kay, is it really you?"

Kaila's smile lit up the lab. It had been so quiet in the lab, when she laughed it startled her and her colleagues, who were now looking at her like she stole something. She pretended not to notice the looks, "The Green people."

"Wow Kay, it's so good to hear your voice." Still shocked at the voice on the other end the phone she said. "This is indeed a surprise."

Kay didn't respond to Kaila, she was wondering how on earth she would be able to get Kaila to come to her home town. It had been years since they were at Vassar together. She was sure Kaila was probably shocked, wondering why she was calling. Although she hadn't seen Kaila in long time, she knew Kaila could still read her. She always could. It was uncanny.

"Kay, are you still there?"

"Yes, I'm here. Are you busy right now?"

"I am always busy, but not too busy for an old friend who I haven't heard from in oh . . ."

"I know, I know," she went on. Kay knew she sounded frantic. She should at least ask how Kaila was doing. But she felt like if she didn't say it now before she lost her nerve she wouldn't be able to do it so she kept talking. "Look Kaila I have something to ask you."

"What is it?' Kaila asked. "What's wrong?" Although Kaila was surprised, no shocked to hear from Kay, she could still, after all this time, feel when Kay was struggling with something. She kept quiet as Kay continued.

"I . . . I want you to come to Mississippi."

Kaila stared at the phone, had she heard right? "You want me to come to Mississippi?" Before she could respond, she heard Kay say. "It's important."

"It has got to be," Kaila murmured to herself. When she and Kay were in graduate school, Kay never talked much about where she was from. Now she not only wanted to talk about it, she wanted Kaila to come to Mississippi. "I'm so happy to hear from you Kay. You sound great, but there's no way I can come to Mississippi or anywhere else for the matter. I'm in the middle of an important research project. It requires all of my time."

"I know. I've been following your work ever since you started at NASA."

Kay was full of surprises. Kaila hadn't heard from her all this time, not one word. She had wondered if they were still friends. "Kay . . ." She started.

"I know and I am sorry." Kay whispered so low Kaila could barely hear her.

Kaila could hear regret in Kay's voice. She truly sounded sorry, but Kaila was not ready to forgive her, yet. It would take her at least another minute. She kind of liked hearing Kay squirm a little. The silence was getting longer. "Okay, I forgive you, but it still doesn't mean I'm coming to Mississippi." Kaila wanted to ask, why now? It didn't sound like Kay. Kaila wanted to know more. Something was wrong. She could feel it. Felt it before, that connection to Kay. Instead of voicing her concern, she said, "Like I told you I have my research and I can't spare the time."

"Okay I understand. I'll talk to you another time when you're not so busy." When Kay started to hang up, Kaila said. "Wait, that's it? You call me out of the blue; ask me to come to Mississippi and now you just say okay I'll talk to you later?" Kaila was getting worried.

"You said," Kay repeated. "You have your research. I wouldn't' want to interrupt you." Kay knew she had to say something. Kaila deserve better.

"You already have," said Kaila. "What's really going on Kay?"

"You wouldn't believe me if I told you." Kay sighed. "I can't talk about it over the phone. Besides you already told me you can't come. I'm sorry for bothering you. I shouldn't have called. You will be forever my friend even if I haven't acted like one."

"Look," Kaila said. "Call me back when I get home." She gave Kay her home phone number and her cell number. "I'm leaving in a couple of hours. What time is it there?"

Kay looked at her watch. "It's three o'clock."

"Well call me at eight your time. It'll give me time to get home."

"You sure?" said Kay.

"Yes I'm sure." When Kaila hung up she couldn't concentrate on work. She was worried. She had thought about Kay over the years since they both left college, but hadn't heard anything from her since. After the phone call, she felt something. "Strange," she murmured to herself as she subconsciously rubbed her hands on her lab coat.

Chapter Eleven

Hanging up the phone Kay thought about the day she first met Kaila.

She had been sitting in the university cafeteria looking at her notes when she caught a familiar, but unpleasant scent.

"Damn, those science majors, why did they have to come straight to the cafeteria from lab? They always smell like formaldehyde." The scent was even stronger today. "Why was that?" she mused. When she looked up, there stood a woman with dark red hair and the bluest eyes she had ever seen looking down at her with questioning eyes. "Yes?"

Kaila pointed to the empty chair next to Kay. "May I sit down?"

Kay wrinkled her nose. The formaldehyde was stinging her nose, but she didn't own the table and she was the only one sitting there so, she said, "sure." Continuing to look over her notes, Kay noticed the time. She had fifteen minutes before she had to leave for an interview with one of her fellow classmates.

"My name is Kaila by the way." Kaila reached out to shake Kay's hand when she sat down.

Kay wasn't so sure she wanted to smell like formaldehyde, but she didn't want to be rude, so she took Kaila's hand. "I'm Kay"

They sat in comfortable silence for few minutes. Kay continued to work on her piece and Kaila pulled out her sandwich she had brought with her. After a while curiosity got the best of Kay. She looked up from her notes. She asked, "Kaila, right?" When Kaila nodded, Kay went on, "I was wondering, what is your science discipline?"

"How did you know I was . . .?" Kaila looked down at her lab coat. She knew it smelled. "Sorry I forgot. When you've been in science labs for as long as I have, you don't notice the smell anymore. I am studying earth science. I want to be a nanotechnologist."

"A what a, what a . . ."

"A nanotechnologist," Kaila repeated, "it's someone who studies things at the molecular level."

"Un, Huh," said Kay, not understanding at all, although, she did love the sound of the word. She repeated it in her head "nanotechnologist." "We do need those I guess." Kaila laughed. "I guess we do. What's yours?"

"I'm in journalism. I hope to work on the local paper in my hometown one day," said Kay.

"You write stories. That's great," said Kaila. "I can't write anything unless it's scientific."

"That's writing, too."

"Yes," said Kaila. "I guess it is." Impulsively, Kaila asked. "Do you want to hang out? Anatomy was my last class." Kaila felt a connection.

Kay looked at her watch. She only had a couple of minutes. If she stayed any longer she would miss her interview. "Sorry," she held up her note pad, "I have to go and do an interview." Funny, Kay thought as she started to get up, it felt like she was losing a moment that she would somehow regret.

"It's okay. It was nice to meet you Kay." Kaila also rose to leave. When she turned to leave, Kay surprised Kaila when she reached for her arm. "Wait." She tore off a piece of paper from the notebook. The kind Kaila had seen reporters use in the movies.

Kay wrote down her cell phone number and handed it to her. "Here, I would like to hang out with you. I will be tied up with my interviewee for a while, but call me later. I should be finished in about an hour. If not, leave me a message. Maybe we can swap stories."

"Sure," Kaila laughed. She could just picture Kay's eyes glazing over when she talked about molecular structure. Kaila had taken the piece of paper from Kay and it was the beginning of a very rewarding friendship.

* * *

Why hadn't she stayed in contact with Kaila? Thinking about the formaldehyde, Kay's nose subconsciously twitched. What was she going to say when she called Kaila later? How could she convince her to come?

* * *

On her way home, Kaila smiled, when she looked at her lab coat. She didn't know it, but she and Kay had been thinking about the same thing.

Walking through the door she saw her husband Tom sitting at his desk with his head buried in a blue print. He was an architect. He owned his own business so he was able to work from home most of the time. What Kaila loved about him was how he cared for her. He always cheered her on in whatever she decided to do. No questions asked. He never complained about her long hours and he did something she had been allergic to all her life. He cooked, and he liked it. As she looked at him, she wondered if she deserved him. He was almost too good to be true. "Now, what made me think that?"

Tom felt her approach and turned around. "Hi you, how was your day?"

"It was great. I got the strangest call from an old friend of mine from college."

"Yeah," he said, which friend?'

"It was Kay. You remember we went to Vassar together."

"Really, I haven't heard you talk about her in a long time."

"I know I was surprised. That's why I rushed home." Kay had sounded so funny on the phone. "I told her to call me later tonight. I didn't have time to talk to her but it sounded urgent so here I am."

"Well if that's what it took to get you here then, thank you Kay."

*   *   *

When Kay called, Kaila had already decided to go to Mississippi. When the phone rang and before Kay could speak, Kaila said, "Okay."

"What?" Kay sputtered here she was all ready to tell Kaila why she wanted her to come and Kaila had already agreed to come. Surprised, she almost didn't hear Kaila next words

"I'll be there. Tell me when."

Still a little off balance she said, "No argument, no whys or what for?" Kay started to ask what had changed her mind but before she could ask Kaila answered.

"Yup"

"So just like that," Kay repeated.

"Yup,"

"Stop saying yup."

"Okay."

"What's with the one word answers?"

"Nothing."

"There you go again."

Kaila laughed. "Okay . . . I mean . . . I'm okay about coming."

Kay was stunned. She hadn't told Kaila anything. What made Kaila change her mind? Then she remembered how close they were at Vassar. Kaila must have felt something. She wanted to ask, but she was just happy that Kaila was coming. She would talk to her when she arrived. So, instead she said, "When you get here I hope you've added a few more words to your vocabulary."

"I'm sure I will," Kaila chuckled. They talked briefly and soon hung up Kay saying they would catch up on years when she got to Mississippi. The rest would wait.

Kaila was still chuckling when she called out to Tom. "Guess what honey? I'm going on a trip and you will never believe where."

Chapter Twelve

While Kay was busy trying to find help, Teresa was still remembering the dream even though she was now fully awake. Kay had been gone for a while. She sat up in the bed as she continued to remember that day in the lilac field. Melana and Meira had told Teresa about the house in the woods after much debating. They had promised to take Teresa there so she could fully understand.

Surprisingly, Teresa readily accepted the fact that she was a part of something greater than herself. Teresa also knew, although it would be years later that Melana and Meira would leave her and she would be alone with the secret. Teresa smiled when she remembered that first time in the ruins.

*   *   *

When they picked her up, Meira said "We must take you to the ruins."

"The only ruins Teresa knew about were the ones that were on the back roads towards the river. "Are you talking about Windsor Ruins?" She had heard about them, but no one ever went there, at least not any of her family. Why would they?

Melana answered. "That's the place."

Teresa shivered as if someone or something had whispered in her ear. The Windsor castle, as it was called then, was built by slave labor around 1859. The ruins had once been a majestic mansion with twenty-nine, forty-five foot columns which housed the Windsor family. It was so enormous the family maintained their own commissary, doctor's office, school and dairy on the bottom floor of the mansion, along with the kitchen and storage areas.

The second story floor plan revealed two parlors, library and, unusual to that period, a bedroom with a bathroom and study. Also, located on this floor was the dining room. Eight bedrooms and an additional bathroom were located on the top floor. Many cultural events were held in the mansion. The mansion was destroyed when a fire broke out in the house after a house guest accidentally dropped a cigarette in debris left by carpenters making repairs to the third floor. All was destroyed except a few pieces of china and 23 of the columns, balustrades and iron stairs.* It was now known as the Windsor Ruins.

Teresa trusted that she would be okay. Melana and Meira never told her anything that she didn't need to know. She nodded and braced herself for what was to come.

*   *   *

The midnight sun shown down on the columns, as they reached the ruins. All three got down from the carriage. Staring, Teresa saw, stuck in the ground like an old tomb stone, a picture of what the castle looked like in its glory. Moss hung from the trees surrounding the remaining columns. Tiny paths, where people once walked, led from the ruins and disappeared into the woods. Teresa could almost hear the people who use to live here. She could also hear the slaves who with bent backs, sweat pouring as they mixed the mortar that built the columns. The picture reminded her of the stories in the Bible when the pharaoh had slaves build stone pillars. Feet churning in the mud with the overseer cracking his whip if they slowed even for a second. Teresa knew without witnessing it, that blood flowed in the soil.

Deep in thought she hadn't realized that Meira and Melana were walking to the center of the ruins, each holding something. It was the hearts that they had told her about, one made of wood, one made of glass. Teresa watched as Meira felt along one of the columns as if looking for something. She touched the wooden heart to small indention in the column, the heart started to glow. Tears formed stars on the surface of Meira's skin as she placed the heart gently reverently as if in sacrifice.

Then, Melana moved to the other side of the ruins and placed the glass heart in another column and the heart glowed. The glass heart began to vibrate and music pierced the air. It sounded like nothing Teresa had ever heard. Suddenly, a stairway appeared.

At the top of the stairs, stood a woman, she was beautiful. As Teresa watched she could see the seasons. Spring felt like budding beginnings, summer felt like love, the fall appeared not like leaves but like hope, like strength, winter contained sorrow.

Melana and Meira bowed and the woman touched them. The glass heart formed and reformed faces Nefertiti, Cleopatra, Aina Irish Queens; they all seem to emanate from the glass heart. Teresa could see creation unfolding. The souls colliding, spirits gliding, she could not tell where one ended and another begun. Melana and Meira stood face to face as the two hearts converged. The two looked as if they were sharing the same souls. They touched each other's hands and they were connected.

*   *   *

The woman focused on them. "You have done well my daughters but there is much work to be done until the circle can be finished. She looked at Teresa.

"Ah, little one, I know you have many questions but for now you only need to know that you are ordained to continue what Melana and Meira have done so far. At once the woman's face turned to sorrow. It was fleeting as she said to Teresa. "You are different in that you are without your twin heart."

"A twin heart?" Melana nor Meira had mentioned a twin. Before she could give voice to her questions, the lady looked at Meira and Melana. "You did not tell Teresa this?"

Melana answered. "We had told her so much; we feared she wouldn't understand that it should have been two of them." Melana and Meira were from different places but part of a whole.

Afraid they had displeased the woman, Meira said. "We are sorry Teresa."

"It is okay," said the woman. As she stood at the bottom of stairs she said, "Teresa, Meira and Melana are twins. One is called the spirit twin and one is the soul twin. Together they are one. Something happened and your half was lost, but fear not Melana and Meira will look after you until you are strong enough to be on your own. However you will still feel like something is missing, even when you are surrounded by family and love ones.

The other half will return and she will come here to the ruins where the first twin souls of the beginning will be. You must also continue to visit the one who resides in the woods, there is where your strength will come." To Meira and Melana she said, "Take good care of she who is without." With that she turned toward the stairs.

Before Teresa could respond the ruins were again as they were. Melana and Meira picked up the hearts. Teresa was overwhelmed. She still didn't understand what she was supposed to do. The ruins were silent again as the women caught their breath. Teresa sat on the ground. When she touched her cheeks there were tears.

They hugged Teresa as she cried. Cried for what was and what was to be. "Now, said Melana, "you know everything that we know. If you choose to accept all this, we," she looked at Meira, "promise you until the day comes when we can no longer be with you, that we will protect you and watch over you."

"You can trust in this, in us. We will teach you everything you need to carry on the work that was started before you were a thought, before we were a thought," said Meira.

The three slowly walked back to the carriage. Teresa's journey had been set and would last until she too would one day return to the ruins for the last time.

The three women returned to the carriage and to a life that Teresa would find rewarding and enlightening.

Chapter Thirteen

Kay was glad to hear Kaila's voice again. She still needed to explain. She knew when Kaila suddenly changed her mind that she had sensed something. It was just a matter of time. Kay got up from her desk to get something to eat. She had forgotten. She wanted to call one more person, Kaitlin. Kay took a deep breath. She took a few minutes to get herself together. Could she ask someone whom she loved and knew loved her back to return to the place which only brought sadness for her cousin?

Kay still hesitated, talking herself out of it. She did this all the time. She was the consummate procrastinator. She talked herself out of a lot of things. If she needed to stop at the store on the way home from work she would get close, but at the last minute, she would keep going as if the car had willed it. She would say, "I can do it tomorrow. I have enough. It can wait." She had many conversations like it over the years. She laughed when she realized she was having one right now. It was late she would call Kaitlin tomorrow.

$$* \quad * \quad *$$

The next day as the curtain closed on the San Francisco Bay, Kaitlin Toussaint's hands moved the brush swiftly across the canvas. From the depths of the ocean, the water beat a long echo refrain. She had painted this view of the bay forever. In the dusk, in the dawn, she painted. She was wearing her favorite San Francisco 49'er football jersey. It was signed by Ronnie Lott, a defensive back who played for the 49'ers in the eighties and nineties. She was thrilled when he signed it. He even let her hold his super bowl ring while he autographed the jersey. She had to put three of her fingers in the ring to make it fit.

The wind blew her short dark hair. She closed her eyes and took a deep breath. Long eyelashes touched her cheeks. They always made her look as if she was asleep. Her face was a round mocha latté color. People

50

said she looked like Jill Scott the singer. When they said this, she would answer, "No, you got it wrong Jill Scott looks like me."

The Golden Gate Bridge was to her left as she painted. The sky was very clear. The fog usually hanging over the bridge was not there. You could see Sausalito and Treasure Island clearly. The mid span towers of the bridge looked like sentries. Golden seemed to be a misnomer, someone's mistake. When she arrived in San Francisco, she thought she would actually see a golden bridge. She laughed when she saw the burnt orange color. She later found out "Golden Gate" didn't mean gold. The bridge was a gate way to California and points north thru San Francisco. The towers looked out over the bay as a silent reminder of its beauty.

She stretched and turned her head. Behind her along the walkway were dozens of bicyclists with those dorky looking helmets. The helmets always looked like they were on backwards. All the helmets on the bicyclist heads were the same color, silver and black. This made the cyclists look like a school of fish with the fin-like bibs sticking out the back.

As Kaitlin looked back out over the bay at Sausalito, she remembered a movie she saw about one of Sausalito's infamous mayors, Sally Stanford. Sally once owned a brothel in San Francisco. Later she visited "Valhalla," the restaurant that was owned by Sally. To her surprise, Sally was sitting on a stool in the restaurant. The 'Bay Area' was a great place to be. You could find anything you wanted, be anything you wanted and it was okay.

Kaitlin's cell phone vibrated in her bomber jacket. Her grandmother Nana gave her the jacket on her sixteenth birthday. When the sound became persistent, she frowned. She flipped open the phone and read the number. She couldn't help but plaster a big grin on her face. It was Kay. "This had better be good," she said into the cell phone.

Kay smiled. Kaitlin was her favorite cousin, "Hey you."

"Hey back at cha."

"I know you're probably painting and from the sound of things in your favorite place."

"Yes, I am," Kaitlin said. "You know, it's that 'Cancer' thing." Kaitlin was not like anyone Kay knew, especially from Mississippi. Kaitlin was like a sea urchin. She loved the water. Kay knew Kaitlin spent most of her time at or near the water and living in San Francisco made it easy. Kay often wondered how this soul, whose light shone so bright, hadn't been snuffed out by all the darkness that had touched her life. Kaitlin had suffered so much loss.

Kaitlin's husband Jake had been killed in Afghanistan two weeks after he was there. Kaitlin was pregnant at the time. When she got the news she went into premature labor. Her little girl didn't live long enough to draw a single breath. Kay was almost tempted not to ask Kaitlin, but she thought maybe this would be good for her. Jake and the baby had been gone for six years.

"Hey," Kay said as she nervously tapped her fingers on her laptop, "I was wondering . . . maybe . . . could you come home." Kay heard Kaitlin gasped. She shivered when the sound reached her, realizing the enormity of what she had asked. If Kaitlin came home it meant seeing Kaitlin's mother her Aunt JoAnne. Her aunt never forgave Kaitlin for running away from home to marry Jake. Kaitlin hadn't seen her mother in over six years. They didn't even talk to each other.

The silence that followed made Kay think Kaitlin had hung up. She forgot about Aunt JoAnne. How could she. Her aunt and Kait had fought a lot before Kait ran away. "That's okay, Kait." Stupid and insensitive, that's me. She changed the subject. "How's the painting going?" Kaitlin still hadn't responded. "Kait, I'm sorry. I forgot sorry. I know . . . I'm so sorry." She didn't know what else to say. "I'll call you back later," she whispered.

*　　*　　*

Kaitlin didn't realize Kay had hung up until she heard the silence on the other end. Staring across the bay, Kaitlin closed her phone.

It had taken some time for Kaitlin to concentrate on the word that had made her close her mind. "Home," it felt unnerving even mentioning the word. Matlin, Mississippi was no longer her home, or it hadn't felt that way for a long time. Kaitlin bowed her head as the tears fell. After a while the tears stopped and she sat on a rock remembering Kay's conversation, which wasn't really a conversation. Kay's voice had brought a smile to her face only to fade when Kay mentioned coming *home*. Her paint brush had stilled. She had lost her place. The last time her paint brush was silent, Kaitlin had gotten the news about Jake. She never thought there could be any greater pain in the universe. When she lost Jake, Kaitlin lost her heart. When she lost her first and only child Alain, she almost lost her soul. She thought she would go right along with Jake and Alain. She didn't think she would ever get her heart, or her soul back, or paint again. But like all great artists, Kaitlin found she couldn't turn her back on that part of herself. If she had, she would never have found her way back from the darkness. Could she do it? Could she go home?

This time the pain lasted only a moment. Kaitlin had promised, as the pain lessened, she'd never go to that empty canvas again. She pushed the memories back into the dark. She looked down at the rock she had been sitting on. It looked worn down by the tides. Sitting there, she felt its warmth against her skin as she touched it. She paused to take a closer look. Tilting her head, she looked at the bottom along the edge of the rock; someone had painted her initials K T M on the side where the stone was partially buried in the sand. She knew they weren't really her initials. Millions of people had those initials and the person who painted them on the rock, Kaitlin would never know. She had sat on this rock half imbedded in the sand every time she came to the bay, but this was the first time she noticed the writing. Why now? Was it a sign?

Kaitlin knew Kay felt bad after the phone call, but she couldn't respond. All these years, she'd refused to talk to her mother. Her mom never understood her. When she first called home after running away, her mother kept talking about what Kaitlin was doing to the family by running away. Telling Kaitlin she was selfish. Why couldn't her mother understand that she was in love with Jake? Kaitlin had always wanted to leave home. She just didn't know falling in love would cause her to leave the way she did. She just wanted to paint and love Jake with everything she had. When she got pregnant, it was as if heaven had open up and made all her dreams come true, but the happiness tumbled down on a wave of despair. Jake and Alain were gone. Her cousin, Kay had come and stayed for weeks while Kaitlin pulled herself from the dark depths. Like the bay her sorrow ran deep, the pain only receding when she was deep into the world of painting and creation.

Kaitlin's thoughts were interrupted by a couple of tourists who wanted her to take their picture with the Golden Gate as its back drop. It was getting colder as the fog slipped over the bay covering it like endless clouds. The sea gulls were skimming just above the water looking for food as Kaitlin packed her things and headed back to her condo. She would call Kay. She was going home.

*   *   *

Kay hung up the phone and turned to watch the moon rise from her window. She had hoped by asking Kaitlin to come, it would give Kaitlin something else to think about. Kaitlin was alone. Kay also knew that if Kaitlin came home, she and her aunt would put away what was keeping them apart. Besides, she needed Kaitlin. She would call her back later and apologize again for her thoughtlessness. She knew the price Kaitlin had paid. She remembered the pain that almost buried Kaitlin when Jake died, then to lose Alain, too.

It was hard the day Kay entered the room where her cousin once sat with the love of her life. Kaitlin stood facing the window her back to Kay. Kay knew Kaitlin was in pain she could feel it as she crossed the room. Like a dark cloud it hovered as if waiting to engulf both of them. The loss of Jake and Alain had stilled her cousin's hands and her heart. Kaitlin was looking at a picture of Jake; sobbing as she clutched it. Kay watched Kaitlin fingers as she touch his face. Kaitlin had no painting of Alain. Alain would never see a sunrise. Could Kaitlin put back the pieces of her heart Kay had wondered.

When Kaitlin turned, she was rubbing her chest as if to erase something invisible. As if her heart was no longer there. Kay watched the light from the window as it fell across her cousin's face, and felt the tears in her own eyes.

Tears coursing down Kaitlin's face, eyes hollow with pain, she stared at Kay as if she was seeing her for the first time. As her tears fell Kaitlin whispered. "He said he would never leave because soul mates never leave." As Kaitlin's knees betrayed her she cried, "He told me ours would be a love that would make "forever" jealous." Kay grabbed her before she fell.

In that moment, Kay had wanted to take Kait's pain. She had never suffered such lost. She didn't know how Kaitlin had survived.

Chapter Fourteen

Bringing her thoughts back to the present, Kay hoped she could somehow convince Kaitlin that it was ok to come home. She would help Kait through whatever confronting her aunt meant. Maybe she could talk to Aunt JoAnne. Kaitlin hadn't even told Aunt JoAnne when she was pregnant. She had only told Kay. She made her promise not to tell the rest of the family. Kay had kept her promise but she knew Kaitlin needed to tell her family, especially Aunt JoAnne. She shook her head. "No. This was between Kaitlin and her aunt." But it didn't stop Kay from worrying about Kaitlin.

She looked at the rolodex again. When her finger fell on Kristin Riley, she frowned. She hadn't even thought about Kristin. Kay and Kristin had grown up in the same town. Kristin however had gone to the only private school and Kay went to the only public school. They would have never met if they both hadn't received a scholarship from the same company. In order to receive the scholarship, they had to attend a ceremony that was being held at the state capital for all the scholarship winners. They were as different as night and day. Both sat in the lobby, that day, waiting with the other participants. Kay and Kristin had ended up sitting next to each other.

* * *

Kay looked over at the girl sitting next to her in the room where they waited to receive their scholarship. Kay had seen her in town. Surprised they were both here at the capitol. Did she win a scholarship, too? She chuckled to herself, *dumb question*. Kay shifted to get more comfortable. The room was crowded. The two of them were sitting so close their shoulders were almost touching so Kay held out her hand. "Hi, my name is Kay."

"I know. I'm Kristin." Kristin had seen her many times, at homecoming parades and at the movies. How could she not, Matlin only had one movie theater. When Kristin saw the look of surprise on Kay's face, she corrected. "I know, I mean . . . I've seen you around. I didn't mean I knew your name."

"I've seen you around, too. Don't you go to Matlin Academy?"

"Yes," Kristin answered. Kristin pointed to the sign on the pedestal across the room from where they both sat. "So, I guess you're here for the Orion scholarship, too."

"Yeah," said Kay. "I wrote an essay on great female African American writers."

"I wrote an essay, too, about . . . about African American female judges."

Kay was stunned, "Really?"

Kristin turned and faced Kay, blue eyes challenging and said "Yes, I did."

Kay didn't know what to say. *Why would she write her essay on African Americans and she won a scholarship for it?* She didn't know whether to be angry or proud. She thought about it some more, then to her surprise, she said, "I think that's great. I have one question, though, why?"

Kristin looked at Kay trying to explain. "I know it sounds strange but I have always wanted to get to know you . . . you know."

Kay let her off the hook. "You mean black people?"

"Yes, and I want to someday go to law school so I picked the subject for my essay."

Kay thought about it. If all people felt like this, the world would be a better place. She asked Kristin. "How was it?"

"It was great. I learned that we were not really all that different in what we believed about right and wrong."

Kay was impressed. "You have to let me read it sometimes. Maybe I can dispel some notions for you."

Kristin laughed, "And maybe I can dispel some notions about us." They both laughed.

They became friends, at least as much as they could be. Even though Kay and Kristin were close, Kristin's mother did not approve. Kay figured it was one of the reasons Kristin left home as soon as she could. They kept in touch over the years, regularly at first, but soon it became a card here and there and then both of them got too busy, or so they thought. Kristin went on to become a lawyer. She had her own law practice in Seattle, Washington. Kay dialed Kristin.

* * *

Kristin held the cup to her lips. Kay had called. She hadn't heard from Kay in a very long time. At least five years. They were both too busy, they confessed to each other on the phone. Too busy for friends, when had it come to that? Kristin didn't want to go home. She pushed back the auburn hair tapered at the neck. Blue green eyes like the Coral Sea stared back at her, as she looked out the window. How she and Kay had become so close Kristin never did figure out. A White girl and an African America girl became friends in Matlin Mississippi. It was the eighties then, but in the small town where she and Kay lived, it might as well have been the sixties. She shivered when she thought of going back. It seemed so very far away. She had once vowed to never go back. She had told her mother until things changed she would remain in Seattle.

Kristin sighed. Kay needed her and that was enough. She hadn't even questioned Kay. The Kay she knew, or thought she knew, would never have asked if she didn't really need her. Kay knew how she felt about coming back to Mississippi. Kristin would wait until she got there to get the whole story. She dreaded seeing her mother again. Her perfect life was about to be shaken up.

Looking out at Washington Lake, the shadows were casting a somber glow. Kaitlin drank her coffee and looked at the tree that had fallen in the last storm. The lightening had spilt it in two. Part of it refused to fall, the other lay on its side, split like an open womb as it lay dying.

Chapter Fifteen

It was almost morning at the center, dawn nearly breaking as Teresa continued down the road of remembering.

After the day they took Teresa to the ruins for the first time, Meira, Melana, and Teresa were inseparable as they covered the country side.

Sometimes, because it was necessary, Meira returned to Dublin. Each time she did, there was a birth that Meira just happened to be a part of. Even though physically separated from Melana, when she touched the babies the gift was passed on. *A midwife's hands* she whispered as each one came into the world. On the other side of the world, Meira could almost hear Melana murmur the same words.

As they got older, it became apparent to Meira and Melana, that Teresa was not only special; she was exceptional. In some ways she was better, even with the loss of her twin. When the student surpassed the teacher it made it so much easier.

Soon Meira and Melana felt their time nearing, they wanted to prepare Teresa. But it never seemed like the right time, so they kept putting it off.

Melana and Meira would one day return to the ruins for the last time. They would become a part of the guardianship. The gift would fade for the older women as Teresa thrived in their care. They followed her progress for many years even when they were no longer able to do what once had been as natural to them as taking a breath. Their job would then be to continue to watch over Teresa. For all their knowing, they also knew Teresa was always longing, yearning for her other half.

Teresa knew the ache of loneness she felt would never be soothed. Melana and Meira never quite filled the void. Teresa hoped she was strong enough for the both of them, the missing part of herself.

After Teresa had her daughter Michaela and when she delivered her grandchildren the ache was at least bearable.

* * *

When her daughter Michaela was born Teresa was so happy. She hadn't realized how wonderful a gift it could be until Melana laid her daughter on her breast. Both of them Meira and Melana were there holding her hands as her daughter pushed through. She had never felt this kind of happiness.

Teresa had wondered over the years, why Melana and Meira never had children of their own. She knew Meira had family because she would return from time to time to Ireland. Meira had delivered some of her own family members.

Teresa had once thought she didn't need any children with all the ones she delivered, but it was nothing like the first time she saw her little girl. It was as if heaven had given her an angel. Although there were times as Michaela grew that maybe there was a little devil in her too.

Her daughter learned well. As did her nieces all of them cut from the same cloth. That also accounted for Teresa and her sisters' closeness. Although it got crowded sometimes, she loved her sisters. She was busy a lot so all those surrogate mothers was a God sent.

Like Meira and Melana not all of Teresa's sisters had children and three of them died so young that they didn't get a chance to bear children. Sometimes she thought it was because her parents had had so many that it wasn't for them to repeat. More than their share she thought. She knew that was ridiculous but she thought about it and had been thinking about it.

Teresa had grown up in a world dominated by women. The women ruled. They were independent and that was how Teresa raised her daughter, to be able to take care of herself. She didn't have to worry about Michaela. Michaela had become a woman with grace and elegance. What she had been worrying about lately though, were Melana and Meira. It seemed in the last year or so they had begun to age rapidly. Something was changing.

* * *

Meira and Melana sat by the fireplace in Melana's house, the light from the fire danced along the walls caressing their faces. Meira had moved in with Teresa when they got too old to practice their craft. At first it had the

59

people of Matlin in an uproar. Somehow, they convinced the town that it was necessary. Since they had never caused any trouble and many of the adult people in the town had been delivered by Meira or Melana, the town folk eventually accepted it.

Both women shuddered at the same time. Looking at each other, Melana took Meira hand. "We have to tell Teresa. It won't be long now. Can't you hear it, feel it. They are calling us."

"I know," said Meira.

"How are you going to explain this to your family?" Melana asked. "You were born across the ocean. What will happen when you never return?"

"The last time I was there, I had a lawyer draw up my will. I have put in it, what my wishes are."

"Still your family must be worried."

Melana was right. They would be worried. Meira wanted to tell them she would be alright and this is where she needed to be. She had to be with Melana. She hoped the will would be enough. Lately she had been writing home. Not telling them everything but that she was happy in Mississippi. Meira's parents had eventually accepted that she would live in the United States for the rest of her life. However when she died her family expected her body would be sent back to Ireland. "I know."

Each one seemed to be reliving some moment in the past. Their faces playing memories like old movie reels. They had been up all night as if they knew it would be the last and as the dawn came, they listened. *Come, my daughters it is time to rest.*

*   *   *

From her window, Teresa watched the sun come up. It had been a long night. The Dawson twins decided to make an early arrival. Smiling when she remembered the look on Mister Dawson's face when he realized is wife was having twins. Teresa had promised Vera, his wife that she would not tell him. Keeping the secret was worth it. She had watched as he held his girls. Teresa never got tired of seeing that picture. She had touched the twins and whispered the words.

Shivering she pulled the quilt she had wrapped around her shoulders. She looked around. What is it? Then she heard it. *Come.* She tilted her head listing again, "Must be the wind." Walking away from the window she moved to the rocker. Closing her eyes as she sat down, *"come."* "No!" she cried. She threw off the quilt and rushed to put clothes on. She ran to the house. Teresa lived just a mile from them. When she got there, she banged on the door. "Melana, Meira!" she shouted. No one answered.

Teresa went around to the back of the house and still she couldn't see anyone. She fished for the keys, had forgotten she had them. They had given the keys to her years ago, so she would be able to come to the house even if they were not there. Teresa threw open the door. She searched the house; the women were nowhere to be found. Trembling Teresa sat in the rocking chair with her head in her hands. When she looked up there on fireplace mantel were the hearts and a note addressed to Teresa. She got up picked up the note and the hearts. She opened the folded piece of paper.

"You mustn't be afraid, Teresa, you will always know what to do. Trust us, trust yourself. We give to you all our love. We will see you again when the time comes. Take good care of the hearts."

M & M

With tears streaming down her face, Teresa clutched the hearts and slowly closed the door as she walked out of the house.

Chapter Sixteen

Matlin, Mississippi 1965

The horses seemed restless as Teresa made her way to the house in the woods. Everything was changing. Melana and Meira were gone only the house in the woods remained the same. It hadn't changed at all. It was same as it was the day Melana and Meira first took her there. There, Teresa felt connected to the past. Like Meira and Melana she was frightened at first. Now, the house, the guardian would be where she would find solace.

One day, a few years back right after Melana and Meira were gone, Teresa noticed the babies she delivered, started looking like people she saw in the ruins. What others believed were only in stories told from another time, Teresa saw in the babies faces. Egyptians, Africans, Irish, Greek, a rainbow of worlds. She was not surprised. She had seen these things in the house in the woods. Teresa had learned from the guardian and the women in the ruins that there were things in this world that couldn't be explained. She knew she would never be able to tell anyone. Even if she could, who would believe someone who had never been out of Matlin?

At first Teresa didn't think she could go on when she discovered the two people who she felt she needed the most were gone. This continued to plague her consciousness. The two of them had been gone for a long time, both gone at the same time, like they could only exist if the other was alive. Months had gone by before she could even bring herself to pass by the house that Meira and Melana had once lived in. She missed them every day.

*　　*　　*

Teresa had wished many times in the years that followed their death that she could see them, talked to them especially when the babies were

62

born with something wrong. With everything that could happen, Teresa hadn't lost any children and as she thought about it, Meira and Melana hadn't lost any either. There were times when she had glimpses of the women but they were buried moments that were fleeting.

Her own sisters were astounded that she had such a following. If you were colored, Teresa had a hand in it. This made her kind of famous. Even some poor white folks asked for Teresa's services, usually in secret. Pride and white supremacy kept most away. Some thought she was strange, but the ones who came to her did not.

One thing that always brought tears to her eyes was the fact although she was the oldest, she had to watch all of her sisters pass away. It was like leaves falling off the tress. She didn't understand. She had cried a river of tears when her baby sister died.

Shaking away the sadness that had enveloped as she rode to the woods, Teresa smiled. She thought about her granddaughters, Kris and Kay.

Teresa's nieces also, thrived. She was so proud that she was able to watch them grow to become successful, independent women. Even when she was busy Teresa tried to carve time for them. She didn't always approve of how her nieces handled things especially how JoAnne had treated Kaitlin after her sister, Maureen died. It was if JoAnne had died along with Maureen. She became this overprotective mother which in the end Teresa suspects was the reason Kaitlin had ran away with that young man she had fallen in love with.

Like always Teresa took a breath to calm the emotional feelings that her memories brought on. Although her mind had been elsewhere, she knew she would never stray too far from the path. Even the horses knew the way to the house. Looking around, she blinked, *maybe not, there was always a first time.*

Panicked, Teresa got down from the carriage and starting running. She stopped in her tracks. "Nothing, nothing, everything was gone!" No sign of the house, no sign of the guardian. She almost fainted. Had she gotten so old that she had forgotten where the house was? That was ridiculous; she had been coming here for years. She could find it blindfolded, even the horses knew the way. Teresa felt like screaming. She sat on the ground for what seemed like hours. She felt raw and open as if her soul had opened up and spilled out. Tears formed but didn't fall. She knew what she had to do.

Clutching the hearts she carried with her always, Teresa ran back to the carriage and tapped the flank of her horse with the reins. Teresa headed to the place she knew would give her answers.

As the she raced to the ruins, her mind took her back to the beginning. Teresa had been transformed that first day in the ruins.

Teresa stood in the middle of the columns and placed the hearts like Melana and Meira had showed her. This time she was really alone and she was frightened for the first time. She felt like she had failed. She looked down at her own hands. They felt strong and fragile at the same time, like the wooden and the glass heart. Teresa stared into the moonlight that blanketed Windsor ruins.

Teresa had called the woman who descended the stairs each time she came, "One bright shining star." It was the only thing she could think of as she waited. Other women had also appeared in the ruins from time to time. Sometimes she thought the other women were Meira and Melana when she came to the ruins after they died. But that couldn't be. They looked nothing like them. The woman never told Teresa who she was. For some reason, Teresa never asked. Teresa felt their presence but not tonight, tonight would be different because only the "One bright shining star" appeared. She spoke, but only to Teresa's soul.

"By passing the world on through others, you have kept the secret of our hands. This is your destiny, your fate," the woman whispered. "We gave you the power to touch life, the very essence of the universe. It will soon be time for you to pass through your hands what we have given you."

"I am old," Teresa said. "What can I do now?" she shivered. She didn't know what to do, but she knew she would do whatever was asked of her.

"For now you will continue to pass this gift until time shifts and expands. One day, you will no longer be able to touch new life. It will slip from your memories, your moments, folding into your consciousness until you are ready to pass this gift to one who will not accept this gift willingly, at first. She will hesitate but her love for you will prevail.

There will be two heartbeats, one heartbeat created the other, but they beat as one, the last of the first, the first of the last.

Your gift of firsts will not pass to your children or to their children, but because of their loyalty to you, the hearts will survive. You must send your daughter's daughter to find them, to find the beginning, of the beginning, the ones who hold the hearts."

Eyes closed, Teresa trembled as the woman continued.

"This journey will begin in the winter of your life, ten years into the new millennium. In that moment of uncertainty, you must find peace with this knowledge. You must be strong. You must have faith. You must remember."

When Teresa opened her eyes again, the woman was gone.

*   *   *

Teresa left the ruins that day knowing that she was truly on her own. She would carry on. For the next years Teresa did what was required knowing that one day she would return.

Teresa was not getting any younger and her hands; she didn't think she could trust them anymore. She looked at her hands. They had started to look like any aging woman's hand. Teresa didn't know how long it would be before progress made her give it up. She was nearly seventy.

"Progress my aunt Fannie," Teresa said as she realized she would not be able to practice anymore. A person had to go to school to be able to become a midwife. She balked. "What becoming? You were one or you weren't." Being a midwife was not something to enter into lightly and sometimes without your knowledge, like she, Meira and Melana you were chosen.

Soon, the town quietly told Teresa she couldn't continue to practice unless she went to school. She was too old to go to school and she was too tired. It was progress that stilled her hands.

*   *   *

For a long time Teresa began to think that the secrets would die with her. She remembered what she had seen and done all those years ago, what the old women had told her. She kept going and kept waiting, hoping time would show her soon.

Teresa's knees began the give out. When she no longer could get around without a wheel chair, she decided she would go to the nursing home or what they called assisted living. She didn't want to be a burden to her family. Later, her sister Belinda came to live at the Center. She was happy for the company even though Belinda could get on her nerves with all that chatter.

Soon Teresa would forget what happened in the house and what happened in the ruins. They became a distant memory.

Chapter Seventeen

Matlin, Mississippi 2010

Kay had been busy all week first with cleaning the house and then calling some of the others. This was getting bigger and bigger. She was afraid. She didn't let on as she called them one by one. One thing though, she got better at the explaining. At first they balk, then they became curious and then they agreed to come. She was surprised when Kaitlin had called her latter that same night. Kay had thought Kaitlin would never talk to her again. Kay had shouted for joy. It was the best news she had heard since she started calling everybody.

Kay picked up the note pad she had been writing on, making sure she had everything and everyone she needed. She also needed to make a list of the things her houseguest would need. She looked around on the desk. "What happen to the pen?" Frustrated, she opened the top drawer to her desk. "Why is it when you're looking for something, you can't find it until you stop looking?" When she closed the drawer, a photo fell to the floor. She smiled when she picked it up, Karina.

Karina was a doctor Kay met in the ER at a local hospital in Italy while she was on an assignment. In a freak accident while doing an interview with one of the locals, Kay had twisted her ankle and Karina treated her. She found out that Karina had been to the United States as an exchange student. They hit it off right away. Karina even invited Kay to her home. And for the rest of the time that Kay was on assignment she had spent a lot of time with Karina. Karina showed Kay parts of Italy that Kay would never have seen. With Karina's help, her article was not only featured in the paper but was also picked up by other newspapers. Kay was scolding herself for not keeping in touch with Karina. What had happened to her?

As she held the picture she wondered. "Should I ask Karina? She doubted Karina would come, but what would be the harm in asking?" When Kay started to shake her head, something made her think about another picture, a picture she had seen at her grandmother's house, the day she and Kyla were cleaning. With everything that was happening she had forgotten. Seeing the picture brought it all back. At the time she had thought it was strange because to her knowledge, Kay had seen every picture her grandmother possessed.

Now thinking back, she remembered in the picture there was a woman. As the other picture formed in her mind, her eyes got wide. She remembered in the picture was a shop in the back ground. Kay recognized the shop. "Had her grandmother gone to Italy?" She didn't think so. If her grandmother had gone, Kay would have known. Her grandmother would have mentioned it.

It was the same one . . . or was her mind playing tricks. The shop in the picture looked exactly like the one she and Karina had gone to by accident. In the shop, she remembered seeing a strange box. She remembered because she was drawn to it. "Jesus, I hope I won't be ready for some home when this is over." She started to shrug it off, but she was a reporter. Reporters always followed their gut and Kay's gut was in overdrive. Staring at the picture again, she picked up the phone. "What time was it in Italy?"

*   *   *

Karina Giovanni was standing in front of the nursery in one of the elite hospitals in Italy where she worked as a heart surgeon. Karina watched through the window at the babies as they were being fed. Just as she turned to walk away, the nurse at the counter told Karina she had a call on her service. Karina always turned off her personal phone so her service was the only way anyone outside the hospital could contact her when she was working.

"*Not now*" Karina looked at her watch. She was about to go off call. She reached for the phone at the nurses' station. "This is Dr. Giovanni."

"*Buonasera* Karina, its Kay."

"*Buonasera! Cara mia!*, you sound so close. Are you here in Italy?"

"No, I am here in Mississippi. And you, let me guess, you're standing in front of the nursery, right?"

Karina laughed. "Yes and no. Yes, I was standing there, but I was just about to go off call when the nurse called me to the phone."

"That's great. Do you have a minute? I need to ask you something." Before Karina could answer, Kay plunged right in. "Do you remember when I was in Italy and we saw this beautiful box in the window of that small shop in the village?" Kay waited a beat. She could almost hear Karina brain churning.

"I remember it quite well," said Karina. "As I remember, you were drawn to it."

Relief sounded in Kay's voice as she went on to explain. "Could you go and check to see if the box is still there?"

Although Karina was surprised by the request, she said, "I will check and see." Like Kay, it was the first time Karina had seen the shop and she had never gone back. "If it is there, what do you want me to do?"

"See if you can buy it, okay? I will pay you back."

"Why do you want it now? At the time you said you could not afford it and even if you could, you did not think it was something you would pay at the price they were asking."

"Well, I think I need it now," she whispered.

"What was that?" Karina asked. What is wrong she wanted to ask? When Kay didn't answer Karina said, "I will do as you wish. If all goes well, I will call you tomorrow."

"*Grazia,*" Kay didn't want to explain on the phone why she wanted the box and she hoped that Karina would understand. She would explain, well she would try to explain, later after Karina retrieved the box. "I know you are about to leave so I don't want to keep you, as always you're the best."

This made Karina laugh. "Next time please inform my Chief, She always says I could be better. *Ciao, Cara.*" Karina hung up the phone. "*Well that was strange.*"

*   *   *

Kay had a feeling when Karina called tomorrow, the news would be good. Kay somehow felt it was important. How important she didn't know. One other thing, Kay didn't believe in coincidences. She will decide later what she would tell Karina; right now she had another call to make. She could almost hear Mozart as she dialed Kenya's number.

Chapter Eighteen

Kenya stretched and yawned in her apartment along "The Mile." It was called that because the views from the window of the downtown apartment stretched for miles. If the skies were clear, you could see all the way to Dallas. The rent was so high in Fort Worth. Kenya wondered how long she would be able to live in her loft apartment.

Kenya was a concert pianist. She had traveled the globe from China to Australia. She didn't know where she got her gift no one in her family had it. When Karina played she lost herself. Today, she was practicing a particularly hard piece.

Kenya shook her head as the sunlight descended below the skyline, the light from the window hurt her eyes. She reached to close the curtains. The windows were open to catch a breeze. It was June and Texas was sweltering. She hadn't turned on the AC because sometimes the chill interfered with her playing. Kenya was willowy but toned. Some would call her skinny but she didn't think so. Kenya didn't pay much attention to how she looked. Her friends, which she had so few of because of her solitude, said she was beautiful. She thought she was just average. Some said she looked like Julia Roberts and Lisa Stansfield.

When the last notes of the melody became silence, Kenya got up to get more coffee. It was past six and she hadn't eaten all day. She always forgot to eat. It was always like this when she practiced nothing would satisfy until she finished. The music captured and held her in those moments. Playing the piano was all she ever wanted to do.

She got her coffee and sat back down at the piano and began to play. She played well into the night. When the phone rang she didn't pick it up, she let it go to voice mail. She smiled when she heard a very familiar voice. She ran to the phone. Breathless she said, "Hello Kay."

"This is a surprise," said Kay "I didn't expect you to pick up. I knew you were probably practicing, so I was just going to leave you a message."

"Yes I was practicing." Kenya realized, for the first time in a while, she was glad for the interruption. Something in the back of her mind had been bothering her. It was like a low hum, ignored but ever present.

"Well, I am glad I was able to catch you in a lull." Kay had known Kenya for a long time. Kenya was one of her first interviews for her thesis class. Nothing ever stopped Kenya from her music. When she was practicing, she was never present. Kay's curiosity was piqued but she didn't have time to think about it. "So how's everything going?"

"Okay, Kay," said Kenya. "What's going on?" By the way Kay sounded, Kenya knew this wasn't a social call and she knew Kay hadn't expected her to answer the phone.

"Well I wanted to ask you something and it might sound a bit strange, but do you think you could come to Mississippi?"

Kenya thought about it, she didn't have any impending concerts she had to do and she did need the rest. Maybe Kris would be there. "I think I can come. My calendar is free for the next month and you won't believe it but, I do need a break."

Kay was shocked. Kenya's music always came first. Kay had prepared herself for an argument, but before Kenya could change her mind, Kay said. "Okay, I'll send you the tickets for the flight."

"No Kay, let me pay. Like I said, I need the rest and besides, you know I can afford it. Please let's not argue about this okay."

Kay knew better than to argue with Kenya. Kenya was very independent and she always paid her own way. "All right we won't argue." They chatted for a little while longer then they hung up.

Chapter Nineteen

Karina stood in the hallway of the hospital after she hung up with Kay. People went around her. Nurses, doctors, EMTs, controlled chaos. She had been standing there for, it seemed like hours. She was glad to hear from Kay. She couldn't help but notice that Kay sounded different, and such a strange request. Yes, she had remembered the box. She would do as Kay asked, but why did Karina all of a sudden feel like running? She looked at her watch, she would just make it.

Karina left the hospital and walked down the street. Although it had been a while since she and Kay visited the shop, if she remembered correctly, the shop wasn't too far. When she turned the corner, there it was. "I thought it was smaller."

She looked at the sign to make sure it was the right shop and walked in, "*Buonasera*," she said to the lady standing at the counter. "Excuse me. I am looking for a box. I saw it the last time I was in your shop. It is rather small." She tried to describe it. She held up her hands as she looked around. "It looks like a small treasure chest. It has emeralds and jade . . ."

"Like the color of your eyes," the diminutive woman said. Karina was startled. She had forgotten that Kay had told her the stones looked like her eyes. "Yes! That is the one." The lady smiled then, "It is in my office. I saved it for you." The lady turned and started towards the back of the shop through a door Karina assumed was the office.

What was she talking about? When she and Kay were there the first time, Karina did not remember seeing the woman, nor had she asked anyone to save the box for her. She and Kay had talked about how beautiful and strange looking it was. The stones etched on the lid of the box were shaped almost like open hands. "Wait! How do you know me? The one time I was here, I do not remember seeing you." The woman didn't answer Karina. She just continued to the back of the store into a small office.

Karina stood there and watched the woman as she hurried to the back. Karina tiptoed closer so she could see the woman. To her surprise, the woman wasn't looking for the box. She was picking up the phone in the office. She had her back to Karina, but she could make out the conversation. Rooted to the spot, not ashamed to be eavesdropping, she listened.

"She is here . . . No not the American, the other one . . ." As the woman held the phone, a glow seemed to flow into the phone. "Yes she is waiting out in the store as we speak." She hung up and picked up the box and went back out to the store where Karina was waiting.

When Karina saw the woman hang up the phone, she rushed back to the front. The woman handed her the box. The lady waved her hand. "No, you do not have to pay me. It is where it belongs."

"What? What are you talking about?" Karina reached in her purse to pay the woman. No way was she going to walk out the store with something she hadn't paid for. It was crazy. When she tried to give the woman the money, the woman pressed the money back in Karina's hand. The woman replied. "You will understand, soon." She practically pushed Karina out the shop and closed the door.

Karina stood there on the sidewalk. What was going on? She turned to go back in the shop but, a "close" sign was now hanging in the window. When she tried the door, it was locked.

* * *

When Karina arrived home she called Kay. She told Kay she had the box and about the strange encounter she had with the woman in the shop.

"Wow," said Kay. She couldn't believe it. "The woman just gave it to you?"

"Wow, indeed *cara*, I did not want to believe it myself. She acted as if she knew me. And when I overheard her talking on the phone she said your name."

"That's impossible." Kay thought about the tape then. Nothing was impossible. Now that Karina had the box, Kay knew Karina was waiting for an answer to what was going on. She cleared her throat. "Karina, I was wondering . . ." She cleared her throat again, although, it sounded more like a cough.

Karina's patience was running out. *"Cara,* what is it you are trying to ask me?"

Kay shrugged, here goes nothing. She started again. "I was wondering if you could bring me the box."

"Bring, you the box?" Had Kay realized what she said? Karina waited. Surely Kay was not expecting her to come to the United States.

"Yes, Karina. I need you to *bring* me the box."

Karina held the phone away from her ear. Turning when she heard someone approach, Karina put her finger to her lips. There was something else keeping Karina from even thinking about coming. Since she had seen Kay, Karina had discovered something about herself. She looked lovingly at the hazel eyes that stared back at her.

"Hello? Karina, are you still there?"

Turning to the phone again Karina said. "Kay you really can't expect me to come to the United States. Besides as you well know I am doctor. I have patients. I cannot drop everything and come to your home. It is impossible."

Kay knew she had to tell Karina something. At least as much as she could say without Karina thinking she had lost her mind. "Look, Karina," she didn't know where to begin, "My grandmother . . . she told me . . . I mean I listen to . . ."

"Just tell me, *cara.* What is it?"

"What I'm about to tell you is as unbelievable as the lady in the shop." She started again. My grandmother was a midwife . . .

"Cara! What are you telling me? You can't seriously believe this can you? And there is a painting that looks like me at your grandmother's home and the shop is in the painting, as well?"

"Yes, I didn't want to believe it either, at first, but remember what you told me about the woman in the shop? How she said she had saved the box for you. That she knew you . . . us. The shop, the painting, the box, these can't all be coincidences. There is something and somehow this all fits."

Karina looked back over her shoulder. She had raised her voice. She was glad she had told Lori to wait for her in the front of the house. She whispered. "Kay, I need to tell you something." Before Kay could reply she said. "Never mind, we'll talk later. I will think about this. I will call you again."

"Okay, Ciao *rina*'

Kay had not called Karina 'rina' in a long time. She turned. What was she going to do? Walking into the living room, she paused and took a breath. "Lori, *mia amor,* I must go to the United States."

Chapter Twenty

Friday June 4th 2010, the day they all arrived

Kaila's plane landed at Medgar Evers International Airport in Jackson. The airport was named for the slain civil rights leader. According to Kay's directions, Kaila had sixty more miles to go to reach her destination. After renting a car she drove carefully down interstate 20. She didn't want to get lost, not in Mississippi. "Small towns how quant," she murmured. Although Kay had given Kaila directions, she asked the car rental company to give her a car with GPS. Kay's hometown was a dot on a map. "This was not going to be easy," she mused. Kay didn't talk much about Matlin when they were in graduate school together, but somewhere Kaila felt a connection to it. She laughed at herself how could she? She had never been anywhere near the south. She hoped those stories she had been told were not happening now, and were long gone. Stories only told in history books, buried in the dark past.

Kaila turned on her windshield wipers, it was raining really hard. The downpour was like a water fall on the window. She thought about pulling over, because she could barely see, then the rain suddenly stopped and the sun came out, as if the rain had never happened. "Okay that was weird."

* * *

Kristin was getting sleepy. Her plane had been delayed because the pilots, who were supposed to fly, didn't show up. They had to wait for another crew. If Kay had not sent tickets for her to fly on AA she would have flown SW She loved SW, same size plane. She felt safe.

* * *

Kenya rushed around the house making sure she had everything. If she didn't hurry she would miss her flight. Living in Texas she didn't have far to go, only one hour by plane. She would get there in plenty of time to rent a car and drive the rest of the way.

* * *

Over the Atlantic, Karina was thinking, she would call Lori to tell her when she had made it. Lori hadn't taken it well but Karina felt compelled to go to Kay. She had called Kay and told her she would come and bring the box.

Karina doubted the distance would be good for them. Lori might leave. Karina knew in her head that wasn't true, but her heart would not let her feel it. It had taken so long for Karina to admit that she cared. Now she was on her way to a place she had never been, to people she never met, strangers really, except for Kay of course. Watching the clouds as the plane started its decent into LaGuardia, her thoughts turned to what she had in her carryon bag.

At her grandmothers' Kay waited anxiously for her friends to arrive. She was slumped in her grandmother's favorite chair. She loved the windows that looked out over the forest part of Teresa's property. The house sat on forty-four acres, most of it timber. A porch surrounded the entire front of the house. A swing for two hung from the roof, swayed in the breeze.

When Kay was a child she thought it was a castle without the moat of course. The house sat high off the ground. Kay and her sister and her cousins played underneath the house. The porch was so tall, that when Kay was young she could stand underneath it without lowering her head. She wondered how it was that her grandmother had acquired this house. From the stories her grandmother told her, Kay's great grandparents were sharecroppers. Hearing the approach of cars, Kay didn't have time to wonder any longer.

She stood and went to the door. As each woman came into the house they all hugged Kay. Their faces were those she had shared her life with. Everyone looked well. When Kaitlin arrived Kay hugged her a little longer than the others. She understood what it had taken for Kaitlin to come.

After introductions and much hugging and kisses, they all sat down at the dining room table. Kay wondered what would happen when they heard the tape. Would those hugs that filled her with happiness and warmth now, be there then?

Kay smiled. Granny's house hadn't been this noisy since the holidays. When everyone was seated, Kay held up her hand.

"I know for some of you it is the first time you have ever been to Mississippi. That you were willing to come says something about the power of friendship and family." She winked at Kaitlin and continued. "I am so glad to see all of you and you must forgive me for not keeping in touch."

"You think," said Kenya. Everyone laughed at Kenya's remarks.

Throwing up her hands, "Okay, guilty as charged," Kay said. After everyone had calmed down, she continued. "I also know every one of you is wondering why. If after you've heard what I have to tell you, and you are reluctant . . . well I will leave it up to you to decide for yourself." Kay rose from the table. "In the meantime, I am sure most of you are hungry after your flight, so I made dinner reservations at a great restaurant in town called Curtains and besides I'm hungry. So if it's okay we'll . . ." She didn't get to finish before they all rose as one shouting. "Let's go!"

Chapter Twenty One

The women sat around the table at "Curtains" eating nachos as they drank margaritas and wine. Kay could hear the waiters as they argued with each other about who would serve them. It was not only how the women looked, but how they were with each other, like they had known each other for a long time, familiar.

The women, observed the owner of the restaurant, seem to be cut off from the rest of the patrons. The owner watched as one man started over but something made him take a step back like a force field surrounded them. He smiled. Each women whose hair, blond, brown, auburn, black and red with highlights complimented each of them individually. They made a lovely sight.

Kay was silent as she sipped her drink. She didn't want to think about what she had to tell them, she wanted to just take in all in. She was glad they were all here and she noticed that no one tried to out shine the other. Not even Kyla which was a first. Kyla always commanded a room. She was an ocean breeze in the morning. She and Kyla were both friends and cousins. Most people couldn't wait to get out of Mississippi, out from around their families, but like Kay, Kyla stayed.

Kay turned to her right where her friend Kristin was drinking a Heineken. Kristin was the sweetest person she knew, all six two of her. Along with all that height, Kristin was smart, beautiful, and electric in the courtroom; a lethal combination. Tonight however, she just looked like the girl next door.

Now her cousin Kaitlin always looked like she just stepped out the pages of Ebony. She had become a true California girl, a daredevil. Growing up in Mississippi you wouldn't think anybody would be a dare devil with things "as slow as molasses in the winter time" as her granny like to say. Then, she remembered all the things Kait got into when she was a kid. Maybe Kait was a dare devil after all. You dared and she did. Kait might look fragile to the outside world, but Kay knew her strength. And yes, she was a well renowned painter, but her strength, her true strength was her capacity for forgiveness. And right now, she thought Kaitlin was the bravest of all of them. Someone jostled her shoulders interrupting her thoughts.

Kaitlin bumped shoulders with Kay. "You haven't said anything since we got here. And right know you look like you were somewhere else. What are you thinking about?"

"About you," said Kay. "I was remembering all those times when were kids. How we would dare you to do something and you never hesitated."

"I went home with a lot of skinned knees as I remember."

Kay punched Kaitlin back. "But you did it anyway."

"Yeah I did, didn't I?"

"Don't I know it," said Kay. "I got blamed for most of it when we were kids."

"Tough ain't it Kay?"

They were both silent for a moment, then just started laughing. The others looked at them like they were idiots. They both said "What?"

"Is this a private joke or can anyone get in on it," said Karina.

"It's not private," Kay said as she sipped her drink. "Kaitlin and I were just talking about when we were kids and how daring she was."

"I remember it too," said Katie, "but I was too little to do what yall did. Although I remember that time we had to jump out of the tree house because of the snake. I don't know how we did it without breaking our necks."

"We were so young and foolish," Kay answered.

Kaitlin started laughing again picking up on her and Kay's earlier conversation. "You remember that time when Kay's doll got caught in the fire?"

"Do we!!" Kyla and Katie said together.

The others stopped talking. Everyone around the table stared at the three of them. "Ok tell us," said Kaila. "Kay never mentions anything about her childhood, so we're all ears."

Kay wondered why was it that every time she and her cousins got together they would bring up this story. Kay flinched. Apparently it still was a sore subject. All eyes were riveted on Kay. Blushing, Kay stammered. "They're not interested . . .,"

Ignoring Kay's protest, Katie raised her hand like one of her kids at school. "Me, Me," she pleaded. "Please let me tell it Kay."

Kay knew she was outnumbered, so she narrowed eyes at her cousins. "Okay go ahead," Kay murmured. *"I must be drunk."*

"Kay got a Barbie doll for Christmas one year and she named her Jasmin," started Katie. "She loved that doll. Anyway, My Aunt Michaela, Kay's mom didn't throw things in the trash. She burned them. She didn't like clutter of any kind. Back then you could burn things in your back yard. Aunt M. always said if she found any of our stuff just laying around she was going to burn them up.

One day when Aunt M. was outside burning trash, somehow Kay's doll ended up in the trash. I don't think she meant to burn Kay's doll but somehow it got in the fire. Anyway, when Kay found out, she came screaming into the house saying 'Jasmin is dead, Jasmin is dead' and crying those big crocodile tears as she held up what was left of Jasmin. The whole side of Jasmin's face was burned. Kay cried until she couldn't talk. Aunt M. apologized to her but nothing soothed Kay."

Kay interrupted. "It wasn't like that."

"Yes it was." Kyla reminded Kay as she took over the story. "Don't you remember the only reason you stop crying was because Kaitlin here suggested we have a funeral for Jasmin. Later that day we snuck into our houses not knowing our mothers had been watching and took their black dresses and hats they wore to church.

In Kay's back yard, there was this tiny hill, it really wasn't a hill it was a mound of dirt that must have be left over from the soil that had been turned in the back yard. Any way we formed a procession and started up that hill. We were singing a song we had heard in Sunday school. What was it?" Kyla snapped her finger. "Yeah, now I remember." Kyla started singing. "Walk with me Lord; come on a walk with me, while I am on this tedious journey . . ."

Katie joined in and finished the story. "Kaitlin picked some flowers which weren't anything but weeds and I got a shoebox. We dug a hole and placed Jasmin carefully in the graved. We mourned and sang for what seemed like hours until Kay felt better. It was hilarious when you think about it and the fact that our mothers skinned us alive for putting on their clothes."

Kay was blushing. "I was traumatized for a long time." She bit her lip and pouted. They all laughed.

Looking at her watch, Kay grabbed her coat and stood. "I think we've had enough reunion." Kay looked over at her cousins, "and telling stories."

The wait staff was starting to clean up. This was a nice lull Kay thought before the storm. She hoped everyone wouldn't bolt for the door when she told them exactly why she had summoned them.

*   *   *

When they made it back to Teresa's, one by one, they tumbled out the cars, dragging as they all headed for the door. When they all entered, Kay closed the door and locked it. Kay turned to her cousins, "you know where everything is. Kristin and Kyla are you staying here or going home."

Kyla didn't want to miss anything. "I think I'll stay."

"I think I will too," said Kristin.

Kay started to ask Kait but she knew what her answer would be. "Okay. Karina and Kaila, you can sleep upstairs in the room across hall from Katie and Kyla." Down the hallway she pointed . . . She went on and on, until everyone had been assigned a room. It felt like they were back in college living in the dorms.

As the women filed pass, they noticed all the baby pictures, tons of them. They all looked familiar but different. The babies looked like they were from all parts of the country the world it seemed. When Karina asked about them, Kay told her unbelievably, "They were all from right here in Mississippi." Karina and Kaila gawked but kept walking.

Kenya stared wide eyed, when she saw all of Kay's aunts. In her family it was just her and her parents. She could only imagine the laughter and the tears that must have filled these walls when they all got together.

Chapter Twenty Two

After everyone had gone to their rooms, Kay went through the house and made sure everything was secure. She stopped by the front window deep in thought. She had asked a lot of her cousins and her friends. Friends she had not seen in years. Some she hadn't even spoken to in all those years either, but in her heart, she knew it was right. She couldn't turn her back on her grandmother.

Her heart beat faster, she needed them to help her, help her granny, and help the world. Funny she thought, then changed her mind, no, not so funny. Somehow she knew she was meant to find them. What if she couldn't? Her world was shifting, changing. Her self—imposed solitary life was about to unravel.

Kay leaned against the window and bowed her head in the still of the night where the silence was all she could feel and prayed. Prayed that her friends wouldn't bolt after they heard what she had to say. And if they agreed, they would all get through it and none of them would get hurt. She lifted her head and with weariness she suddenly felt, headed upstairs to her own room. Closing the door, she noticed the maroon backpack in the corner. Its torso covered in patches from over forty countries. How her backpack had gotten there she wondered. She must have brought it to the house to show her grandmother all the places she had gone. It had been a while since she traveled. Why hadn't she taken it home?

Kay lay down on the bed, rubbing her hands along the threads of the quilt. All the beds had quilts on them. All her aunts made quilts. Staring at it, she realized it was the one her grandmother said was given to her by the midwife called Melana. The quilt was midnight blue like the ocean. She felt along the "ticks." They were called ticks because of how the yarned was tied in small knots and sewn in straight lines on the patches of the quilts. The ticks looked like tiny trees.

Kay got up and lit the candle by the bed. Granny loved candles as much as she loved the quilts. When she struck a match to the candle the room became a soft glow. The shadows played along the walls of the room. Kay always felt as if her grandmother's house, this place was really her home. She felt so much love. It seeped in every corner of the room. Every time she entered, she felt the same hope on a wave of happiness. She had felt something else, too, but didn't know what it was and she wasn't quite sure what it meant. She was scared, she admitted to herself. She was about to lay down again when she heard someone knocking.

*   *   *

"Kay, are you up?" Karina whispered at the door.

"Karina?" Kay swung her legs to the floor and walked to the door and peeked out. "Come on in." Kay stepped aside and allowed Karina in. Karina came into the room and sat beside Kay on the bed. She held up the box. "Cara, have you forgotten what you told me to bring with me."

She had forgotten, almost. "Let me see." The box was the same as when she first saw it. She looked at Karina. "Is the shop the same as when we were there before?"

"Yes, it is the same." Karina handed the box to Kay and she placed the box in Teresa's cedar chest at the foot of the bed and locked it. It would be safe there. For some reason, she wasn't ready to reveal it to the rest of them. "Thanks for bringing it to me Karina. I really appreciate you coming."

Karina didn't question Kay as she locked the chest. She knew Kay had her reasons for not showing everyone the box. "I would not have missed it. It seems so unreal when you told me. What did you tell the others?"

"I didn't tell them a whole lot, but they were willing to come anyway."

"I have wanted to come to see you for a long time," said Karina, "so this is good." *And I need to tell her about Lori.*

Kay didn't think Karina would believe it was so great once she heard all her grandmother had said. Kay gave her friend a hug. "Again, I'm glad you're here."

Karina was glad too, but she needed to tell Kay about Lori while she had the nerve. She didn't know where to start, so she just sighed, here goes nothing. Kay . . . *Cara* . . . I"

"What is it *rina*? You're shaking."

Karina grabbed Kay's hand and blurted out. "I have fallen in love."

"That's great, who is he? Is he from Italy, of course he is, Venice is the city of love and romance."

"No, Cara it is not a he . . . she . . . I mean . . . her name is Lori." She sat waiting in judgment.

Kay tightened the grip that Karina had on her hand, and wrapped her arm around Karina's shoulder. "I might live in Mississippi, but it doesn't mean I'm homophobic. You took care of me when I was hurt. You invited me to you home and we became friends, although I haven't been much of a friend lately. It doesn't matter to me. I love you. I don't judge my friends or anyone for that matter. Besides, you can't help who you fall in love with. And seeing the happiness on you face she must be some kind of special."

Yes she is. So relieved, Karina hugged Kay back and kissed her cheek. "*Gracias, ami,* I love you too. I think I will . . . Kay do you mind if we keep this to ourselves for now?"

"Sure." Karina stood and started for the door and turned. "Thanks again," she said, as she closed the door.

Kay watched Karina as she slipped out. She got up blew out the candles, smiling as she turned on her side, "*wow, I didn't see that coming*"

* * *

The house was quiet, but thoughts of the women inside were playing back in the darkness.

Kaila heard ringing. It was her cell phone. She turned over. Kenya, who she was bunking with, seemed to be asleep. Who could be calling her at . . . she looked at her watch 3:30 in the morning for God's sake. She sat up with a start, stared at her cell phone ringing. She flipped it on. "Hello," she whispered.

"Hey baby," Tom said. "I'm sorry for calling so late, but you didn't call when you got there. When I called your cell and you didn't answer, I got worried."

"Oh honey, I forgot to turn it back on when I got off the plane. Then Kay took us out to dinner and I didn't remember." She never forgot. Kaila looked over at Kenya "That's all right, you can call me anytime." She suddenly felt sad. She missed him. Very seldom were they apart.

"I miss you, too" Tom was reading her mind like always. "I just wanted to tell you I love you and I'm glad you made it okay."

Kaila caught her breath. She was hopelessly in love. She always felt him.

"Hey, have fun and call me tomorrow, okay?"

"I will. I promise, love you." Kaila closed her cell phone happy she turned on a side and was soon sound asleep.

In the other room, Kristin was trying to get comfortable in a strange bed. Why didn't she go to her mother's house? She knew why. She wasn't ready to face her mother.

*   *   *

Unbeknownst to the women in Teresa's house in another part of the country Kris Mitchell was tossing and turning, trying to get comfortable. The dream was so real. She had felt them. Kris shook her head. She needed all the rest she could get. She had to convince herself to go back home, face her mother, and somehow prove to herself that she was okay. She would know tomorrow when the car reached its destination. She had decided to ask her grandmother if she could stay with her. She hadn't talked to her family in a long time.

Kris knew she could never keep her emotions hidden from her grandmother. Teresa saw too much, too smart for her on good. This time though she hoped to pull it off. She hugged her pillow and hoped for a sleep filled night.

Chapter Twenty Three

"Did everyone have a good night's sleep?" Kay asked the next morning as she stood in the kitchen. She had gotten up early and made coffee. Everyone nodded except Karina. She looked like she hadn't slept at all. "There is coffee and if you want breakfast help yourself. I tried to get what I thought you would like. After breakfast we will listen . . ." Before Kay could finish, someone was knocking at the door.

Kaila was nearest the door, so she got up and went to answer. She looked through the peep hole. "There's a woman at the door," she told Kay. "And she doesn't look too happy."

Puzzled, Kay went to the door. When she opened it she looked past Kaila. Kay couldn't believe her eyes. There standing on Granny's porch was the last person she thought she would see. Maybe she just happened to be in the neighborhood . . . not a chance. Kris never just happens to be anywhere, there was always a reason. She didn't do things on the spur of the moment. Kris had been gone from home a long time, why had she suddenly showed up?

Kaila looked at Kay and whispered "Who is that?"

Kay started to say something, but Kris strolled past her like she was expected.

"Well, well, well, cousin," said Kyla. "What brings you back to this neck of the woods as you so eloquently called it when you slammed the door never to return?"

Kris knew her cousins were staring at her like they had seen a ghost, a nice looking ghost. Kris was tall almost six feet. She had played in the WNBA. She had finished first in assists and free throws. When Kris was in high school she broke all kinds of records that so far, no one was even close to breaking. Although older, Kris had the body of thirty year old, broad shoulders, nice figure. She looked around the room. What were her cousins and these strange women doing at her grandmother's house? Where was Granny? The only person she recognized besides her cousins was Kenya and she hadn't seen her since Kenya went to Texas. She, Kay and Kenya had all been friends once. She suspected that Kay and Kenya still were.

"What are you doing here?" asked Katie.

"I could ask you the same thing. What's going on Kay? Where is Granny?"

Kay didn't answer her because she was shocked that Kris didn't know where Teresa was. Why didn't she know? It wasn't like Kris lived in another country. She turned to the others watching, heads moving back and forth between Kay and Kris like they were at a soccer game. "Everybody this is my sister Kris."

Everyone said hi.

Kris could feel the tension in the room. She had questions and she knew Kay was reading her. She looked over at Kenya but didn't say anything else. Maybe latter she would talk to Kenya.

"You know you are welcome here, after all this is your grandmother's house, too." Kris acted as if she didn't hear Kay. She backed back out of the door.

"If it's okay with you Kay, I think I'll go get my things." She turned and walked out the door. *That went well.* Again, what were all these people doing here?

Kay watched her sister leave. Kris had come home. Why did she come to Granny's? Why not mother's? As she watched her sister go back outside, Kay said, "Everyone please take a sit in the dining room. I need to call my grandmother." She hurried upstairs. Before Teresa could say hello, Kay blurted out. "She's here."

"Whose here?" Teresa smiled. She knew who Kay was referring to.

"Granny did you hear me?"

"Yes, I heard you. I'm old not deaf."

"I know that," Kay laughed. "I just thought you would . . . wait a minute you knew all along didn't you, you little sneak. You knew Kris would show up." When her grandmother didn't answer right away, Kay hesitated. "You did, didn't you?"

"Yes," her grandmother answered. When Kay didn't respond, she said. "Kay honey, are you still there? Maybe I have lost my hearing," she chuckled.

"Oh no Granny you haven't. Granny, did you tell Kris you were at the Center? When she came in the house she acted like she didn't know. Why didn't anyone tell Kris?" Kay suddenly felt guilty. She hadn't said anything either. She figured her mother or her grandmother had said something. "I guess I made this announcement for nothing," Kay said.

"No, you did right to call. I knew but it was only a feeling. I wasn't certain. And I don't know why Kris didn't know. I guess I thought your mother would have told her. I am sure it will work out." Changing the subject, Teresa said, "Have you played the tape? Kay?"

Why didn't Kris not knowing about their grandmother bother Teresa? Kay wondered. "What? Uh, no, I didn't play the tape. It was late when everyone arrived yesterday. I was just about to play it when Kris came walking through the door."

Teresa knew Kris would be upset when she found out that she was at the center. Why hadn't anyone told Kris? Not only that, after Kay played the tape, Teresa didn't know how Kris would react.

"Granny, I had better get back down stairs," said Kay. "I'll call you when we're ready to come see you tomorrow." Before Kay hung up, she said to Teresa, "There aren't any more surprises are there?"

Teresa chuckled. "I think you've had enough surprises for now."

"You're right about that, said Kay. "Bye Granny." Kay hung up the phone and sat on the bed. Well I guess we are *all* here. Kay was tired not physically but mentally. Kay picked up the recorder and placed the tape inside. Again she hoped when the women downstairs heard the tape, they wouldn't all head for the door.

*   *   *

When Kay walked into the room, everyone looked up at her expectantly. She noticed the seat at the head of table was not occupied, she smiled. Kris had returned and was standing next to the only other empty chair facing her cousin Kaitlin. "Okay, now that we are," she looked at Kris, "all here . . ." When Kris took her seat, Kay placed the tape recorder in the middle of the table."

Kris sat down. What was going on? And why did Kay have a tape recorder? She almost opened her mouth to ask, but thought better of it. She had seen the look on the faces of the women now sitting around the table. It was if they were bracing themselves . . . for what she didn't know. She wondered if she was welcomed. Kris didn't let on, but she was glad she had come home. She thought maybe that was the reason she had been having those dreams. She loved Kay. After all, they were sisters. Even though Kris was the oldest, she had always looked up to Kay. There were a lot of hurt feelings when she left. She had a lot of making up to do. She looked over at Kay again; *yes she had a lot of making up to do*. Kris brought her attention back. She almost missed what Kay was saying or the way Kris hand trembled.

"Again," Kay said. "I want to thank all of you for coming. I know I sounded mysterious on the phone." When Kay looked around the room everyone was nodding. "I hope when you hear this you will understand why I asked you to come."

She sat down and pressed the button that said "Play." Ninety minutes later there was only silence around the table. It was so quiet when the tape clicked signaling the end, everyone jumped.

*   *   *

They sat there, mouths open, the silence echoing off the walls of Teresa's house. This revelation had them clamoring for answers to questions they never asked. No one had one.

Kay spoke first. "I know it's a lot to take in . . ."

"A lot," Kris said. What was going on, first all these people and now this? She couldn't keep quiet. "Do you know what granny is asking you to do? And why isn't she here since she recorded this." She didn't know what to think. She almost fainted when Kay turned on the recorder and she heard her grandmother's voice. *Oh God what's happening? This is crazy and only a lunatic would even attempt it.* "Kay you don't really believe this do you?" She was almost yelling. What could her grandmother be thinking? She couldn't wait until she showed up.

Kay held her hand up to ward off Kris's rant. "Since, I don't remember inviting you; I don't see why it concerns you. Kay knew she was being harsh with Kris and knew Kris was, according to her grandmother, was meant to be here, too. She was still mad that Kris hadn't been home in years. And that she hadn't bothered to find out where Granny was.

"Although I hate to agree with my prodigal cousin," said Kyla. "It does sound crazy, not to mention bordering on illegal."

Loosening the lump in her throat Kay tried to break the tension. "Well . . ., we have Kristin," said Kay. "She's a lawyer."

Kristin didn't say anything at first. She was an observer. In the court room she always watched everyone. She could read people. She had to. Without this skill, she might as well hang up her shingle. "Look, I do not, I repeat, I do not want to end up getting anybody out of jail."

Kay looked around the table at all the faces. Faces she had known, some since birth, but all a part of her own landscape. Kay finally said, "Can't you feel it? When I called to ask you to come, didn't you feel compelled to come?"

Kaitlin had felt it. She remembered the rock with her initials on it. Her heart jumped and she waited for the pain. To her surprise, she didn't feel it. Kaitlin looked at Kay. When Kay looked back, *are you okay*? Kaitlin nodded.

Kaila mused. She had felt something, too. "I might have felt something, she said to Kay, "but who's to say it wasn't just my imagination. I have never in my life been to Mississippi or any of my family. I need facts. I'm a scientist. As a matter of fact, I probably should get back to NASA and continue my research project."

"Kaila, you of all people should know anything is possible," said Kay. "In the sixties a man landed on the moon. Before that happened, people thought it was just a fantasy, now look at NASA. They are sending unmanned shuttle craft to Mars. Shooting rockets into the moon, and what about the International Space Station, so don't tell me it's not possible."

"That's different," Kaila said. "We've been studying space for a long time. There are published reports and documented evidence to back up those reports."

Kaitlin interrupted both of them. Looking confused she asked. "Why didn't she tell our aunts, our mothers?"

"Yeah, why didn't she?" said Kyla. "All our lives, we've been told our grandmothers were all close."

"I don't know," Kay said. "I will ask her when I . . . when we see her. Granny can be stubborn, but she is not one to imagine things."

"I listened to the tape like the rest of you," said Katie. "I don't have a clue what it all means and I'm supposed to be the gifted one," she teased.

Kay took the tape out. No one had touched it. Clutching it she said "I think we're all here because we were chosen."

"How can you know?" said Kenya. "You were the one that called us."

Kay remembered how she felt when she started calling them. Somehow she knew she had to. She had been hiding behind her work for a long time, alone and sometimes lonely. Right now she felt like running back to that place. She pushed those feelings to the back of her mind. The women around the table, needed to be here, at least she hope she had made the right choices. By the way some of them were acting, maybe she hadn't. She had to convince them. She would talk to Kris later. Kay looked at them so intensely until they all moved back just a little, not even aware that they had. "Didn't you notice it?"

"What?" They all said at once.

She had been surprised that no one else had noticed it. "Our names, everyone at this table name begins with K." Their mothers, their grandmothers, none of their names began with K, but everyone here all had the same letter K.

They all started talking at once, but Kay held up her hand, silencing them. "I'm not asking you, or anyone else around this table to break the law. But, I am asking for your help. If not, I know Granny will understand if you didn't want to do it. We can forget all about it and go out and have a reunion with friends and family." Kay didn't sound at all convincing.

"Yeah right, we've just heard that if we don't do what your grandmother asked, the world is going to turn upside down. And you just stand there shrugging your shoulder," said Kristin.

"I do know how important it is," said Kay, "but I will not ask you to risk your lives, or your livelihood if you are not willing." Kay sat back in the chair waiting. It was fight or flight. She didn't have to wait long.

"I will help you," Karina said.

"You can count me in too," Kaitlin added.

Inside Kay shouted. Thanks, thanks for persuading her *"Jake"*

Kaila sat thinking about what Kay said. Her research, but what if it was true what Kay's grandmother said, shoot it didn't compare to this. She would ask her project team to take over the research, for now. Besides, she hadn't had a vacation since last year. This was as good a time as any to start. Kaila looked up at Kay "Make it so Number One."

Kay laughed, *well, that's three.*

Not to be out done, Kyla raised her hand. "If their doing this so am I."

Kristin realized she needed to say something. All she could think about the remark that Kris made about it being illegal. It was funny or not so funny. She imagined walking into the Matlin County Jail and demanding the release these women from incarceration.

Kristin mother's face suddenly flashed in Kristen's mind. Had her mother changed at all? Twisting her hair she thought, "Everybody changes at some time, right?" Well, she didn't come back here for mother. She came for Kay. She wanted to be a part of whatever Kay was purposing. To be a part of whatever this was. She looked at Kay. "Count me in too."

Kay looked at Kristin and winked, *five*.

When no one else volunteered, Kay said, "Maybe when you have met and talked to my grandmother maybe that would help you to make up your mind." They all nodded. "Okay, I guess we should go." According to the clock over the kitchen sink, it was almost eleven and the residents at the nursing home would be getting ready for lunch soon. Kay wanted to get there before then. She knew they'd all wanted answers, but with her grandmother, you never knew. If everything she said was true then, it was important for them to meet Teresa.

They all started out the door when Kris grabbed Kay's arm. "Kay, wait where are you all going?"

"We're going to the Community Center."

"Why are you going the nursing home?"

"That's where she is."

"That's where who is?"

"Granny, that's who, if you called home once in a while you would know this." Kay headed for the car.

Kris wanted to cry. Why didn't she know? She followed Kay out the door. "How long Kay?" Kay left Kris standing outside. She got in her car and closed the door, signaling everyone to follow. Kris didn't think she could face her grandmother, but she got into her car and followed them anyway. "Maybe . . ."

Chapter Twenty Four

The women pulled up at the nursing home, and got out. One by one they looked around at the place. Kris parked her car but didn't get out. She watched everyone go in. Kay looked back at her. What did she see on Kris's face, disappointment or understanding? Kris didn't move. It was all she could do to process everything. "I'll just wait right here," she said to herself.

Kay had to press a buzzer to get in. The nurse or receptionist opened the door. As soon as they started through the door, they saw dozens of old people and some that didn't look so old.

There was no way they could all fit in Teresa's room, so Kay went to ask the administrator to see if they could use the conference room. Kay's family used it once when all of them decided to show up at the same time. Kay came back saying it was okay. While the others were directed to the conference room, Kay went to get her grandmother.

No one said a word as they waited for Kay. The room was none descript except a picture of Martin Luther King and Medgar Evers, two of the most famous civil rights leaders in the nation, hanging prominently on the walls.

Kristin stared at the picture of Medgar Evers. She remembered her parents talking about him. Telling Kristin, "See what happens when you try to change things that don't need changing." Looking at the pictures reminded her of why she hadn't come home.

They all turned towards the door as Kay pushed Teresa into the room. Those who had never seen Kay's grandmother looked stunned.

*   *   *

The women kept silent and watched the woman with the silver hair flowing down her back. A caramel and coca latte was Kaila's first thoughts of the elegant woman sitting in the wheel chair. When she smiled, her eyes sparkled like topaz. Shell shocked she didn't know what to say. Teresa didn't look like any ninety six year old person she had ever seen.

Trying not to stare, Karina was prepared to see a dowdy old lady. Teresa, they had been told, was ninety six. How could this be, Teresa didn't looked anything like she imagined.

Teresa smiled as she watched their faces. *I guess they were looking for some old lady.* She looked at them as they kept staring. She imagined what some were thinking, how . . . ? Teresa had thought the same thing about Melana and Meira when she first met them. They looked even younger.

Kay and the rest of her cousins were the only ones that didn't look like they were in a time warp. They were used to it. Kyla and Katie got up from the table and kissed Teresa on the cheek and returned to their seats.

She leaned forward and called each of them by name, even Kaila and Karina.

They all looked at Kay. Kay threw up her hands "I didn't tell her anything." She was as surprised as the rest of them.

Teresa looked around the room and frowned. Kay waited, she knew what was coming. Teresa eyes bored into her. "Kay, where's Kris?" Kay fidgeted as she answered her grandmother. "Kris is in the car . . . she didn't get out. I think she's upset because she didn't know you were here."

Eyes still boring into Kay "Go get her. She still needs to hear this."

"I didn't even know she was coming," said Kay. "How am I gonna . . . what if she won't come?"

"Don't you worry, she'll come," was all Teresa said. Kris got up. She'd never disobey her grandmother.

*   *   *

Outside, Kay knocked on the window of Kris's car. Talking through the glass, Kay said, "Roll down the window Kris." Shaking her head like a bobble head doll, "I can't. Tell Granny I'm not coming in, I'll come by later." Kris felt so bad. Her grandmother in a nursing home, what happened while she was gone? She heard Kay's voice *"If you had come home sometime, you would have known."* Kris wanted to cry.

Kay pulled on the door handle. "Come on Kay, you need to come inside. Granny is insisting and you know how she can be. She will clam up and won't say anything."

95

Reluctantly, Kris rolled down the window. "That's fine by me. Remember I wasn't a part of this."

Kay shook her head. "Not fine, you've got to come in. She wants to see you." Kris was scared. Kay could see it in her face. She knew Kris must be feeling guilty for staying away and now when she finally returns, Granny was here. "Don't you want to know how she's doing?" Kay voice got softer. "Come on Kris, it's going to be okay."

Kris shook her head as she opened the car door and got out. Bracing herself, like she was heading for the firing squad, Kris ducked her head and followed Kay into the center. When Kay dragged Kris in the room, what she saw surprised her. Everybody was talking to her grandmother like they were family. Her grandmother had done it again. Teresa had a way about her.

Kris started to sit down, but remembered her manners. Still too shocked to say anything, she kissed her grandmother on the cheek. Teresa patted her on the shoulders. Kris sat down in the seat next to the door. Her face said she was hoping for a quick exit.

Kaitlin sat watching the exchange between Kris and her aunt wishing her own grandmother was alive. She knew if Grandma M was alive, she would have buffered her against her mother. Her grandmother would have liked Jake and she had no doubt that she would have fell in love with Alain.

Katie on the other hand, was having the time of her life. She looked around the room. This was way better than a book and a dirty movie. She knew her aunt would say what she wanted in her own time. One thing Katie remembered about Teresa was that she had the patience of a saint. Somehow, Katie had gotten that temperament from Teresa. As a teacher, she had to be. If patient is a virtue, then her aunt was as virtuous as they came. She couldn't wait to get started.

Kay was watching her grandmother. She hoped Teresa would get on with it.

*   *   *

Teresa was glad she asked Kay to help her. She thought *I will not die with this on my soul.* She looked around as the women stared at her expectantly. Teresa had helped to bring her nieces and their mothers into the world, helped to take care of some of them, too, until she was unable to take care of herself. Kay had chosen well. Teresa knew she would. Teresa tapped on the table. "I know what I have asked you to do," Teresa addressed those seated around the table, "will be both challenging and difficult."

"That's an understatement," said Kris.

Ignoring Kris's remarks, Teresa continued. "I know you're wondering how you will accomplish this." She spread opens her arms as if she was giving them hugs. "All of you . . . oh my," she said suddenly remembering something. "My purse I forgot, Kay could you run to my room and get it?"

When Kay returned with the purse, Teresa looked relieved. Kay handed it to her and sat down. From her purse Teresa reached in and pulled out a key. "This is the key to my safe deposit box at the bank. What's today?" She was not asking, just thinking aloud, but someone answered.

"Saturday," said Kenya.

The bank was closed. She turned to Kay. "First thing Monday morning I want you to go to Matlin National and use this key to open my box, remove the contents. I'll call Peggy and send a note with my signature to let her know you have permission to open it." Peggy or Mrs. C was what most people called the president of the bank.

When Teresa handed over the key to Kay she said, "Again, I am thankful that Kay has such wonderful friends who are willing to help her or to at least hear her out. I know everything that you have heard so far sounds unbelievable. If it had not happen to me I would not have believed it either. As I said on the tape I was so young when I . . .," Teresa waved her hand "Well you know all of that so I will leave it to you to decide. If you decide to help her, I will be here to help as much as I can." She turned to Kay. "You can take me back to my room, now." Teresa had said all she would say. It was now up the women in this room.

Karina, Kaila, Kristin and Kenya all stood and walked up to Teresa. One by one, they hugged her and kissed her cheek. This surprised Teresa. Maybe they wanted to see if she was real. Kay and her cousins were equally surprised by the looks on their faces. It was as if Teresa had already captured the other women's hearts.

Teresa watched the women as they filed out the room. Kris was trying to get pass the others. Teresa had seen the look on her granddaughter's face. She stopped Kay and summoned Kris before she could bolt out the door. "Kris, please come here." Dutifully Kris stood before Teresa. Teresa whispered as she put her hand on Kris's arm. "It's going to be all right. I'm sorry no one told you I was here. I would have tried to find you myself if I had known. I'm just glad you're here now. I love you. And Kris, trust this, trust yourself."

Kris tried not to cry but tears formed anyway as she nodded, "Ok." When she turned to leave, Kris looked over her shoulder at her grandmother and mouthed "*I love you too.*"

Kay, who was close enough hear them, wasn't so sure everything would be alright. She kept quiet as she pushed her grandmother back to her room.

*   *   *

After everyone left the Center, Teresa sat looking at the walls again but this time she was happy. She was so happy to meet all of Kay's friends. She was also happy to see her great nieces, especially her granddaughter Kris. She knew everything would be okay now that she had passed this on the Kay. It had only been two weeks ago when Teresa started to remember. For Teresa, it was a lifetime ago, memory just waiting to be unlocked from her consciousness.

Chapter Twenty Five

Matlin, Two weeks ago

Startled, Teresa sat up in the bed. Everything, all of it, came back, the house in the woods and the ruins. What had been asked of her in the ruins that night had all come back. She knew what she had to do. She wouldn't be the one to finish what she and the others had started but she understood that night that it was not for her to finish.

Teresa grabbed the note book that she kept by her bed and tried to write it all down, but her hands once steady as she brought firsts into the world, now shook. She needed to find another way. As much as Teresa hated technology of any kind, she knew it was the only way she could explain.

She paged the nurses' station and when one of the nurses came to Teresa room, she asked the nurse to let her use a tape recorder. At first the nurse hesitated shocked. Teresa convinced the nurse by telling her she wanted to record the history of her family, while she was still able to remember. Oral history was the way Negros had passed their history down from generation to generation. All though still a little wary, the nurse relented. The nurse returned with the tape recorder and showed Teresa how to use it.

Time stilled as she talked into the machine . . . She was no longer in the tiny room.

*   *   *

She searched frantically for the guardian. Nothing was there. It was as if the house in the woods had never existed, that Teresa had imagined it all. Only darkness resided in the place where all life had been illuminated. Her hands had started to hurt the pain almost unbearable.

Teresa cried out achingly, silently mourning the lost. She felt empty for the first time in her life, the hollowness invading every cell of her body. She looked up to the sky with tears falling in pools on her clothes.

Teresa hung her head as she headed to the ruins. Even though automobiles were everywhere she rode in the carriage. She would never bring a car to the sacred place. The light had gone out and the trees stood still nothing would be as it was before. She was sure of it. She dried her tears and lifted her head.

The women in the ruin had erased Teresa's fears that fateful night when she had received the message. The message she must now pass on to her *daughter's daughter.* Teresa had looked back at the ruins that day knowing she would never return, not in this life anyway. She didn't have to, hers would be only to hold destiny intact. Teresa left the ruins that day, knowing *the woman in the woods* would return.

*   *   *

Teresa pushed the stop button on the machine. Kay would make the journey. She would be the one to find them. Teresa also knew Kay would be shocked and scared at first, but her granddaughter was always a curious child and that curiosity would help her make the decision.

Teresa gripped the wheelchair, she hated being out of control. She had to prepare herself for whatever was coming. First though, she had to prepare Kay. Teresa placed the tape and the recorder inside the night stand and looked over at the empty bed once occupied by her sister Belinda.

Chapter Twenty Six

There was much discussion after Kay and the others returned to Kay's grandmothers,' but it was decided that Kay alone would to go to the bank. Kay didn't want too many curious eyes on her friends.

As she left the house the next day she knew her friends were in good hands; her cousin Kyla would take care of them and Kris too, once her cousin got over Kris's defection.

Kay looked around as she entered the bank on Main Street. She knew all the people who worked at the bank. Some she had gone to school with. Like everything else in town, things were past down from generation to generation. The tellers, the loan officers all were daughters and sons of the people who worked there before.

Once in the bank she went directly to the office of the bank's president. Ms. C as everyone called her had been president of Matlin National Bank since Kay was old enough to know that's where people put their money. She peeked in the office of Ms. C's secretary, "Hi Wanda."

A blond head looked up at Kay. "Oh hi Kay, Ms. C is waiting for you, go right on in." When Kay raised her hand to knock Wanda said, "You don't have to knock."

Kay knocked anyway. She always knocked even when doors were open. Her mother and so did her grandmother told her. "Doors open didn't always mean come in, so out of respect for the person on the other side of the door always knock. Then you'd know for sure if you were invited." She knocked on the door frame. A women who didn't look a day over sixty looked up and smiled at Kay, "Hi little one."

Why couldn't people stop calling her that? She was a grown woman. Living in a small town can be a pain she thought. "I am just fine Ms C. "My grandmother . . ."

"I know," Ms C said. "Teresa called me earlier. She told me to personally escort you to the safe. Teresa and I have been friends for a long time despite the age difference. She knows I would have done it, even if she hadn't asked. But as she so dutifully told me over the phone, she just wanted to make sure her wishes were carried out." Ms C shook her head as if remembering some long ago moment. By the way she smiled when she looked at Kay, it was a pretty happy one.

Ms C asked Kay to sign the log and she followed her to a room in the back of the building. To Kay surprise, Ms C didn't go to where the boxes usually were; instead she proceeded to another room further in the back. Funny Kay didn't remember this room. She was sure of it because she also had a safe deposit box at the bank.

Ms C kept walking. When they entered the room, along the back wall, was a dozen small boxes. On closer inspection she saw that the numbers on the boxes were spelled out in Greek letters. As she watched she remembered that there were no numbers on her grandmother's key. She didn't think anything of it at the time. She just assumed the number had just worn down. She was trying to understand why, when Ms C coughed.

"Do you have the key?" Ms C asked.

Kay held up the key. When Kay started to hand it over, she noticed the key ring for the first time. It looked like it was made of some strange metal; she didn't have time to digest this information before she gave it to Ms C.

Ms C opened the box and was bending down to retrieve the metal box inside. To Kay surprise, the box was not the pea green long narrow box like the one she had. It was red, red like rubies. Ms C didn't say anything when she handed over the box. She asked Kay if she needed a private room to view the contents. Kay nodded.

When Ms C closed the door to the room, Kay sat down and just stared at the box. She thought *Pandora's Box* as she studied it. The box was heavy. She took a deep breath and opened it. The box was warm. This startled her. She let the lid snap back into place and stared at it for a while longer. "Okay Kay, get it together. It is only a box, albeit unusual, but it's still a box."

When Kay finally had control of her nervousness, she lifted the lid again. Something was wrapped in material that made her think of rose petals, velvet rose petals, was a book. It looked like a bank book. When she opened it a shiver ran down her back. It was dated back to the late 1800. "How could this be," she mumbled. She looked at some of the amounts.

At least she thought that's what they were. There were rows and rows of numbers.

Where did her grandmother get all this money? She picked up the book. Underneath the book Kay saw them. There they were the hearts, one wooden heart one glass heart. She closed her hands around the hearts and put them along with the book in her bag. Her grandmother had told her when Kay had wheeled her back in the room that she would know what to do when the time came. She put the bag on her shoulder and walked out the door to wait on Ms C to come and let her out the area.

*   *   *

When she made it back to her grandmother's, everyone was waiting anxiously for her. Kenya was sitting by the fireplace with her feet on an ottoman. Kaitlin and Kaila sat on the couch facing the television neither where really watching. It looked to Kay like the television was watching them. On the other side of the room Kyla and Karina were playing scrabble

Kris was sitting on the edge of the chair facing the kitchen. The same one she had sat on since she arrived. She looked like she was about ready to bolt. She wasn't smiling just looked bored.

Kay wasn't fooled. She knew Kris. She knew that look. It said "I am ready to go back home and I'm sure as hell wasn't going to do what she wants . . ."

When Kris realized Kay was staring she tried to smile but it didn't quite make it to her eyes. When Kris smiled, truly smiled her whole face glowed. Her eyes would be shiny and crinkled. It made her look like a little girl. Kay missed Kris's smile but she knew it would probably be a long time before she would see it at again *she hoped not.*

"What?" Kris asked.

Kay shook her head," Nothing." She was glad her friends were willing, well most of them, to help her. It was a testament to the power of friends especially girlfriends. She knew she would not attempt this alone.

They watched Kay place the bag she had brought from the bank on the table. She emptied the contents. They all gasped the same reaction she had had earlier. They looked at the book as if it would come alive. Kay had removed the hearts.

Carefully Kyla picked it up. Her eyes got wider as she turned each page of the deposit book. She didn't say anything. Kay kept silent and slowly one by one, they each picked up the book, first, the eyes, and then the silence. You could actually hear the shuddering of the leaves as a breeze floated into the house. When Kristin opened the book she asked. "Are all these numbers deposits?"

"I think they are." Kay examined the book, again leafing through the pages. She still couldn't believe it. When she got to the last page, it looked odd. The page was folded at the corner. She unfolded it and discovered it was two pages. The corner was folded the way people use to do when they didn't have a stapler. Folded in a triangle and torn in two places half way down the triangle creating a sort of flap and then it was folded backwards. This made a neat clip but the paper was torn which would not be acceptable today. She carefully unfolded the flap and slid her finger into the hole, out popped out a smaller piece of paper. On it someone had writing a name.

When she went back through the pages she noticed all had hidden piece of papers. Carefully they took all the pieces of paper out and placed them on the table. Below each name there seem to be symbols or something. They were studying the notes, when Karina cleared her throat they all jumped then laugh at how they reacted. "Okay," Kay said, "we need to find out what this all means."

"Why didn't your grandmother tell us about this," Kaila asked.

Kay suspected her grandmother didn't know about this little surprise or did she? "I think if she would have known, she would have told us."

Katie, who was the historian of the group and had studied ancient languages in college, picked up one of the pieces of paper. When Katie looked closely she thought she saw a picture of some kind. "Hey Kay, does Aunt Teresa have a magnifying glass?"

"I think she does." Kay went to the sitting room where her grandmother did her sewing and found the magnifying glass in her sewing bag. The bag was where it always was on the small table near her grandmother's rocking chair, she paused as she remembered lying on the floor near the fire and listening to her grandmother as she sang while she sewed. She grabbed it and brought it back.

Katie took the glass and held it to the paper. When she looked she saw tiny hands. She was almost sure. She showed it to Kay. "Don't you see what it means?" said Katie"

"No," they all said.

"Aunt Teresa was a midwife. And if you were listening, so were the two old ladies that she trained under." Kay looked at the paper again. Then she handed it back to Katie. "What are the other symbols representing?" Below the hands were more numbers.

"They look like dates to me," said Kenya.

"No they . . ." Kristin picked up the magnifying glass, closed one eye and peered. "Look, here see how they seem to form shapes."

"Wait a minute," Katie pulled out her iphone. She started tapping. Soon she found what she was looking for. "It's places." She picked another piece of paper from the book. "Kay, remember Aunt Teresa would read to us when we were little."

"So," said Kris, "she always read us stories."

Well remember how when she read this one book she would say how it reminded her of places and she would start writing in a book.

"I remember now," said Kay"

Katie handed the book back to Kay. "Was it this book?"

Kay took the book and looked at it in earnest, "Maybe." While everyone was trying to figure out the book, Kay was wondering if she should show them the hearts. Seeing the hearts, Kay knew her grandmother was not crazy. Everything she said was real.

Chapter Twenty Seven

"We need a plan," said Katie. "We need someone to search the Internet and any other resources available." Feeling the excitement in her voice, Katie started talking faster. "First, we need to figure out what those symbols are on the bank book. Two, we need to replay Teresa's tape again to see if we can make sense of some of the things. If we are still unsure, we can always clarify it with Aunt Teresa. Kay, do you remember if there is a Mormon church in Mississippi?" Katie was in her element.

"Whoa cousin," Kyla said to Katie. "Where's all this coming from. We haven't heard a peep from you all this time and now you're acting like a dynamo. What lit your fuse?"

Katie didn't know why but she had been on board from the start. Being a teacher she was naturally curious. Kay had summoned all of them there *except for Kris* and it felt right, that all of them needed to be here, even Kris. Then she thought, "Who was she to start taking over?" She looked over at Kay and then at Kyla. Embarrassed, she said, "sorry if I sound like I'm taking over."

Kay didn't hesitate. Grinning she said, "Go ahead dynamo you have the floor."

"Thanks." With Kay's approval, Katie continued. "As I was saying, the reason I asked is because the Mormons kept records of the entire census dating back to the early 1800."

"We don't have a Mormon church here," said Kyla. Kay agreed.

"I know where one is," said Kaitlin. "There's one in Oakland. Remember Kay, last time you were in San Francisco, I showed it to you when we were on our way to the football game, the 49'res against the Oakland Raiders."

"Oh yeah, I do remember seeing the church when we got off the subway."

"We're in Mississippi," Kenya reminded them.

"I'll just have to go back," Kaitlin said.

"But you just got here," said Kay.

"I know but someone has to go and what better person than me."

Kay knew Kaitlin was right.

"I might as well go back with her," Kaila said. "I live in Santa Cruz." She could go see Tom. She missed him and she could also check on how her research was going. Funny how she and Kaitlin lived so close and had never met before this weekend, then she thought, what's funny about that she didn't even know any of her neighbors so why should she know Kaitlin.

Kay looked at the both of them. "Are you two sure?" When Kaila and Kaitlin both nodded their heads, Kay realized it made sense for those two to go. So she agreed. "Okay it's settled," said Kay. She looked on the table where the book was. What better use for the money. Pretty clever of you granny, Kay knew this was part of the reason Teresa sent her to the bank.

"Don't forget," said Kenya. "According to the tape, we also need someone to find out about the church with the hand pointing to heaven. When does it open? We just can't walk up to the minister and say "by the way, can we go up into the hand. And by the looks of it, I don't think it's hollow. This might pose a problem."

"Blueprints are public records," said Kay. "We can go to the court house and look at property records from that time."

"How are we going to look up records without arousing suspicion," Kris asked. "Remember this is Matlin. No one's gonna not see that something is going on? The people in this town barge into other people lives enough as it is." *That's why I had to get out in the first place.*

Kyla looked at Kris. "Who asked you?"

Kyla was itching for a fight and Kris wasn't going to scratch that itch, so she went on. "You can't go to the bathroom without someone knowing about it. And if they don't know the facts, they will make it up. How do you think we are going to keep this a secret?"

"Granny kept the secret and no one found out about it," said Kay.

"How do you know this? We haven't started anything yet," said Kris. *Now where did that we come from? Am I going to help?* Deep down Kris wanted to help but she was too proud to say it.

"What do you mean "*we?* No one asked you to come," said Kyla.

Kay held up her hand. "All right you two, that's enough. We have company and we haven't begun to understand what this all means. We need to concentrate all our energy on what needs to be done." She turned to Kris. "I guess this means you're going to help."

"I didn't . . . mean. Sorry."

"I've lived here all my life. I know how small minded and narrow vision people can be." Kay admitted. "I don't how Granny kept it a secret."

"We won't be able to ask anyone because everybody that was involved are all gone, the women Melana and Meira, which means your grandmother is the only one that can help us," said Karina.

""We'll think of something, besides Granny wouldn't have asked if she didn't think we could do it."

Finally Kay stood. "Let's go to bed. Tomorrow is another day." She knew they didn't have much time. She still hadn't told them about the hearts.

Chapter Twenty Eight

The next day Kyla stretched as the sunrays laid a summer blanket across the bed. The light caressed her face as she looked out the window. The house was quiet. She tiptoed down to the bathroom, trying not to disturb the household. On her way back, she saw Kris coming down the hall. Kyla turned trying to avoid her. She had almost made it, when Kris called out to her.

"Good morning Ky. How are you?"

"I'm fine and don't call me Ky, only Kay and my mother are allowed to call me that." She kept walking.

"Wait Ky . . . I mean Kyla." Kris was stung. She didn't know it would hurt so much. There was a time when she could call her Ky. "I know everyone is mad at me for not coming home."

"We aren't mad at you; at least I don't think I am. You are the oldest but it was Kay. She's the one who watched out for Aunt Teresa when she was sick and you didn't even know she was at the center."

"I know I wasn't there for her Kyla, but it doesn't mean I don't care."

"It sure didn't seem like it when you left. Now you come back here as if nothing has happened, beside no one knew where you were. You certainly didn't try to contact any of us. Don't you know we were all worried about you? Oh we didn't say it, but we all were"

Kris hung her head and stared at the floor. She knew she talked a good game but she knew better. She always used this tactic even when she played basketball. She just plodded right in. It didn't work then and it wasn't working now, at least not with her cousin Kyla and she was sure it wasn't working with her sister. Kay must think she had flipped out or something.

Kyla could see that Kris was really sorry, so she said, "Hey cous you know we're family and we should forgive each other. I'm sorry if I was hard on you but, I missed you." Kyla grabbed Kay in a big hug, "Let's get down stairs so we can go with Kay to the courthouse." Kris hugged her back. "Yes, let's do that"

* * *

All the women went to the court house, trying to gather information on the church with the golden hand. As they walked down the street, they looked like the poster child for diversity, all colors all sizes. This was a very strange sight for the small town. There were not many shades of gray in the town. You were either black or white. They were walking arm in arm.

People were staring. Kris shook her head it was 2010. Would the town ever change she wondered. Kris loved people, all kinds, didn't matter what color. She had returned to this God forsaken place and now she was pulled into her grandmother's crazy story. Kris didn't want to believe it, but . . . She shivered.

At the Center her grandmother had told her that she loved her, but she knew in her heart Kay was Teresa's favorite and Kris somehow didn't measure up. Her mother always told her it wasn't true. Granny told Kris she loved them both the same. Kris knew better but she pretended it was okay. Kay hurried to catch up. She had fallen behind the rest of them.

As they entered the courthouse they instinctively knew to follow Kay's lead, even Kris. They filled the tiny court house lobby. Kaila and Karina were looking at each other. They were really strangers but somehow they had gravitated towards each other creating a united front because they had never been to Mississippi. Kaila lowered her voice and whispered. "Do you really think we can do this?"

"I don't know," said Karina, "but Kay seems to think we can."

"Yeah, but," Kaila whispered back. "Kay is from around here. She knows these people. She's talking about breaking into a church."

"She didn't say we would," said Karina. "She said we needed to go to the church."

"And the people," said Kaila. "I don't know about you, but I think they look as conservative as they come. They bleed red state, religious right. How do you think they are going to take us snooping around? I'm sure . . ." Before Kaila could finish, she heard Kay raise her voice to the clerk, who looked like he couldn't be much older than fifteen.

"What do you mean we can't see them?" Kay shouted. "They are a matter of public record." Kay was a reporter and she came to the court house a lot asking for information to support her stories. She still looked over at Kristin for confirmation.

Kristin nodded.

Kay's eyebrows were knitted like small darts and her target was the young clerk. Kaila and Karina both whispered, "uh oh," they both hadn't seen Kay in a long time but they knew her well. She would not take no for an answer.

"Why don't you have records of them?"

"Ma'am," the clerk started . . ."

"And I'm not a ma'am. I'm Kay Mitchell and you know me."

"I know you ma'am, I mean Kay, but that's what it says."

By now the noise level had increased exponentially with the increase in Kay's frown. A lady came up to the counter. She looked like she might be the supervisor. She looked at Kay and smiled.

"What I can I do for you Kay?" She looked surprised by all the people who were with Kay. She knew Kay's cousins but who were all this other women?

Kay calmed down as she recognized the woman. "Hi Paula," Kay said. "I need to see some blue prints and this person says they burned up. Oh, sorry where are my manners, let me introduce you to my friends."

As she did, Paula nodded. "Now, Kay you know a few years ago there was a fire and some records did get burned." Paula looked at the paper that Kay had given the clerk. "Let me take a look and I will get back to you."

Kay knew Paula wanted to know why she was asking about the blue prints, but she also knew Paula wouldn't ask. Kay wasn't satisfied but she relented. Once Kay put on her reporter's hat, she would be impatient to see it through. Kay knew it would take some time, but did her grandmother have time. She turned to the rest of them, "Let's go."

"Wait, Kay" Paula said," let me . . ." before she could said anything else, Kay turned and said, "I'll be back."

Everyone in the courthouse watched as the women walked out the door.

When they got outside the court house, Kaila touched Kay's arm. "Why don't we go to the library? You do have one?" She was only kidding but Kay looked at her and said. "We might be a small town, mind you, but we do have a library."

"I was just kidding shish."

Kay had tunnel vision when it came to getting at the truth. She looked at everyone. She noticed that most of them had been quiet throughout the incident at the court house, including her cousins. "What's up with you guys?"

They all started laughing.

"Look Kay," said Kyla. "I have known you all my life. I know how you are and I see everyone else does too. So until the storm blows over, the rest of us agreed to just ride it out."

"You guys really, I'm okay. It's just that . . . Okay you do know me." The storm had calmed.

The women didn't have any luck at the library. The people at the library said the same thing. The blueprints for the church had been burned.

Kay was frustrated. They had to get into the church and the only way they could find out what was in the hand was to go into the tower that held the hand. Minutes after returning to Teresa's, the phone rang. Kay picked it up. "Hello."

"Hi Kay, this is Paula. As luck would have it the blue prints hadn't burned after all. Do you want me to bring them to you?"

"No," Kay said. "I'll come and get them." The one thing Kay didn't want is someone getting curious about what was happening. When Paula asked what she needed them for all Kay said was that she needed them for a story she was doing.

In the meantime Kaitlin and Kaila started packing so they could leave for the airport the next day.

Chapter Twenty Nine

Kaitlin didn't think she would have to return so soon. She looked at the California coast line as the plane began its descent into the San Francisco Airport. San Francisco was only about twenty minutes from Oakland. This made Kaitlin the natural choice to go to the Mormon Church.

While on the flight Kaila, who was also returning to help, told Kaitlin she had flown out of San Francisco because she couldn't get a flight out of San Jose or Oakland.

After arriving at the airport they both headed to the baggage claim to pick up their luggage. When the bags arrived, they proceeded to the parking garage.

Usually Kaitlin didn't take her car when she flew. She rode BART. This time though, she didn't know when she would return and wanted to be sure she had a ride when she did. She turned to Kaila. "Well, I guess, I'll see you tomorrow then."

"Wait, is it okay if I go to your house? I think we need to talk some more. Since I'm already in San Francisco, I might as well find out where you live. This way I won't waste any time trying to find it tomorrow." Funny, Kaila thought. She had been all ready to rush home but . . . something made her want to go with Kaitlin instead.

Kaitlin was surprised. From what Kaila had told her on the plane about her husband Tom, especially with the dreamy look on her face, she thought Kaila would be anxious to get home. "Okay, let's find my car first, and then I can drive you to yours. Then you . . .," Kaitlin laughed. "You get the picture." When both retrieved their cars, Kaila followed Kaitlin out of the garage.

Kaitlin lived near the Presidio in one of the newer condos overlooking the bay. Kaitlin put her key card in the slot and the gate to the condo opened. She honk at Kaila and pointed to an empty space beside her parking spot. The space belonged to her neighbor but she was out of the country. She had told Kaitlin if she had company, they could use her spot. Kaitlin pulled into her parking spot and turned off the engine. She sighed, home. She grew up in Mississippi, but for her, San Francisco was home. It had been a long time since she had company, male or female.

They rode the elevator to the sixth floor. The doors opened up to soft colors and warm light. The carpet was so deep, Kaitlin couldn't see her feet. There were plants everywhere. At the end of the hall was a sitting area with what looked an atrium, maybe it was the mirrors that lined the walls which made it appear that way.

"Wow, if the hallway looks like this," Kaila said, "I can't wait to see the inside of your condo." Kaitlin opened the door and waited until Kaila filed past, then she closed it.

"Oh my," Kaila said. ""What a great view of the bay."

"Yeah until the fog rolls in, then you can barely see the towers on the Golden Gate Bridge." The sky was clear however, so the bridge looked majestic.

Kaila kept looking around. Although she admired the view from Kaitlin's condo, she had seen the bridge for most of her life. When she turned from the view there on the far wall, Kaila's eyes settled on a painting. "Kaitlin, uh Kaitlin," she grabbed her arm and squeezed. "What . . . how," she pointed to the painting, there they were, all of them. She held on to Kaitlin. She felt faint.

Kaitlin blushed. She didn't think she would have any company soon. She had forgotten about the painting. "Okay," she confessed. "I couldn't believe it myself." She hesitated for a minute wondering if Kaila would believe her story. "I painted this picture from a dream I had. I know it sounds crazy but I had this picture in my mind for a long time. One day I decided to put in on canvas. When those same faces all showed up at Aunt Teresa's, I was shocked, too. So much had transpired, that I didn't think to mention it." As if reading Kaila mind, "yes, I also know it doesn't make sense that I could have forgotten about it." Changing the subject, Kaitlin said. "Would you like something to drink? I'm sure I have something."

"What? No, nothing right now," Kaila was still reeling. How could Kaitlin forget something this important? She had questions lots of questions, but Kaila obviously wasn't going to tell her more, so she didn't ask.

Kaitlin kept talking as if she didn't notice Kaila's shock. "I think tomorrow or the next day will be soon enough for us to go to the church." Kaitlin looked at the clock on the wall in the kitchen, it was getting late. Kaila had a long drive. She had to go all the way to Santa Cruz from San Francisco.

"Listen," said Kaila. "Why don't you stay the night? I'm sure your husband won't mind and he would probably worry about you anyway, the long drive and all. And if you stay, we can go to the church sooner rather than later."

Kaila was trying to collect herself. She tried to concentrate on Kaitlin. Finally she was able to understand catching the last thing Kaila said. Tom would be worried if she left now and it would be better if they got to the church early, before the tourist. "Okay," she said to Kaitlin. "I'll give him a call and let him know I won't be home until late tomorrow." She flipped open her cell phone and punched the number one on her speed dial.

Tom was surprised that she had come home and then sounded disappointed when she told him she was staying at Kaitlin's. Of course she had to explain who Kaitlin was and why they were going to the Mormon Church, without revealing what was happening in Matlin. This was the first time she had to keep something from him. She explained to him how it made sense that she stayed in the city. It wasn't like Tom, he almost sounded jealous. Now she wasn't sure how he would react when she told him she needed to go back to Mississippi. It was the first time he had ever seemed annoyed with her.

Kaila also called the lab to check on how the research was going. It was late but she knew someone was always there. A scientist never knew when a breakthrough would happen so most tried to stay close to the whatever project they were doing.

Kaila shook her head compared to what was going on in Mississippi right now; her research was child's play. Kaila was a scientist and facts were all she knew. She always needed the truth of things. Now she wasn't so sure. The things she had heard in the last two days had shaken her. She now knew she knew nothing. If what Kay's grandmother told them was true, she would have to question some of her beliefs. It had to be a rational explanation for all of it she reasoned, but she didn't know what that was. She would find out.

When Kaila hung, up she found Kaitlin huddled over her computer intensely watching the screen. "What's up?" Kaila asked.

"I was just getting ready to look up some information about the church. How was everything at home?"

"Everything's fine."

Kaitlin raised her eyebrows. What happened? After the conversation on the plane and the dreamy look Kaila had on her face, Kaitlin thought Kaila would be smiling from ear to ear. Kaitlin could tell Kaila was madly in love with her husband. "I heard you calling your job, everything alright at NASA? I think what you do is so cool. You help send astronauts to the stars."

Kaila laughed out loud. "I do not. There a lot of people responsible but I'm not one of them. I'm just a lab rat."

"Yes you are," Kaitlin insisted. "You study the things the astronauts bring back with them. You get a chance to explore, as Star Trek Leonard Nimoy would say, "Space, the final frontier."

"Yeah, I guess I am," Kaila agreed. "It is great. I've met several astronauts. I even took pictures with them. NASA also gives pictures of the crew to all the NASA employees."

"Hey, I'd like to have a crew picture."

"You," Kaila said, "can come visit me. Just tell me when you want to come and I will give your name to security and they will issue a visitor's pass."

"That would be fantastic," Kaitlin said as she turned back to the screen.

Kaila looked over Kaitlin's shoulder. "Did you notice that all the places we are researching have the same pointed steeples?"

Kaila stared at the screen. "You're right," she agreed. "We should call Kay and tell her."

"I'm sure Kay has already figured it out."

"You're probably right, After all, they are places of worship right?"

"I guess," Kaila said, "but they must have something else in common besides that."

*   *   *

Kaila turned to Kaitlin, "about the painting? When did you have the dream?"

"I see you're going to force me to talk about it, huh?"

"Yes, remember I'm a scientist. Usually there is some explanation for things, but for the past few days, I have been at my wits end. First, Kay calls out of the blue after years of no communication, telling me to come and I drop everything without question. I come to a place that I have never been before introduced to strangers . . . don't get me wrong, I loved seeing Kay again and I liked Teresa from the start and you . . . everybody. I felt something when we were all together." She took a breath "Second, I hear this fantastic tale on the tape telling us we need to go to the Mormon Church to look for something or someone. Now here we are back here sitting in your living room and on the wall is a picture with those same faces. Am I losing my mind?"

"Okay, Okay, believe me I feel the same way." Kaitlin looked over at the picture. "It was recent, before Kay called me. I was so unnerved by her call, I couldn't think of anything else."

"Oh," said Kaila. She had sensed something in Kaitlin when they were at Teresa's. It wasn't her business, but she was still curious. It looked like pain on Kaitlin face but it had been fleeting. "I'm sorry what were you saying?"

"I was just saying I need to tell Kay right away." The painting was important. Where could she have possibly seen these people before? She and Kaila lived in the same state and she was Kay's friend. By the way the both of them had talked at the house, they were very good friends. She didn't know anything about her. But she remembered Kay never talked much about any of the women. Maybe she had mentioned her college friends but Kaitlin didn't remember.

"It's okay," said Kaila. "I am pretty sure Kay has enough going on." Kaila spotted the picture of a man on the coffee table. She reached to pick it up when she heard Kaitlin.

"No!"

Kaila snatched her hand back as if the picture was hot.

"I'm sorry," Kaitlin walked over and picked it up. She knew she needed to move the picture. If this had been three years ago or even last year, if someone had merely mention his name she would have fallen apart. Now she smiled." What happen just then was just an automatic response."

Kaila looked at Kaitlin. She was sorry she had even looked at the picture. She tried to apologize but Kaitlin raised her hands.

"It's okay." Kaitlin didn't know why but suddenly she wanted Kaila to know. Somehow she knew she and Kaila would become friends. So she cleared her throat and told Kaila what happened.

When Kaitlin finished, Kaila just sat there she couldn't form the words. My God she thought to lose so much. She couldn't even imagine her life without Tom. How did Kaitlin do it and to lose her only child too, Kaila just looked at Kaitlin. When she opened her mouth nothing came out. She touched her cheek she was crying.

"Please don't cry," Kaitlin said. "It's been six years now." Besides since Kay's phone call, something inside her was healing. She didn't know how her mother would react. Her mother was out of town, for this Kaitlin had been grateful. She didn't know how she was going to explain nor could she explain. She just knew some day she would have to face her mom. She was stronger now and she knew as long as she had her cousins, especially Kay, she would be okay. Kaitlin pulled tissue from the box on the coffee table and handed it to Kaila.

Kaila sniffed and took the tissue.

"Look. You have got to stop crying okay," The pain was not there. Kaitlin knew she would be alright. She realized as she watched Kaila dry her eyes; she could talk about it now and not break into a million pieces.

"Hey I think it is about time we went to bed. We want to get to the church as soon as it opens." She showed Kaitlin where she would be sleeping. Kaitlin watched as they headed to the guest room. She was happy for the first time in a long time. "Yes," she whispered. "I'm going to be alright Jake."

*   *   *

When Kaitlin got in bed she couldn't get to sleep right away, so she just stared at the ceiling. She was glad for the distraction and the fact she was able to return home and not half to see her mother. When Kay asked about the Mormon Church, she jumped at the chance to get back to San Francisco, but it would be short lived. She looked at the picture of Jake again. This time when she looked the tears didn't come they stayed just at the tips of her eyelashes.

Kaitlin knew she had been wrong for not telling her mother about the baby and about so many things in her life but this journey they were on made her rethink things.

Kaitlin pulled out the tiny receiving blanket that she kept under her pillow, it had been six years and she knew she needed to put it away but she still couldn't bring herself to do it. She would one day.

Chapter Thirty

Back in Mississippi, Kay was putting together a journal of sorts so they could keep track of what was being done; she dreaded the questions the rest of the family would soon be bombarding her with. She braced herself for the onslaught but she had to tell them something. As if she had conjured her up the phone rang.

"Hi Kay, this is your mother. I see a lot of comings and goings at mothers. What's going on?"

There was heartbeat of silence before Kay answered. She had concocted a story and she hoped it would be believable. "Mom you know Granny's birthday is coming up soon, right?"

"That's funny I was just sitting here thinking about what to get her, before I called."

"Well, I decided to give her a party of all parties."

"You know your grandmother can't get too excited child. Why would you give her a party?"

Kay shook her head, her mother had no idea or she pretended she didn't. Her mother always acted like Granny was some senile old woman. Of course Granny was old she would be ninety seven on her next birthday, but she was not addle. It always made Kay upset with her mom. Her granny was strong in her own way and she would be delighted to have a party. The Center was not a prison and her grandmother was allowed to come home if someone was there with her. "Mom, granny can have a party and I am going to give her one."

"I know Kay she is my mother." Michaela wasn't calling to argue with her daughter. "What are all the others doing there? Some look like strangers to me."

"They are to you I guess, but to me they're my friends and I invited them to come and help me plan it".

"They didn't need to come all this way; they could have just done this over the phone or by email."

"I know,' Kay sighed." I just wanted to see them." She dreaded what was coming so she just blurted it out. "Kris is here"

"What! Kris is here?"

I guess she didn't know. She would have to warn Kris that she had told her mother. Her mother was silent for a long time. "Momma Are you still there?" Kay said into the phone. Her mother sounded like she was laughing. This was not the reaction she had anticipated. "Wow this is a surprise I would have thought you would be tearing over to Granny's house demanding Kris come out the door." Her mother finally answered her.

"A few years ago maybe," said Michaela. Kris had made it very clear that she never wanted to return. Michaela had been following Kris career ever since Kris left home. Although Michaela was still surprised that Kris had actually come home, she knew her oldest child was just waiting for someone to ask her to come home. Pride has many arrows and sometimes those arrows can hurt when you least expect it. She knew Kris was hurting. Michaela also knew Kris was too prideful to admit it.

Kay was still waiting for an answer. Instead her mother said. "I remember the day she left, she told me she would never come near this place again. If she ever did she would have to be destitute and holding a cup waiting for someone to drop change in it." Michaela knew Kris was a long way from destitute; as a matter of fact Kris was doing quite well.

Kay laughed "I remember, so don't you think it was a surprise to me too when she showed up on granny's doorstep. One other thing mom, no one told Kris that Granny was at the Center. Why?"

Her mother suddenly sounded serious, "I don't know why." And Michaela didn't. "How is she Kay? Is she alright?"

"Kris is fine. I'm sure she will get around to seeing you eventually."

"We'll see." Changing the subject, Michaela said, "If you think its okay with your grandmother then by all means, go ahead and have a party. I was thinking of what I wanted to do for her birthday myself. Anyway, let me contribute something I don't want mother to think I don't care."

"It's okay, mom, Granny knows you do." Kay's family wasn't very affectionate. When Kay and Kris were growing up they hardly ever sat down to the table to eat together each in their own world. It had always been that way. Kay wanted to change all that and maybe what they had to do would bring her and her sister closer. She couldn't think about it right now there were other pressing matters. "Hey Mom, I got to go. Party plans remember?"

When Kay hung up with her mom, she smiled. Her mother would get the word out and the party plans would be all over town. She didn't have to worry about anyone else nosing around. Her mother would take care of that.

Kay reached for the journal again. She hadn't heard from Kaitlin and Kaila, but she knew they would call her as soon as they could. She was hopeful they would find something; she wondered why the Mormons kept all those records. No matter she turned to her computer and continued to write. She would stay close to home in case anyone got suspicious.

Paula had brought over the blueprints from court house of the church with golden hand reaching up. They all took a look at the prints and then handed them over to Kyla because she and Kenya had volunteered to go to the church that evening. Kyla had gotten permission from Sister Marie to go into the church. Sister Marie taught Humanities at the college where Kyla worked. Kyla had been surprised that Sister Marie had so readily agreed, so had Kay.

Chapter Thirty One

When Kyla and Kenya arrived at the church, Kyla looked up at the golden hand reaching towards the sky. She had grown up in Matlin and to her knowledge she had never been inside. It was a Catholic church and her family was Baptist, so she never had the inclination to visit. Now Kay had sent them to see something that was . . . if Aunt Teresa was right, inside the arm. The steeple reminded her of the statue of liberty that stood in the middle of Stanton Island calling out "bring me your poor and huddle masses." Yeah right now it was saying "bring me your rich and all your money."

Kyla laughed to herself because the hand on this church stood as direction for saints. They were now going inside to try to find a way to the top. Kyla wished she had one of the mini man shuttles at NASA that Kaila had talked about. Maybe they could fly up. And one more thing and it was very important they could get caught and in up in jail. She was scared.

Kenya looked as if she wasn't quite sure what to do. After hearing the tape she was scared to even think about the consequences of what they were doing. Jesus, she shook her head and looked up at the hand. She laughed *maybe it should be pointing in the other direction.* This thought shook her, so she concentrated on what they were doing. "Sneaking around in a church is sacrilege," Kenya murmured.

"What," Kyla said.

"I said sneaking around in a church is sacrilege."

"You think I don't know that. Keep your voice down, according to what we found, the caretaker will be walking around soon and if we don't find what we are looking for we might get caught."

"You really believe what your aunt said?"

Kyla looked at Kenya. "Don't you?" Kenya didn't want to believe but she had to know.

"Kay believes her so that's all that matters."

They tiptoed up to the altar. Kyla silently unfolded the blueprints on the communion table. She shook "*on the communion table.*" On the side of the table in carved letters, read "In Remembrance of Me" She started to curse when she remembered where they were. She swallowed the lump in her throat and continued to look.

In the meantime Kenya was looking around where she assumed the choir stood as they sang hymns. She was awed by the beauty of this church. From the stained glass windows of angels with wingspans so wide she knew they could almost cover the sun, to the picture of Mary in prayer. She looked at the pipes from the biggest organ she had ever seen in her life. They looked like they were growing out of the floor. Her fingers started to tingle, she wished she could play it, but right now all she could get out was "Sacrilege", she repeated again.

Kyla turned around and put her finger to her lips. "Will you please be quiet?" She was concentrating so hard right now she didn't have time to be scared.

Kenya realized for such a small town they had a lot of churches, every denomination and on the same street. It was even called Church Street. They were only interested in one though. The one they were nervously standing in. She believed in the goodness of God and hoped he wouldn't strike her and Kyla down in a flash of lightening. She looked up and said a small prayer that He wouldn't.

Kyla was concentrating so hard that when Kenya touched her she almost screamed. "What's wrong with you?" she asked as she tried to calm down. Her heart rate had kicked up double time.

"There, over there," Kenya pointed to the door right behind the choir stand. According to the blueprints, behind the door should be where the stairs lead to the hand. *How are we going to get up there?* The cone shape steeple looked tall from the outside. It looked even taller on the inside. When Kenya opened the door all she saw was long dark winding stairs.

Kyla turned trembling to Kenya. "I'm scared."

"What?"

Kyla needed to confess before they went any further. "I forgot I'm afraid of heights." Kyla had been afraid of heights for a long time. It was one of the reasons she went to college close to home. Flying on airplanes was not her idea of fun, even the top rows of the college stadium gave her the willies.

"Well you had better become unscared because I can't do this by myself." Kyla just stood there she couldn't move. "Look I got your back. I will hold your hand all the way to the top." Kenya didn't know where she got her own sudden burst of courage. A minute ago she was scared out of her wits.

Kyla shuddered again. She had to find a way to climb those stairs. She couldn't let Kay down. She swallowed her fear as they ascended the steps.

They had almost made it to the top when they heard music. Kenya turned to Kyla "Did you remember to close the door?"

"I thought you did." Both were looking at each other each silently accusing the other. Kyla hands tighten as she gripped Kenya.

Kenya put her finger to her lips telling Kyla to be quiet. It felt like forever but eventually the music fell silent. They waited a few minutes longer then all they heard were their own heartbeats. Breathing a sigh of relief they kept climbing to the top. When they got there Kenya was speechless.

Kyla just gawked. She looked at the magnificent sculpted hand. She took out her cell phone so she could take a picture. According to what they had been told there would be a symbol of some sort where the thumb crossed the last three fingers.

Kenya looked. She almost missed it. Right at the bend of the thumb she saw it. It was a Hebrew word, "Bekor". Kay's grandmother was right. How did Teresa know? Kenya wondered but right now she was getting nervous.

Kyla took the picture.

"Let's go before someone finds out we're here."

Kyla couldn't move. She had made it up to the top and was even able to take a picture. Now she knew it would take an act of God to get her back down. Well they were in a church, she joked to herself, but it wasn't funny, not funny at all.

"Did you look down?" Kenya asked. "I told you not to look down."

"I didn't," Kyla lied. She had looked. It was like looking into a spiral maze, from a Hitchcock movie, steps leading nowhere.

Kenya put her hands on Kyla shoulders and squeezed. "Look at me. We are going to climb down these steps and you're coming with me."

"I can't," Kyla said as tears started to fall. She was terrified.

"Why did you come when you knew you were afraid?"

"I know. It was dumb. I should've told Kay before I volunteered, but I was embarrassed."

"You have nothing to be embarrassed about. A lot of people have phobias." However, now was not the time? Kenya had a phobia, too, or maybe it was a nightmare. She always feared that one day she would be sitting at the piano doing a concert and when she touched the keys, nothing would happen. No sound. She couldn't think about that now, she had to get them down. She started singing. She knew Kyla liked to sing too. She had heard her in the shower from the hallway at Teresa's. Kyla had a beautiful voice. She squeezed her shoulders again.

Kyla jumped. "What are you trying to do make me fall down the stairs and break my neck?"

Kenya looked into Kyla eyes. Kyla listened to the soothing sound of Kenya's voice. Kenya kept singing and soon Kyla joined in. The acoustics in the arm was beautiful. Kenya held her hand and slowly they walked down.

Kyla was so in awe by the sound she and Kenya were making, she hadn't realized until they had made it to the last step. She had made it. There were still tears in her eyes. Kyla looked at Kenya and found the reflection of her tears mirrored in Kenya's. She smiled then.

"Hey let's get out of here." She couldn't wait to tell Kay she had done it. She suddenly stopped. Kenya almost tumbled over her.

"Hey, why are you stopping?"

"Sorry." Kyla realized this was why Kay wanted her to come. She was sending her to help Teresa but she was also helping her to face her fear too. They eased into the main part of the church and slipped outside again, none too soon because the caretaker was making another tour. They laughed all the way back the house.

Chapter Thirty Two

Kaila and Kaitlin drove to the Mormon Church the next day. Kaila stared at all the greenery as they rode up the twisting road that led to the church. They needed to look at the records to see if they could find any information on Meira or Melana. Kay expected them back in two days.

The Mormon Church was located in the Oakland Hills. The church could be seen from miles around. Whenever Kaitlin went to Oakland for a game or just to visit, she traveled by BART, and every time she exited the train, she would stand on the platform for a minute as she looked towards the east towards the rising sun. Kaitlin was awed how the light fell across the steeple of the church. It glowed like sapphire. She was always curious. Now she would see it close up.

Kaitlin had read on the internet that The Family History Library housed in the church held over two million rolls of microfilmed records, 400,000 microfiche, and 300,000 books. It also housed an extensive collection of written manuscripts including family histories, local histories, indexes, periodicals, and aids to help in genealogical research. The immense collection of genealogical material covered most of the world. The Library's United States holdings include records from thousands of county courthouses and state and regional archives, plus all of the U.S. Census records from 1790-1920.

If they were going to find out anything, Kaila was sure it would be somewhere in the Mormon Church. Kaila wondered how they were going to look through all those records and find what they were looking for. Teresa had said they would know when they found it. Kaila wasn't too sure. At this point she wasn't sure of anything.

When they made it to the church, it looked like no one was there. They tried the doors. They were locked. Kaitlin was sure she had the time right they couldn't be closed. They knocked again. A tall woman with a flowing white dress came to the door. "Yes may I help you?"

"Yes," Kaitlin said. "We need to go through the census records to see if we could find . . ." Kaila bumped her. Kaitlin had to think. Kay had given them so little to go on, just a family name. "Ah I mean we are doing a genealogy study and we would like to see if we can find information here," she told the lady.

The lady had them fill out forms so she could locate the microfilm for them. They didn't know actual dates because Teresa had said she didn't know how old the ladies were she could only guess. It would take some time to do the research. They settled in for the hunt.

They filled out the request forms. "It will be a minute," the lady told them. They sat down on the most comfortable chairs they had ever seen. The chairs caressed them like a hug as they sat down. Kaitlin looked out at the visitors building. There were many things to see. Kaitlin had never met a Mormon. That was crazy. What do Mormons look like? That was just like saying what do Baptist look like? She grinned. She did know a Mormon, sort of, wasn't Steve Young the former quarterback for the 49'crs a Mormon? Well she didn't know him exactly she just cheered for her favorite team. She remembered that long touchdown play he did back in the nineties when the 49'ers were a power house. She had just arrived in the bay area then. She was so excited. She was a big fan, still was, even if they were losing now. She was sure they would be back. All they needed was another quarterback.

Kaila bumped her again. "What?"

"The lady," Kaila whispered. "She's on her way back."

"Here you go," The woman said as she showed them where the microfilm was housed.

They got up. "You take this part," said Kaitlin. "Kay said to try and trace the name as far back as we could. Remember," she said to Kaila. "Melana was Negro her ancestors like mine were salves. Some didn't even have names, just male and female. Sometime they guess the ages and sometime they were called breeding stock." This was going to be very hard.

"We know Meira was from Ireland and Melana from, Mississippi," said Kaila. "According to what we heard on the tape, it was sometime in the 1800's. Didn't people keep family bibles back then?"

Looking through the microfilm, Kaila was struck by how the birth and death read; "Male age 25, breading stock" Female 18 field hand" owner Thomas plantation. She wanted to understand but couldn't wrap her mind around it. She looked over at Kaitlin

After awhile they were frustrated. They had been searching for hours and hadn't found anything, not a clue. It was getting close to closing time; they would have to come back tomorrow.

Kaitlin stood up and stretched her back. As she turned to sit down again, the woman, who had directed them, was staring. She was use to people staring. It was her eyes. They always changed colors, whenever she changed emotions. Hazel when she was happy, steel gray when she was angry, and when she was pondering, like she was doing now, the irises where hazel and the pupil soft brown, "Yes?"

The woman seemed startled that Kaitlin spoke. "Ah, yes did you find what you were looking for?"

"No we didn't," said Kaila. "Maybe tomorrow," she murmured.

"Okay well . . ." The woman looked like was going to say something else, but she turned and left.

"That was odd," said Kaila.

Kaitlin agreed. It was odd. "It's late and according to the brochure the church will be closing in five minutes," said Kaitlin. They took off the visitor passes and returned them to the man sitting at the desk. When they turned to leave, the security man held is hand up. He was looking at the log they had signed when they came in.

"Wait," said the guard, "are you the ladies who came in earlier today."

"Yes," They answered.

He looked at the log again. "Kaitlin and Kaila Langley, right?"

They both nodded. "What is it?" said Kaitlin.

"Ms Marshall told me to give you this."

"Who is Ms. Marshall?" Kaila asked.

"The woman who showed you the microfilm the one in the white dress," The man at the desk replied.

When they looked at what the man had in his hand, they gasped. It was tiny hands. There were words in them but they needed a magnifying glass to see it clearly. Kaitlin squinted as she turned the hands over trying to read what it said. Did people always write this small?

"Where is she?" Kaila asked.

"She left right after she told me to give this to you." They didn't say anything just rushed out to the parking lot trying to catch the woman.

Outside they looked around. The parking lot was almost empty. They went back inside to see if they could get some information from security man at the desk. It would be impossible. No one gave out personal information. They would definitely be back.

When they made it back to Kaitlin's house, Kaitlin called Kay to inform her of what had transpired.

Kay was surprised too. The tape had sent them there, she thought, to look for someone from the past, but maybe they were supposed to look for someone in the present. It was all confusing. They were no further than they were when they left. "Let's see what it says," said Kaila. Kaitlin found a magnifier in her desk drawer. They examined the piece. It looked old.

"Hey you know it looks like the hands on the church at home," Kaitlin said.

"It sure does," said Kaila. Although it was Kaila's first time in Mississippi, she had noticed the church with the hand pointed skyward. She also remembered how Kay had reacted when she couldn't get the blue prints from the court house and smiled.

They saw the words and symbols but they still didn't know what it meant. "I better put this up," said Kaitlin. "We can look at it some more in the morning. Besides we're going back to the church tomorrow. Let's hope the woman will be there." Kaila was startled when Kaitlin suddenly frowned.

"Wait," said Kaitlin. "Weren't you supposed to go home today? I'm pretty sure your husband Tom is expecting you. I can go to the church by myself."

Kaila hadn't talk to Tom since last night. He would be worried. She and Kaitlin hadn't really gotten any answers from the church just more questions and the mysterious hands. They really needed to go back. She was torn. She needed to talk to Tom. He would be upset at her if she didn't come home. She debated with herself and made a decision. "Excuse me Kaitlin I need to call Tom."

When Kaila pulled out her cell phone, Kaitlin went to the kitchen to give Kaila some privacy.

Chapter Thirty Three

Karina was standing with her cell phone suspended in her hand as she watched Kay walk into Teresa's kitchen heading for the coffee maker on the counter. "I need to leave," Karina blurted out. She had just hung up with Lori. Lori had sounded frantic.

Kay turned to face Karina. "What? But you just got here," said Kay. She walked closer to stand next to Karina. "You brought the box," Kay whispered so the other women couldn't hear. "You said you would stay and help."

Karina saw the disappointment in Kay's eyes. Yes, she had agreed to help find whatever it was Kay's grandmother wanted them to find. She also liked Teresa. There was something special about the older lady. When Teresa had looked at all of them in recognition Karina had been shocked at first, but she felt okay about it but didn't know quite why.

"I know. I know I have a part in what's happening here. I can feel it. It's just . . . It's just." She couldn't get the words out so, she just looked down at her feet.

Kay touched Karina's arm. "I know my grandmother sounded cryptic. When I first heard the tape, I thought Granny had gone around the bend. She is asking a lot of me . . . of us."

"That's not it. I need to go back. I need to see Lori. She's just called me." Karina swallowed. "I didn't even call to tell her I had made it to Mississippi. Kay I have to go but I'll be back."

Kay wasn't so sure. She couldn't ignore the panic in Karina's eyes. "It's alright Karina. Go on, go back and do what you need to do." No matter how disappointed Kay was she wouldn't hold Karina to her promise.

Karina was surprised. "But I thought you wanted me to stay."

"I do, but not at the expense of you. Gone on back, you're only a plane flight away."

"Are you sure?"

"Yeah, go on get out of here. Your place will be waiting for you if you decide to come back." Before Karina left the room, Kay asked, "You are coming back?" Kay knew she sounded selfish but she needed Karina.

"Yes I will be back, *cara.*" Kay watched as Karina turned and hurried up the stairs. She wasn't so sure.

As Karina hurried up the stairs to pack she flipped open her phone. She needed to call the airlines to see if she could get a flight out tomorrow.

"What's going on Kay? Why is Karina running up the stairs in such a hurry?" Katie asked from the door of the dining room where she had been sitting watching the exchange between Kay and Karina.

"She's going home," said Kay as she grabbed a cup out of the cabinet and poured some coffee.

"She came all this way and now she's going back." Katie hadn't heard what Karina and Kay were saying in the kitchen but their body language said it was intense.

"Something came up. She'll be back in a couple of days."

"A couple of days, don't we need to hurry? Maybe we should ask Kris to help."

"No, I've known Karina for a long time. She'll be back," Kay didn't sound all that convincing. "Let's just wait before we decide"

"But there's no harm in asking." After Katie said the words she suddenly wasn't so sure. Her cousin Kris had been acting nervous since she arrived unannounced at her aunt's house.

Kay grimaced *yes there is.* She shook her head. *She had to talk to Kris sooner or later.*

*   *   *

When the plane landed the next day, Karina breathed a sigh of relief. When she grabbed her bags from the carousel, Lori was standing there. Karina had called letting Lori know she would be returning. At first Lori tried to persuade her to stay but Karina knew better. She could hear it in Lori's voice. Karina looked at Lori and smiled. "Hi."

"You're here." Lori said with a nervous look on her face. After talking to Karina on the phone, she hadn't been sure of anything, hadn't been sure of anything since Karina had left Venice without explanation. She suddenly felt guilty. Before she could apologize for her actions, Karina grabbed her hand shaking her from her thoughts.

Karina held tightly to Lori's hands. "Before you say anything let's get out of here." She tightened the grip on the bags. "Come on." They headed to the airport parking lot. Karina didn't want to discuss things in the airport. They got in the car and headed home. After a few minutes, Karina took Lori's hand again. "I must return to Mississippi."

Lori dropped Karina's hand like it was hot. Putting both hands on the wheel she said. "You didn't tell her, did you?"

"Yes. I did. Listen Lori, when I told Kay about us, she was fine about it, even happy for me . . . for us, said a person couldn't help who they fell in love with."

She wanted to touch Lori wanted to take her hand again but she didn't dare. "I came back to explain . . . to let you know I want . . ." Hell, Karina didn't know what she wanted. She didn't try to touch Lori again.

When they arrived at the house, Karina noticed the grass looked dry. "The grass needs watering," she mused as they turned into the driveway. She needed to call the gardener. Startled, why was she thinking about grass? She and Lori hadn't said anything to each other since she had blurted her intentions. Karina had stared out the window the entire way home.

Once inside, Karina went straight to her bedroom and put her bags in the bedroom closet. She was too tired from the long flight to unpack anything. When she turned, Lori was standing behind her. She almost stumbled over her. Karina saw tears in Lori's eyes. Lori quickly wiped her face. She walked away from Karina and headed for the living room.

Karina followed. When Lori sat on the sofa, Karina sat down next to Lori. She started to take Lori's hand, but after the reaction she got in the car, she thought better of it. So instead she put her arm along the back of the couch. "Can we talk about it please?"

Lori blurted out. "I don't want you to go back to the US."

"I have to return." It did not matter to Karina if she and Kay hadn't talk to each other for a long time, Karina still wanted to help. She was excited too. She had taken off from the hospital so she would be able to leave, which was no easy feat. The only reason Dr. Baxter okayed it was because Karina's boss knew she owed her time off. Because of an epidemic that caused a lot of people to get sick, Karina had stayed at the hospital for days. She took a risk of Lori pulling back but she touched her arm, when she didn't she tried again, she looked at Lori. "Let me explain."

Lori watched Karina. She wanted to understand what was so important that Karina had to return to America. Before Karina could say anything else she said. "I'm afraid."

Karina saw the emotions that played across Lori's face and what she saw there made her heart stutter. "Why are you afraid?" Lori look hesitant and Karina didn't think Lori would tell her. Karina could not stand it she had to touch Lori so she brought her hands down from the couch and took Lori's hoping this time she wouldn't take them away. She couldn't help it she needed the contact. "Tell me," Karina said.

Lori squeezed Karina's hand it felt good. She said "I am afraid you will not come back."

That wasn't the answer Karina expected. "Lori," said Karina. "My work is here, my family is here. Most importantly you're here. I am just helping Kay out. We go a long way back." Karina tried to assure Lori but she didn't think she was doing a great job of it. She wanted to tell her everything that was happening. She was glad Kay had called. What could she say to Lori to make her understand how important it was to return? Suddenly she had an idea. She squeezed Lori's hand again. "Let's do this. I will talk to Kay and maybe, if you want to, and you can get away from your job, you can come with me."

Lori was stunned. Karina looked at her expectantly. She didn't know what to say so instead she said. "I know you are tired after your long trip. Let me fix you something and we can talk about it later."

With relief Karina nodded. It was true. She was tired. What was she thinking when she offered to take Lori? She knew Kay couldn't stop her from bringing Lori but Kay might not want her to know anything. She had told Kay about Lori, but the others, what would they think? She could tell them they were friends. That doesn't make any sense. Why would she be bringing a friend with her? "Okay we'll talk later." She followed Lori into the kitchen.

*   *   *

Later that night, which was morning in Mississippi, Karina called Kay. She and Lori had talked and Lori had agreed to at least see how Kay would react when she told Kay. Karina hoped Kay would understand because she realized that she really wanted to bring Lori with her. "Hi I made it."

"Yes I see you have," said Kay. "I am glad you made it safely." Kay couldn't help it she needed confirmation. She felt things would not be right if Karina wasn't a part of it. Before Karina could say anything Kay asked "You are coming back?"

"Yes, *cara* I told you I would." Karina chickened out. It would be time enough to tell Kay before she was scheduled to come back. "Well, I know it's early there so I will not keep you just wanted to let you know that I made it"

"Okay," said Kay, "see you when you get back." Kay hung up wondering why Karina sounded like she had said no.

Lori was standing in the door to Karina's office by the time Karina hung up the phone. She knew Karina hadn't said anything to her friend. She had not been trying to eavesdrop but she had been on her way to the bedroom. Karina had gone to her office to make the call and it was on the way. Lori was disappointed. What was she going to do if Karina decided they weren't important enough? She stood there and looked into the eyes that haunted her. When Karina didn't say anything Lori just turned and left the room.

"Lori, wait. Let me explain." She hurried after Lori. But how could she explain when she didn't understand. However if she was going to bring Lori, she had to tell Kay something.

Chapter Thirty Four

"Kenya and Kyla have been gone for a while," said Katie to Kay as they all sat around the living room, "I hope everything is going okay at the church. I'm starting to worry."

"I know, me, too said Kay. "I'm sure they will let us know if they were in any trouble" *I hope.* As if somehow the conversation had summoned them there, Kenya and Kyla came running through the door.

"We got it!" Kenya and Kyla shouted at the same time as they came rushing in the door. "It was right where Teresa said it would be," said Kenya. They showed the rest of them the pictures they took in the church. They were breathless. Kyla and Kenya gave each other a high five. They had gotten away without the caretaker seeing them.

"Great," said Kay. "I also heard from the gang in San Francisco and they have run into a mystery all on their own." Kay told them what Kaitlin and Kaila told her over the phone.

"Wow." Kristin said. "This is getting stranger and stranger."

"You got that right," said Kris. When they all started talking at once, Kris held up her hands. "Wait a minute, one at a time. Okay Kenya, you start first."

After Kenya told them what happened, Kyla downloaded the pictures to Kay's computer and printed out pictures for the rest of them. "See here," Kyla pointed at the markings.

Katie the gifted one peered at the symbols. "I think they're Hebrew."

"How do you know?" said Kenya.

"I studied languages when I was in school. Let me check it out to make sure." Katie started surfing the Net.

They were the same markings on the book. Why were they on the book in the first place? They had discovered other marking inside the book but this was the only one her grandmother had mentioned on the tape.

Where they supposed to find all the markings? Maybe her grandmother had left something out. Kay didn't think so. She was sure her grandmother would have remembered. Maybe the other markings are other clues put there for them not her grandmother. It was possible. Meira and Melana didn't have all the answers and it seems that her grandmother didn't have all the answers either.

Kay looked at everyone and said "We need to find out what the other symbols are. Kristin let's look at the book some more to see if we can find out something. In the mean time we're going to need some money so we can go wherever the other clues lead us."

*   *   *

Half listening, Kris sat in the corner brooding. She had come home on a whim and now she felt like she was being ignored. She thought she would feel better after she had seen her grandmother, but she felt worse. Maybe she deserved it. She had been practically estranged from her family. She watched the excited faces as they tried to figure out what was happening. She couldn't bring herself to say it, but she was kind of excited too. "I guess I'll go for a walk. I'm not needed here," she murmured.

"Wait, Kris;" said Kay. "Where are you going? We have a lot to do . . ." She didn't get to finish. Kris had closed the door. *We have got to talk.*

*   *   *

Kay stood staring as her sister walked out the door, she called out to Katie. "Hey Katie, will you tell everybody I need to go to my house for a minute." She needed to think. Think without anyone around.

Katie turned around, "Is something wrong?"

"No, I think I will go by my place for a minute. I need to check on things. I took leave from the paper but, I still need to check on a story I was following. All my notes are at the house."

Katie wasn't convinced but she said okay. Kay slipped out the back door before anyone could ask where she was going.

* * *

Sitting at her desk Kay closed the desktop. It was true, she did have to check on the story, but she knew she had plenty of time and it could have waited. Too many missing pieces of the puzzle, she could see why her granny failed to do what she said needed to be done. What was the connection? If what the tape told her was real, then everything she believed was messed up.

She realized it would take longer than she had originally thought. All the things they experienced couldn't be explained. However, she believed there were no coincidences. She knew the mind was a powerful weapon. Meira, Melana and Teresa touched so many lives. She was sure some of them had to be special.

Warring with her own beliefs, Kay laid her head on the desk. Her arms tucked, cushioning her head. Kay was torn. She pretended to be something she was not. She knew she needed to be brave. She once thought she was fearless, but lately she wasn't so sure. Except for Kyla she had isolated herself from the rest of her friends and family. No one noticed because she had never let on. Her eyes closed as she drifted off.

"Everything will be alright my daughter. You will be brave when the time comes." Kay woke with a start. "What . . . Who is it?" Shivering, she stood up. Looking around the room, all she heard was her heart beating and her breath as she let out shaky sigh. "I'd better get back."

Chapter Thirty Five

Kris walked to edge of the driveway and looked down the street. If she walked to town, maybe she would see some of her old classmates, not that she missed them or anything. She was just bored.

Walking down Market Street, Kris saw nothing much had changed since she had been away. There were a total of five street lights on the main street. There were only two groceries stores. The Piggly Wiggly which Kris realized was the same store although the 2010 version but still the same place where Melana and Meira had met one another. "Maybe her grandmother wasn't crazy."

One thing that still stood out was the statue of the confederate soldier. It was erected right in the middle of town. She shook her head. "When was this town going to come out of the dark ages?"

Kris stopped in front of the volunteer fire department building. "I wonder if Ellis is still around." She had dated Ellis for a short time when they were in high school. She didn't bother to say goodbye to him when she left. She was in a hurry to get out of Matlin. Of course they were not dating by the time she left. Kris didn't want any ties, nothing to miss. She hadn't let on, but she did miss her family.

She went inside and asked for Ellis. The dispatcher told her that he was in the back with one of only two fire trucks. She walked up to him and tapped him on those same broad shoulders that she remembered. Startled Ellis turned. "Who," . . . then he smiled. "Do my little old country eyes deceive me? I didn't think I would ever see you again Ms Kris."

Kris smiled back, yeah *me too*. "What are you doing here among the country bumpkins?" He asked.

"I never thought you were a bumpkin." Kay laughed. Some of the boredom she had felt at her grandmother's was lifting.

"That's not what I heard," he teased. "Are you staying at your moms, maybe I'll drop by and we can have lunch."

"I'm staying at Granny's"

"It must be kind of crowded with all the cars I saw parked in front of her house." Kris shook her head one of the downside to living in a small town. "I think Kay's planning a party or something for Granny. So, what's going on with you?"

Ellis recognized that the subject was closed so he answered. "Nothing much same as always in this one donkey town," Ellis laughed out loud when he realized he must be one of the donkeys because he was still in Matlin.

Kris laughed too. She needed a good laugh. "Hey how about showing me around the station?" She asked him. "Nothing much to see in this one . . . never mind," he said.

Kris had run out of conversation. Asking him to show her around was just an excuse. She wasn't ready to go back to the house. She politely followed him around as he showed her the two fire trucks. The building was as old as the town. Matlin was one of the towns that survived when the south burned.

When she looked back at Ellis, he had put his hands in his pocket. She could hear him jiggling his coins. "When did you start doing that?" she said, pointing to Ellis's pocket. "Getting old huh?"

Ellis laughed at Kris then pulled out two coins. When Kris looked at the coins, she was shocked. The coins were of two African Americans, Booker T. Washington and George Washington Carver. They were in profiled both facing left. When she looked closer she realized the coin said "In God we Trust" on the back it said "half dollar." "Where did you get these? Are they real? Can you spend them?"

"My grandmother gave them to me and yes they are real and yes you can spend them, I think." although he would never spend them. "My grandmother told me that she had gotten them from someone. I think she said her name was . . . what was it now? Yes, now I remember she called her Melana." Ellis didn't notice Kris's small gasp, so he continued. "She told me when she was young she would pass by the lady's house and that it always smelled like honeysuckles. I was as shocked as you are when she gave me the coins, so I looked up the coin's history, not sure myself if they were real or not."

Ellis told Kris the story of how the department of treasury was commissioned to make so many, but they only ended up making half and those they did make ended up not being circulated because the south didn't want to use them. Someone had even tried to burn them up. "Can I hold one?" Kris asked.

"Sure," Ellis passed her a coin.

When she looked closer there right below Booker T Washington's jaw were the same symbols that she saw in the pictures from the church, she had pretended not to be interested but she had looked at the pictures too. She asked, "You mind if I borrow this?"

"Sure you're not going to run off with it, are you?"

"No I just want to show Kay she is . . . ." Kris caught herself "I'll bring it back." Not bothering to explain.

"Keep it. Think of it as a coming home gift."

"Are you sure Ellis? It must be worth a lot of money. I can't take this. I can bring it back."

"No it's ok I have more." Ellis assured her. "We were friends once." He winked at Kris. "More than friends, I want you to have it."

"Thanks. Ellis" She reached up and kissed him on the cheeks. "Maybe we can have that lunch after all. Oh, and thanks for the tour. I think I'll go on back to grannies. I'll catch up with you later." Right now she needed to show Kay what she had discovered. She turned and rushed back to the house, leaving Ellis standing on the sidewalk staring back at her.

Kris pulled up short before she opened the door to the house. *Maybe I will show Kay later.* Now why did she say maybe? Was it because of how they had ignored her? Her cousin Kyla was not all that happy to see her. "Maybe I should hold on to this for a little while." She realized it was foolish. Teresa was her grandmother, too. She loved her as much as Kay did, even if she didn't say it. She would show Kay later. In the mean time she would keep it in her purse.

Chapter Thirty Six

Katie wanted to follow her cousin. It wasn't like Kay to act so strange, but she hadn't lived at home in a long time. She and Kay talked with each other a lot but, lately she felt that something was bothering Kay. Watching her hurry out the door just now made Katie feel something was wrong. She shrugged. She knew Kay would tell her eventually. She went upstairs to Teresa's sitting room and sat down in her aunt's favorite chair. That's when she noticed a photo album.

Katie picked up the album and started looking through it. It was one of Teresa's old photo albums. She had seen pictures of Teresa all around the house. She liked to look at the old photos. Most of them looked like they had been taken at a carnival. She saw pictures like these in the malls. The black and white photos looked more brown than black.

Her mind wandered as she turned the pages. She was thinking about her class back in Atlanta. Although she wasn't in a hurry for school to start, she still missed those innocent small beings.

One picture caught Katie's eye. It was a picture of Melana and Meira. They looked so young. She wondered when the picture was taken. She bet Aunt Teresa dated all her pictures. She pulled back the clear filmed that was covering the picture. When she turned it over she was shocked. This couldn't be. The women must have been at least seventy by the date but in the picture, the women looked the same as the other pictures Katie had seen of them. She ran down the stairs "Look." She shoved the book in Kyla's hands.

"What is it Katie?" Kyla asked. "You look like you've seen a ghost." Katie's eyes were wide with shock.

"I was looking at Aunt Teresa's album . . ." Katie's hands were trembling as she held out the album so that Kyla could look at the picture.

"Where did you get this," said Kyla.

"It was on the book shelf in Aunt T's sitting room."

Kyla had been in and out of her Aunt's house for as long as she could remember. She knew every nook and cranny and she didn't remember this album. When Kyla looked at Katie she had the strangest look on her face. "Are you sure?"

"Yes I'm sure there it was in plain sight."

"I don't remember this album." Kyla reached for the album. "Look at this picture?" Katie pointed to the page. Kyla shrugged. "So, it's a picture of Melana and Meira." Katie removed the picture. "The date Ky, look at the date."

Kyla read the date. "This couldn't be right . . . could it?" Her aunt had left out a lot of things. What Teresa had said, so far, was so fantastic until she didn't think anything else could top it. Maybe her aunt's house was haunted. She held the picture to get a closer look. "We need to show this to Kay."

"Uh . . . Kay's not here?"

"Where is she? She was just upstairs she couldn't have gone out. I would have seen her."

"She told me she needed to go home," said Katie. "When I asked her why, she told me she needed to check on a story."

"And you believed her?"

"Yes." Katie lied. Whatever was going with Kay was Kay's business, *for now.*

Kyla knew Katie didn't believe it, but she said nothing. "Let's go show the others." The rest of the women were in the dining room sitting at the table going through some of the book again.

"You think its okay? Maybe we should wait until Kay gets back," said Kyla.

"Maybe you're right." Katie put the album back where she found it and she and Kyla went into the dining room.

Kenya looked up. "Where is Kay? She's been upstairs for a long time. I'm starting to worry."

Chapter Thirty Seven

The Mormon Church

The next day Kaitlin and Kaila where back at the Mormon Church. They hoped the woman who left the hands would be there. When they got out the car, they went straight to the front desk. It was a different person at the desk than the one who had given them the hands.

"Excuse me, there was lady here yesterday, who helped us with some forms and the instructions," said Kaitlin. "She was tall, long blond hair." Kaitlin raised her hand as she tried to describe the woman. "When we saw her yesterday, she had on a long white dress" Kaila added.

"You must be talking about Ms M." the young lady said. "She's not here right now. She comes in late on Tuesdays. She should be in around ten."

Kaitlin looked at the clock that hung on the wall behind the desk. It said 9:15. Forty-five minutes, they would wait. "Do you mind if we wait for her?"

"No go right ahead." The young lady pointed down a hallway. "There is lobby through those glass doors on the right. You can wait for Ms M there."

When they entered the lobby area, they plopped down on the most comfortable chairs Kaila had ever sat in. The beige leather fit right in with the décor. Earth tones, Kaila loved those colors. There were plenty plants. *Very green* Kaila thought. From the vibrant colors of the plants Kaila knew someone took real good care of them. She loved plants, too when she didn't kill them. She always forgot to water them. She didn't have a green thumb hers was a kind of off white. She cringed as she remembered the many times she had come home from a trip to find them dead or dying. She didn't like killing anything. She just couldn't for the life of her, do any better. She also noticed there were floor to ceiling windows in a semi-circle a panoramic view. You could see the Bay Bridge and Emeryville. It was beautiful. God must be pleased.

Kaitlin was busy looking at the sculptures that were along one side of the room. They looked like they were very expensive. When she looked closer she laughed. "Do not touch" written in bold letters was on a sign next to each one. Yep they were expensive. Both turned when they heard someone cough.

"Hi I see you're here again. Didn't you find what you were looking for?"

"No we didn't. We came back to . . . when we were on our way out the man . . ." Kaitlin started to explain. Before Kaitlin could finish, the woman put her fingers to her lips to silence Kaitlin. "We'll talk in my office."

Kaitlin and Kaila followed the woman down the hall. They waited as the she opened the door and put her brief case down. The woman sat down at her desk and pointed to the chairs facing it. "Please sit. I know you have questions."

Before the woman had a chance to speak again Kaitlin reached in her jean pocket. "Why did you leave us the hands?" She handed the hands back to the woman.

The woman nodded and took the hands "I know it looks strange."

The whole situation was strange. They didn't know this woman but she seemed to know them. Kaila and Kaitlin waited for an answer.

The woman placed the hands on the desk and leaned back in her chair and rested her hands in her lap. "First, let me introduce myself. My name is Maura. I have been working as the administrator in the Census department of this church for a while.

Before I started here, I use to be a historian at the University of Maryland. I studied women's history. One day I was studying and gathering information on midwives. I wanted to see how far back the practice went. Well as I was doing the research," The woman got up and went to a bookcase and took down a framed picture. "I came across this." She held the picture for both to see. Kaila and Kaitlin looked at the pictured. They were stunned. It was Meira or Meira's twin.

The woman pointed to what looked like a pendant worn by the women in the picture. She said, "If you look real close, you can see a symbol. I tried to trace back its origin but I hit a dead end. I didn't pursue it any further because I had other issues to attend to. So I put the picture up for safe keeping. I would return to it later. But later never came. Later I left the university because I wanted to try something else.

Then one day it seemed out of the blue, I decided I wanted to come to California. It sounds strange, but it almost felt as if I was destined. I started searching for jobs, in northern California. When I saw a vacancy for a administrator here, I was intrigued. The Mormon Church holds so much history. To make a long story short, I applied and here I am."

Kaila and Kaitlin looked back at Maura. "What about the hands?" Kaitlin said.

The impatient of the young, Maura thought. She wondered what they would think when she told them the rest. She continued "One day I was looking through some old books that have been in this church for hundreds of years and I saw the same picture, recognized it.

The book talked about the pendant I gave you and it also talked about the woman in the picture. I was so excited. I started looking for the woman in the picture and it led me to Ireland. I went there and that's where I found the hands. They were at an estate auction. I bought them. I tried to find more, but as you can see I was not successful. That's where my search stopped.

When you two showed up and asked about looking up . . . oh I apologize, I peeked at your documents and saw the name Meira and I knew what I had found was connected to what you were looking for."

The room grew silent. "Can you tell us anything else?" said Kaitlin.

"That's as far as I got. I wish . . ." she didn't finish instead Maura got up and walked around her desk and hugged each one. Kaitlin and Kaila didn't know what to think. They hugged the woman back. But neither spoke.

"I have to get to work now. Again, good luck." She opened the door and Kaila and Kaitlin filed out.

As they turned to leave Kaitlin thought she heard the woman whisper *"Beso bo"* She looked at Kaila. The look on Kaila face told Kaitlin, Kaila had heard something too. "What . . . did?" Both looked back but the woman had closed the door.

Chapter Thirty Eight

Kay snuck back into her grandmother's house without being seen. She went upstairs. She didn't want to explain her sudden departure. She wasn't there two minutes when someone knocked at the door. Shaking her head, she said "Come in." Kay looked up at Kris standing in the door. "You don't have to stand there in the door. I won't bite."

Kris hesitated but when she saw the sparkle in Kay's eyes she went in. Kris closed the door. "Can I sit down?" she asked.

Kay patted the bed. She had so much on her mind. It was flying off in different directions. She had heard from Kaila and Kaitlin. She was satisfied that they were okay so she waited for Kris to speak.

"I need to talk to you Kay." Kris was the oldest, but right now she didn't feel like it. She always felt this way around Kay. Kay was the smart one. Kris was the physical one. That's why she was able to win a scholarship to Georgetown and then she got drafted by the Maryland Ducks in the WNBA. She had been so excited. She was leaving home. She was making money in something she loved. When she blew out her knee she was let go. She stayed in Maryland.

Kris had a good life but she was lonely. She had been gone a long time and she knew her mom was upset with her because she never came home even to her family's funerals. She didn't like attended funerals. If she could miss her own she would. Now she sat there on the bed wondering if she could make it right. She didn't know where to start. Before she could say anything, Kay said "I missed you." Tears formed in Kris eyes as Kay hugged her close.

Kris cried for all the years she spent apart from her sister and her family. The way she found out about her grandmother, she still couldn't believe that Teresa was in a nursing home.

Kay let Kris cry. She knew this was hard. She lifted Kris's head from her shoulder and looked in her eyes. "You don't have to say anything. Whatever kept you away doesn't matter. It never matter at least to me it didn't. All that matters is that you are here now. I also want to tell you how sorry I am that you had to find out about Granny the way you did. Honestly, I thought you knew and just didn't want to come home."

Kris wiped her eyes on sleeves. "I really didn't know and that's the truth. I also know I haven't been the big sister you needed," said Kris, "but I am going to try to be."

"You have always been the big sister." Kay felt bad because she had thought Kris had been whining and now she saw Kris was just scared, scared to say what she felt. She was like this even when they were small. She hid her emotions well. She understood why Kris left home.

As if reading Kay's mind, Kris said "I never felt loved here." It was hard for her to admit this before, but now because of what was happening, she felt she needed to. She needed to clear the air, especially with Kay. She would talk to her mother later.

Kay sat listening she knew Kris had more to say.

"I didn't think anyone cared."

"Even me?" asked Kay.

"No, never you, momma and granny," Kay knew how Kris felt about her relationship with Teresa. She took Kris's hand. "Granny loves you too."

"I know . . . at least I think I knew it, but I guess I was too busy trying to run until I couldn't see it. I'm so sorry Kay. I love you and mom and granny. I just never knew how to say it. When I found out how good I was at basketball it took the place of love." Kris had put everything she had into it. "It felt good for a while, but I knew it wasn't enough and when my knee blew out I felt like a failure and I felt ashamed."

"Why?" said Kay.

"Because I didn't know who I was after basketball. I loved all the attention playing gave me. After that I didn't think I had anyone. Oh I had other friends and relationships, nothing like family but what was I going to do?"

Kay hugged Kris again. "Look we are going to start over. The past is the past, okay. I'm so glad you are my big sister and I always have." Tears formed in Kris eyes again but she refused to cry.

Kris smiled then and hugged Kay back. She dried her tears. "There is something else I wanted to tell you earlier but you weren't here when I made it back to the house. I was walking uptown." She had left the house feeling sorry for herself. "I went to the fire department and I saw someone I use to know."

"You mean Ellis?"

"Yeah, how'd you know?"

"Didn't you and he date?" Kay didn't know him very well because she and Kris had different friends they didn't associate with the same people with Kay being the oldest they rarely shared each other's friends, except Kenya. She knew Ellis worked at the fire department but they were really just acquaintances. She wondered how that could be in a town this small. She shook her head listening to Kris.

"Yeah when we were in high school, but we broke up, or rather I broke up with him. I didn't want to be tied down. I was in too big of a hurry to leave home. Anyway we were catching up on old times." Ellis hadn't changed a bit. "When I got ready to leave after our visit, I notice he was jingling the money in his pocket. I teased him about it, telling him he was getting old jingling coins like old men do. He told me he had a lucky coin. When he showed it to me I was surprised."

"Why," said Kay, "one coin looks like another."

"Not this coin." Kris pulled out the coin.

Kay looked. "Why . . . it's . . ."

"I was just as shocked as you. Imagine we are on coins."

"Let me hold it," said Kay. She looked at the coin. "What . . . how?"

"I will tell you the story of the coin later, at least what Ellis told me. But that's not the real surprise," although it was a wonderful surprise. "Look," she pointed to where she had seen the writing. "Do you see it?"

Kay turned the coin over in her hand. "What?"

"Right there under Booker T Washington jaw." Kay looked closer, her eyes widening. "It's . . ."

"I know it's the same symbol on the hand in the pictures Kenya and Ky brought back."

"I thought you weren't interested," Kay teased.

"Well I wasn't . . . Okay, so I lied." She looked embarrassed. She hadn't known how Kay felt especially the way she had come home unannounced.

"I knew you wanted to be a part from the start," Kay teased. "Seriously Kris, I didn't want to ask you earlier because I knew how you felt about everything and you have been gone so long."

"I felt something Kay and suddenly I wanted to come home. I didn't know how to say so as usual I barged in. When I saw you and Kenya, my cousins and the other women I knew I wanted . . . no I felt I needed to be here."

"Well you are here and we are going down stairs to show this to the rest of them, except the ones that are off following other clues."

"Wait Kay, that's not all. Ellis also told me that his grandmother gave him the coin and that she had gotten it . . . get this, from someone named Melana."

"You know what this mean, don't you Kris? It means that this coin is a part of it too. Wow. Let's go show the rest of them."

The women were all surprised by the coin Kay showed them. When she said that Kris had discovered it, they were really surprised. Kay had said that everything was fine with Kris and that was the end of the subject.

* * *

After the excitement about the coin died down, Kris looked over at Kenya. "Let's go outside and sit in the swing." Kris always liked her grandmother's big green swing that hung from the porch ceiling. When she was little she would sit in the swing and imagine she was the star center on the Orlando Magic. Oh she knew it was a boys' team but she still thought about it.

"Okay." Kenya was curious. She and Kay and Kris had been friends once. But after Kris went off to school, something changed. She always wondered why. Kris seemed to be upset when she and Kay were together. Any attempt on Kenya or Kay's part to include Kris back then failed. Kris led the way outside and they both sat down. Kris gently pushed the swing and it swayed as she turned to Kenya. "I'm sorry for treating you the way I have been since I got here."

"It's all . . ."

"No, it isn't. I acted like a jackass."

"Come to think of it," Kenya laughed. "Yeah you did."

Kris sputtered. "You didn't have to agree with me."

"Okay, is there something called a Jill ass?"

Kris burst out laughing. "Okay, okay I was acting like one. Look Kenya I was jealous of you."

"You were Jealous, of me? Why?"

"Not jealous of you, jealous of you and Kay. You and Kay seem to be so close. Was it ever like that with us?"

"It could have been Kris, but when I left for New York you acted like we were strangers. It was Kay who called me when she found out that I was playing in the New York symphony and again when I moved to Texas. It was Kay who kept in touch. You never said a word."

"I know, I know. I have always been insecure. Kay is my little," not so little; Kay was as tall as Kris, "sister and sometimes it feels like she's the oldest."

Kenya didn't try to discount what Kris was saying she understood all too well. "Don't worry about it. I forgive you." Kenya knew how hard it was for Kris to admit her feelings.

"I'm going to try and do better," said Kris. When this is over, whatever *this* was Kris thought, "and when you get back to Texas, I'm going to call you every week until you get sick of me."

"Oh no you don't, you know how I am about my music. But maybe once and a while check on me. Especially when I get so caught up until I forget to eat or sleep."

"You can count on it," said Kris. "Now, let's go inside and help solve a mystery."

Chapter Thirty Nine

On Monday Karina called to let Kay know when she would return. "Hi Kay I will see you on Thursday. I hope it's not too late to help."

"No," Kay assured her. "You would not believe all the things that have happened since you've been gone."

"I can imagine. Uh look Kay is it alright if I bring Lori back with me."

Surprised, "Sure, but you know what's happening and I . . ."

"I know you can't afford to trust people you don't know. But Kay, I can't leave her here. I won't tell her anything if you don't want me to."

"I will leave it up to you 'rina, but, you know my grandmother kept this a secret for a long time. And I don't want to disappoint her. I know I can trust you to do the right thing. See you on Thursday."

Ciao Cara ami, Thursday" Karina hung up the phone. She turned to Lori. "It's going to be okay." I hope. Karina waited on Lori to respond. Lori just nodded.

*   *   *

Thursday, Karina returned to Teresa's house and as she had told Kay—she was not alone. A woman who looked about the same age as Karina came in the door behind her.

When Karina and Lori stepped into the house, she looked around the room, all eyes were riveted on her and Lori. "Everyone," she grasped the woman's hand. This is Lori. Lori nodded at everyone. "She . . . She's a friend of mine. We . . ." Karina couldn't finish. Kay saved her.

Kay held her hand out. "Hi Lori, I'm Kay. Everyone Lori," the women nodded and acknowledge Lori. Kay continued "When Karina returned home, she discovered that she had forgotten Lori was going to visit her," Kay said. "Being the gracious host that Karina can be, I know because she was so gracious to me when I was in Italy. Especially after my accident, she couldn't abandon Lori. And she didn't want to disappoint me so she asked Lori to come to the states with her." She turned to Lori. "Welcome to the US and welcome to my home, or rather my grandmother's home." Lori shook Kay's hand.

Kay knew Karina would explain later. Right now Kay needed everyone's attention. After Kay shook Lori's hand, she noticed Karina whispering in the woman's ear and pointed up stairs. Lori nodded and started towards the stairs. She hadn't said a word.

When Lori was out of ear shot, Kay said "Okay we have one successful mission. And according to the gang in San Francisco, who should be here tonight, they were somewhat successful too."

Kay went on. "According to the tape, we need to go, to the MLK museum Memphis and to the Holocaust Museum in Washington. Do I have any volunteers?"

Kristin raised her hands "I'll go to Washington."

"Okay," said Kay. "Who else would like to go with Kristin?"

"I'll go," said Katie. She was very excited.

"Ok. Now who will be going to Memphis?"

"I want to go to Memphis," said Karina. Unaware that Lori had come back into the room.

Lori just stared back at Karina. *You're leaving me here?* Karina looked away. How could she do this to Lori leave her here with strangers. Kay had told Karina over the phone it was okay to bring Lori. She told Karina it was up to her how much she wanted to tell or if she wanted to tell Lori at all. Karina decided she would tell her about the box. Karina wanted to go to Memphis. She had known Kay long before she had met Lori. Long before she knew what shape her love would take.

Suddenly Karina remembered. Kay had not said that Lori could stay at Teresa's; she just said it was alright to bring Lori. Was she being to forward in assuming Lori would be staying here. The nearest hotel was over thirty minutes away. Karina didn't want them be that far away. "Can Lori stay here?"

"Yes, of course," said Kay. She looked at the rest them. "We'll take good care of Lori." They all nodded. "You don't have to leave until tomorrow. It shouldn't take any longer than a day to get what you need so, you have enough time to get everything settled. Well that's leaves one more person to go to with Karina."

"Maybe I can go," said Kyla, "since Kenya and I were so successful."

"No Ky," said Kay. "I need you here to help us decipher some of the other symbols."

Before she lost her nerve Kris raised her hand. "I'll go with Karina." The rest of the group looked stunned, but Kay was proud that Kris had volunteered to help.

Karina looked at Kay's sister. She didn't know how to respond. She didn't know Kris and from the tension in the room when Kay arrived, she didn't know what to think.

That went over well Maybe I need to respond. "Look, I realize what you all must think of me, but Kay is my sister and Teresa is my grandmother," said Kris. "You don't have to worry about me not holding up my end." She looked at Karina. "Besides I know Memphis and I've been to the MLK museum before."

"And Memphis is not far from Matlin," said Kay.

"We can take my car," said Kris.

Way to go Kris. "Okay," said Kay. She winked at her sister. "It's settled." Karina and Lori headed upstairs while the rest of them went back to work deciphering symbols and plotting their next move.

*   *   *

There was silence in the car as Karina and Kris drove to Memphis the next day. This is ridiculous thought Kris. Somebody needs to say something. "Uh, Karina how did you and my sister meet anyway?"

Karina was looking out the window so she didn't hear Kris. She had been quiet for so long she had to clear her throat before she answered. "Oh Kay and I met when she was in Italy. She told Kris how they met in the emergency room at the hospital where she worked. "Kay mentioned that she had a sister that played basketball but, that's as far as the conversation went."

So Kay never talked about her to any of her friends. "I know I was a bit abrupt when I came in the house the first time, but I am trying to come to terms with my grandmother being in a center. And right now, I'm trying to make up for my absence and help out. That's why I decided to volunteer to go to Memphis. Your friend Lori . . . ?"

"Yes," Karina said. "What about Lori?"

Kris saw the look on Karina's face it said *closed subject.* "Nothing, I think we're almost there." The sign said Memphis forty miles. They both fell silent.

Chapter Forty

Kris and Karina arrived in Memphis and checked into the hotel. When they went to the MLK museum, it was closed. They got out the car and stood beneath the balcony of Lorraine Hotel, the place where Dr. King was assassinated. After Dr. King's death the hotel was turned into a museum. Kris shivered.

"What is it?" Karina asked. She had seen a strange look on Kris face. Karina realized she was standing beneath a great part of American History. Even in Italy she had heard about this great American. It was one of the reason's she wanted to go with Kay's sister. As she had told Kris on the way to Memphis, Kay hadn't said much about Kris. However because of what they were doing she knew she would eventually get to know her. She waited for an answer.

Kris said, "Oh it was nothing." She opened her cell phone. "I'd better call Kay and tell her we made it," said Kris. When she called Kyla answered the phone. "Tell Kay, we made it safely and are now trying to figure out how we are going to get in into the room."

The room which she and Karina had to get in was where they kept parts of the original bus from the Montgomery Boycott in 1955. The bus also had a replica of Rosa Parks sitting on the front seat. Kris had seen plenty pictures of that scene with Rosa Parks head turned slightly as if looking into the future. Her hands clutching the bar that separated white from colored. Kris often wondered what was she thinking as she sat there. A glass window had been installed so you could see into the room but the door to the room remains closed.

After speaking to Kyla, Kris hung up the phone and said to Karina. "Let's go back to the hotel." Karina nodded and they both got back in the car.

When they arrived back at the hotel, Kris said to Karina "It's too late to do anything to night. Let's get something to eat. There is this great barbeque place where a statue of Louie Armstrong stands in the middle of Beale Street. You have heard of him?"

"Yes I have," said Karina. "Shall we?" They walk outside and like the whole south in the summer time, it was ninety five degrees, hot and humid. The air was so heavy they were sweating as soon as they left the hotel.

"Let's hurry this heat is almost unbearable," said Karina. They walked fast and when they entered the restaurant the both of them sighed.

"Thank God for air conditioning." They both laughed as they waited to be seated. Sitting with elbows on the table, Kris looked over her menu and asked Karina, "Have you had southern cooking before?"

Karina shook her head. "What do you suggest?"

Kris laughed, "Too many choices." She was about to tell Karina about the food when Karina whispered from behind her menu. "Someone is staring at us."

"What . . . ?"

"Do not turn around; she will know we know she is staring at us."

Kris didn't turn around but she hissed. "Are you sure?"

"Yes I am sure do you not think I know when someone is staring or not?"

"I don't know," said Kris. "Do you?"

"Yes."

"Okay so she's staring. This is the south. People stare."

"I know but she . . . never mind." They gave their order to the waitress. They were both silent for a few minutes taking in the place. It was like walking into the seventies. All the old R & B singers like Aretha Franklin, Smoky Robinson, The O 'Jays, The Temptation and there was even a picture of Elvis Presley which looked out of place but maybe not the man played in Memphis. She also saw pictures of Rosa Parks. There was even one autographed by her. There was also the scene on the balcony of the Lorraine hotel when King was assassinated.

When the food came they both dug in. Karina put her fork down to catch a breath. She had to slow down. When she picked up her napkin to wipe the barbeque sauce off her mouth she saw the woman again and again she was staring. She didn't say anything to Kris. She picked up her fork again and kept eating.

*   *   *

Kris and Karina finished eating and patted their stomachs in intense satisfaction. "They might have to roll us out if we sit here any longer." Kris said.

"You are right about that," said Karina. "I think I am going to, how do you say, "burst a gut. I will have to run for miles to get rid of all the food I have eaten since I have been here."

They paid the check and headed for the door. When they got outside again it was dark outside. Karina started fanning herself. It felt like she was having hot flashes and she was definitely too young to have those. When she looked over at Kris she was fanning too, "whew let's do a quick walk." It was almost ten and the heat was still sweltering. They started down Beale Street. There were a lot of small shops. If Karina closed her eyes she could imagine the sounds of Venice.

Too hot, they headed back to the hotel. When they got back to the hotel they both rushed to the room. Kris hurriedly slid the card in the lock. Before she could get the door all the way opened, Karina pushed past her. Kris just laughed "Girl I didn't know you could move that fast."

Karina turned the air conditioning up high, "How do you live here?"

"Don't turn it that high. It's going to be freezing in this room in a minute."

"How can you say this," Karina said. "I need air, until I stop feeling like someone is roasting me, it stays that way for now."

Kris turned to close the door on the floor there was a note. *"Kris and Karina please meet me in the lobby at eight am"* signed *the woman at the restaurant.*

Kris frowned. Karina looked at her. "What is it?"

Kris handed the note to Karina. "I bet it is the woman who was staring at us," said Karina. "But how . . . the woman knows our names, I am calling Kay. We are getting out of here right this minute. I will pack."

"Wait Karina we can't leave. Kay sent us here we don't . . . at lease I don't want to disappoint . . . Kay trusted us to do this. Feel free to leave but I'm staying."

"How do you know this woman is not some deranged person?" said Karina.

"Remember what we heard, all the things my grandmother said the coin I got from Ellis. Why is this so hard to believe?"

Karina nodded her head. Now that she thought it, this wasn't so hard to believe. She just didn't like all the mystery that was surrounding all of this.

"Besides," Kris said, "the woman asked us to meet her in the lobby which is a public place. People will be going in and out of the hotel. There will be people at the checkout and check in counter, bellman, the concierge and the . . ."

"Okay I get the picture. But if she makes any sudden moves *Vado a ponte la sua.*"

"What are you saying?"

Karina started to laugh. When she got excited, her native tongue spilled out. "I said I am going to 'deck her"

"You are not going to deck anyone. Remember where we are there will be no decking." Kris said. Karina surprised her. Kris was starting to like Kay's friend, even with all the mystery surrounding them, along with the mysterious Lori. She saw how Karina looked at her when she mentioned Lori.

"Well . . ." Karina thought about it. "Okay, but I will be watching her very, very closely for any sudden moves." Kris smiled. "Okay, Karina Li watch her."

"I do not know this Lee person you say, but if he decks people than I like him." Karina had to laugh at her own antics. They lay down anxious for tomorrow. Maybe their problem was solved. The others had help why wouldn't they. They both were soon fast asleep.

Chapter Forty One

The Holocaust Museum Washington DC

Kristin had been to the Holocaust museum once and thought once was enough. She had cried throughout the tour. At the beginning of the tour they all got Passports of people who had died in the Holocaust. It had almost been too much. The silence inside was loud. If silence can be loud, according to Anne Sexton the poet, it could. She described the silence as a place where words flowed like miscarriages, flowing into the silence.

Kristin looked at Katie. Even though she only knew Katie through Kay, she also knew how smart Katie was. She and Kay were much older than Katie and by the time Katie had graduated from high school Kristin had been gone from Matlin for a while. She liked the child like enthusiasm she saw in Katie and knew, although what they were doing was quite serious, that it would also be fun, albeit a little scary.

When Katie entered the Museum behind Kristin the ghost of history seemed to follow, all those people perishing in the concentration camps. Katie had traveled to Germany once to visit Tulane, a sister school to the one where Katie taught. When she had toured the concentration camps, she saw how dead everything was. Nothing lived. No life at all. When she told her cousin Kyla about the camps, Kyla had said, that it reminded her of the stories about slavery-one genocide to another.

Kristin and Katie whispered and tiptoed around. "Why are we tiptoeing?" said Katie.

"I don't know," said Kristin. They both laughed nervously. They needed to find, the diary of Anne Frank not the books, they could get them in any library but they had to get a look at the original.

When they found the diary, it was surrounded by protective glass. Kristin looked at the diary and thought about Anne Frank's courage and to be so young.

They had deciphered the symbols on the bank book. It led them here. The messages said, on the page where Anne Frank made her last entry would be a mark, another lamppost in the journey. But the dairy was opened in the middle. How were they going to see what was on the last page. They both looked at each other.

"What are we going to do now?"

"Let me think," said Kristin." That's when she heard the tour guide.

"Ladies and gentlemen today is your lucky day. One of you will be able to look at the Diary of Anne Frank up close."

"All right," Kristin said.

"Not all right," said Katie. Although Katie was secretly enjoying herself she still didn't know what was going to happen. And when did she and Kay's friend Kristin get this close? When she had seen Kristin at Aunt Teresa's she had noticed a pained expression on her face, but looking and hearing the excitement in her voice now reminded her of her students.

Kristin ignored Katie "They *are* going to let us see."

"What the tour guide said," Katie repeated, 'one of you meaning any of the fifty people in this tour would' what she didn't say was that it would be either one of us."

Kristin knew better. She knew in her heart that one of them would be chosen.

"Like Teresa said on the tape," Kristin reminded Katie, "there was always something guiding the midwives, so why wouldn't that something be guiding us."

Thinking about it, Katie agreed. "Okay, come on we have to put our names in the box."

They hurried over and signed their names. Katie closed her eyes and prayed to whatever guide Kristin was so sure of. She crossed all her figures and toes. She would have crossed her eyes too if she could but she was too scared. When Katie was little her grandmother told her, after she had teased the neighbor about his cross eyes and showing grandmother how they looked, if she crossed her eyes again they would get stuck, her punishment for teasing. She was a grown woman and she still believed her grandmother. So she just closed them tight. She was so busy doing this until she didn't hear her name when it was called. Kristin elbowed her.

"Oof, what'd you do that for?"

"They called your name. Over here! Over here!" Kristin shouted. Pointing at Katie, Kristin shoved her up to the front of the crowd. The woman looked at Katie.

Katie nervously looked through the glass at the diary; she had read the story of Anne Frank. It was required reading when she was in high school and she had had her students read it, but to be this close to history she thought she was going to faint. She walked up to the curator who was there to escort her.

Kristin realized the woman had been there as they had walked through the museum.

The woman touched Katie's arm. She jumped. She felt a current. She thought she had somehow rubbed her shoes on the carpet.

Kristin looked at her frowning; she mouthed "What's wrong?"

Katie shrugged her shoulders, but when she turned around the curator winked at her. "What," she almost blustered. Everyone was watching, so she kept quiet and followed the woman to the diary where it stood on the glass base. Katie was so nervous. When looked down, she thought the book was vibrating. She blinked. When she looked again it was still.

The curator turned to the others and said. "Today we will actually allow this young woman to see the rest of the diary. We usually don't allow it to be disturbed because of its fragile state but today we will." She whispered to Katie, "You are not allowed to touch it so I will turn it for you. Do you have your cell phone?"

Katie was so shocked she couldn't speak. The lady stared at her and asked again. Katie didn't find her voice so she just nodded. The woman had on special gloves that allowed her to move the pages. She turned to the last page and then hid Katie from view for only a second, long enough for Katie to take the picture. She whispered "now." Katie took the picture then the woman stepped around Katie as she looked at the page.

The people were asking what it said. Katie looked at the people waiting for her answer and she said to the crowd" In remembrance of me." They all applauded as Katie stepped back into the crowd. People took pictures of Katie as she walked. She shook her head. Was she famous now? She didn't think so. By the time those people made it outside she knew they would have forgotten. When she walked back to where Kristin was standing, excitedly she said. "You would not believe what happened."

Before she could tell Kristin, the curator put her finger to her lips. This silenced Katie. She bowed her head and she could swear the woman eyes were glowing.

Kristin was shaking her. "What happened?" Was that all it said "In Remembrance of me?"

"I will tell you when we get outside." Kristin pulled her away from the people and found an empty bench on the side of the museum.

Kristin grabbed her armed. "Now tell me what happened."

"The curator she . . ." Katie couldn't get it out.

"Snap out of it Katie and tell me."

Katie began again. "The curator . . ."

"Yes, you said that already."

"When . . . she touched me to take me into the where the diary was. I felt something."

Kristin looked at her funny. She had felt it too and like Katie she thought it was some kind of static electricity.

"She knew," said Katie. "She knew why we were there. She purposely stood in front of me so I could take a picture of the page."

"Wow said Kristin. Do you think . . . Naw, it's not possible." But there they were and they had gotten what they came to get.

Chapter Forty Two

Back in Memphis

Kris stretched and yawn she looked at the digital clock on the night stand between the beds. The red block numbers said 6:00. "Shoot, we have two hours before we have to meet the lady from the restaurant." Kris wondered how the woman knew where they staying. Maybe she followed them to the hotel. Maybe Karina was right and the woman was deranged. She shook her head. She was going on her instincts which had served her well so far. She looked over at Karina. She looked like a small child. Blond hair spread across her pillow. They were so different, from different cultures. Things had changed a lot. If they had been in Memphis when Dr. King was alive they wouldn't be staying in this hotel and if people saw them together they would have been called agitators. Not only that, they would be face down on the ground with the water from a fire hose pushing their bodies into the grass. Kris shivered when she thought about what all the people went through. Most of them were kids, so much younger than she and Karina. She yawned again. "I guess I'll go in the shower." She looked back at Karina. She was sound asleep.

Karina heard the shower running. She pushed herself up from the pillow. Like Kris predicted, it had gotten cold in the middle of the night. She had gotten up to turn the air down. She thought she was in Alaska. She was still leery about meeting this woman, but in the light of day she was not as tempted to deck the woman. She laughed to herself she couldn't imagine decking anyone. She knew she was just bluffing. When Kris came out the shower she said "I see you are up early."

"Not so early. We have to meet the woman downstairs and I for one want to meet her on a full stomach, so if you want to go to breakfast too, you had better get going. It is almost 6:45."

Karina looked up. "*Yikes* I had better." She grabbed her clothes out of the suitcase. Neither had bothered to unpack since they figure it would only take them a day. However it proved to be a little daunting. First they had to meet this mysterious lady and then figure out a way to get in the room. Maybe Kris was correct maybe the woman had the answer.

"Are you going in the shower or not?"

"They made it to the dining room Kris grabbed a blueberry muffin and Karina got the honey and raisin muffin. They both nuked their muffins and got some juice and sat down at the table.

"Well this didn't take long. We could have stayed upstairs a little longer," said Kris.

"But we do not want her to be waiting on us we want to be waiting on her." Karina looked at her watch it was 7:30. They had thirty minutes to wait. She noticed Kris didn't wear a watch. She asked. "Why do you not wear a watch?"

Kris looked down as if she hadn't realized it herself. "Oh I haven't worn a watch in years. It feels like a shackle to me, bound by time.""

Kris punched her as they headed to the lobby. When they got to lobby the woman from the restaurant was talking to the person at the desk. When she saw them she turned and smiled. "Hi . . ." before the woman could get anything else out. Karina interrupted her.

"Why were you watching . . . ?" Kris nudged Karina before she could continue and whispered. "Remember no decking."

"Okay. Excuse me," said Karina. "You have us at a disadvantage, you know our names but we do not know yours. May I start this conversation by asking who are you and what do you want with us?"

"My name is Myra. If you don't mind, let's continue this out on the patio. It's early so it shouldn't be too many people there."

"Okay, which way is the patio?" Karina started to ask the lady at the desk.

"I know the way," Myra said. "Follow me."

"By all means," said Kris. Karina and Kris followed the lady to patio. They sat down on wicker chairs that faced a beautiful garden. The sky was clear and it looked like it was going to be a beautiful day, hot but beautiful.

Kris started. "What is this all about? I am not use to being summoned and especially not by a stranger."

"I know why you are here and I was sent to help." The woman said as she looked out over the garden.

Both Kris and Karina's mouth dropped open. "What . . . you . . . how . . .," Karina stuttered. Kris nodded her head. "Yeah what she said." They were both speechless.

Karina found her voice first. "I do not know who you are and you cannot possible know why we came to Memphis. We could very well live here."

"How did I know you were staying in this hotel and what your names are?" the woman replied.

Kris chimed in. "You could have followed us and since we did see you at the restaurant, you could have got our names from . . ."

"From where?" the woman interrupted Kris before she could finish.

"Well . . . Kris didn't have an answer for it but given time she could think of some reasonable explanation. For now she would just see what the woman had to say, so she sat back and kept quiet as the woman started to explain.

"First of all," said Myra, "I did see you at the restaurant and I knew you were the ones she told me about."

Okay this is getting weird Karina thought. She asked. "What are you talking about and who is she? As a matter of fact who are you and why have you asked to see us? If you don't tell us right now, my friend," she pointed at Kris, "and I are leaving right now." Karina started to get up.

"Wait!" the woman started, "I don't really know her name, I just know." The woman answered. She touched Karina hands and there it was the spark. Karina slowly pulled her hand back. She didn't want the woman to know she felt something, but Myra smiled and Karina knew that Myra had felt it too.

Kris just looked back and forth at both of them. Something had passed between the two. "I know you are trying to get into the room where they have the replica of the bus that Rosa Parks rode in the day she was arrested. I'm here to get you in there."

"How," they both said as they leaned forward both all ears now. Kris and Karina had forgotten they were supposed to be wary of the woman.

"There is a security person that works there and she will let you in."

Kris shook her head. "You have got to be kidding me. You expect us to walk up to a security person, whose sole purpose is to protect the museum and say what? Myra sent us. No wait, maybe there is a secret password we need to say."

Karina interrupted Kris's tirade. "Where are you going to be and how will this person know us?" She was beginning to realize whatever this was would change her life forever. If she could she would do whatever it took, to see it through. Lori's face flashed in her mind but she ignored it.

"Wait a minute, Karina, wasn't it you who just last night was talking about decking?" Kris said as she looked at the both of them. Why had Karina changed her mind? All of sudden it dawned on Kris that they were really going to do this and some stranger was going to help them. At that moment Kris wished Kay was here.

Myra went on as if she hadn't heard Kris. "I've talked to her already. She knows to let you in." Myra wondered if she was doing the right thing. It had been a while since she had been called upon to help.

"We just got here . . .," Kris clamped her hand over her mouth she still didn't trust the woman. The whole thing they were doing for granny was weird but Kris decided right then to go along with it so she kept quiet and allowed the woman to finish.

"You see I am originally from Mississippi," said Myra as she tried to explain why she had followed the women here.

Okay so much for keeping quiet. "So you're from Mississippi," said Kris. "I bet there are lot of people here from Mississippi, doesn't mean anything."

"I know Teresa."

Karina, who had been quietly listening, looked at the woman to see if she could tell if the woman was lying. By the intense look on the face of the woman she couldn't tell if she was or not. When the woman touched her she had felt something, a connection, she hadn't quite recovered yet so she kept quiet.

"I know it sounds crazy," Myra said, "but I did come here to help you. I will give you the security's person name and her work number at the museum. You don't have to believe what I am telling you, but please at least go see her."

Karina reached in her purse for a piece of paper and took down the information. Afterwards she looked at Kris to see if she was okay with it. Kris nodded. Putting the paper in her purse she said. "We can't promise we will go or even call this person but we will consider what you have told us."

The lady rose. "I have done what was asked of me so I wish you luck." She shook both of their hands. They felt her. She turned then and left. Kris and Karina sat back in their chairs and just stared as the woman left the room. Karina said. "Do you think she is telling the truth?"

"I don't know but I know both of us felt her hands."

"Yes you are right, I felt it too," said Karina.

"Alright suppose," said Kris, "and I'm just supposing, but what if she's telling the truth and we don't go see this person how else are we going to get in." Neither one had thought any further than yesterday and didn't have a clue.

"I say we go see this woman. We can always pretend we just needed to be sure of the times of the opening up of the museum. That doesn't sound suspicious does it?" Karina asked.

"If she is telling the truth, then I say we go for it," said Kris, "if not we go to our plan."

"What plan?" said Karina.

Kris laughed. "Okay, so we don't have a plan". Kris and Karina headed in the direction of the lobby. Kris looked at the clock in the lobby. It was almost ten. "We had better get going. According to what Myra told us the woman is on the day shift."

Karina stopped in her tracks. "Are you saying we are going to try to get in that room in broad daylight?"

"No, we are going to see the woman, that is all we are going to do for now."

"Okay," Karina said. "Let us go." When they got to the museum people were lined up around the block from the hotel.

When they finally made it to the front, Kris asked for the guard. The woman was tall like Kay when she thought about it the woman looked a lot like Kay. As if reading her mind, Karina was staring with a slight frown, eyebrow arched as if she was thinking the same thing.

They had to see if the women, Myra was telling the truth, but what were they really going to say Myra sent them like they were some kind of spies. Kris murmured a small plea. "Please don't let us have to break in this sacred place."

They approached the women. Before they could confront the security person, she said. "You have finally arrived. Myra told me you would be coming."

Karina mused. Maybe we will get what we want to after all. When the woman told them to come back later after the museum closed and that she would let them in, Karina asked. "How do you know who we are? We could be anyone."

"You're not anybody." She touched Karina hands. "Is everybody like this?" By the time they finished her hands might have blisters but when she looked at her hands they were as normal as always.

The woman turned to Kris. "I see there is still uncertainty."

"Don't you think we have a right to be? First this woman at the restaurant leaves a note. Then when we meet her she tells us to come see you. Now you tell us to come to the museum tonight."

"Some things you just have to trust," the security guard said as started towards the door. Her grandmother voice was in Kris's head. *Trust this Kris.* Ignoring her grandmother's words, "Some things I do, like the sky is blue and I am brunette that's not faith that's what you see with your eyes."

"That is true," said the security woman. "But I am not talking about what you see with your head . . ." She pointed to Kris's heart. "It's what you see there."

Kris turned to Karina as if asking if she believed the woman. "Yes," Karina said, "We will be back."

Chapter Forty Three

That night Kris and Karina went back to the museum. The security woman was where she said she would be. The guard put her finger to her lips and gestured for them to go inside. She closed the door behind them.

Kris jumped when she heard the door close. Maybe this wasn't such a good idea after all. She started to panic. They were breaking into a museum. Actually, they weren't really breaking in. However, it felt like they were desecrating the past. Shivering, now, all Kris wanted to do was get in and out without embarrassing herself.

The silence that engulfed them as the light from the door went out, made Karina hesitate for a second, all of sudden it was real. Shaking her head she followed. They silently walked through the museum.

When they got to the room Kris stood at the glass. She could almost hear the bus driver telling Rosa Parks. "Get up let me have those seats," and Rosa Parks refusing to move.

The woman whispered, "Go on." When Karina and Kris started toward the door, they looked back, the women remained outside. Kris asked. "Aren't you coming?"

"No, I was only asked to help you into the room." Karina frowned. "But . . .," the woman shook her head. Gathering her courage Karina reached for the knob, "we can do this."

The security guard opened the door and Karina and Kris walked in. Karina didn't want to touch anything so she walked slowly around the room. It was if she could smell the charred flesh of the bus. She had read about the Montgomery Boycott but actually seeing the remnants of the bus made her wondered if she had been here during that time, which side would she have been on. After all she was not African American. Karina considered herself a good person and she didn't believe she would be any different. And she loved Kay. And under the circumstances she found herself with Lori, she knew she was not that far removed from prejudice.

For Kris, it was as if Rosa Parks was watching. She had been so emotional when she came here for the first time. She listened to the speeches and stories of the Movement in the headsets as she walked through the museum. The room seems to vibrate with sadness, sorrow and redemption. Kris felt all those emotions . . . the driver angry, the people on the bus screaming for Rosa to get off, and then cheering when the policeman took Miss Parks into custody. Now she was about to go beyond the words as if going back into history itself. She shook her head as if to shake off the past, a past she was not born to but felt just the same. Turning, she saw the look on Karina's face, she mouthed. "What's wrong?"

"Everything," Karina said. "We need to get out of here. It's like looking into ones soul. You know people leave their imprint wherever they go." Before Karina could get the rest of what she had been thinking, she heard footsteps. "Did you hear that?" whispered Karina.

"Let's get on the bus. Hurry" said Kris. When they tried the door on the bus, they were surprised to see it open easily. Everything looked so real. Karina hesitated. She could feel them. "I can't."

"Well if you don't want to end up in jail or worse on the front page of the newspaper with the caption "Crazy women break into the MLK museum." Kris didn't finish. She grabbed the hem of Karina's jacket and pulled them on the bus. Kris was breathing hard. The sound got louder, Karina starting praying. "If you left some imprint, Mrs. Parks, please let it be a way out." Someone was jiggling the door.

"Hey you two what's taking you so long?" It was the security guard. "I' m not supposed to be on this shift remember, the night security will be suspicious. If you don't hurry up, you are going to have to stay here until tomorrow when I come in for my shift."

Kris hurried to the door. "Give us five more minutes. We had just started looking at the bus when we heard something."

"Okay, sorry I scared you, but you need to hurry," she repeated.

Sweating both kneeled. "I don't see anything," said Karina.

"Well, keep looking it has to be here." Kris felt along the edges underneath the seat where the tiny metal tag said "For Whites Only", she saw it. The Symbol and the hands, she took a picture. "I got it, let's get out of here." They hurried off the bus and out the door. The woman let them out the back, which led to the street. Just as they made it through the exit, the night security guard was rounding the corner.

171

They ran to the next corner. All three women started grinning and couldn't stop. The security guard looked at them. "I'll tell Myra you got what you came for. You did get what you came for?"

They both nodded. "By the way who . . ."

The guard held up her hand. "I'm not important. It is you two who are the important ones. So, go."

Kris and Karina rushed back to the hotel. When they made it back, Karina deadpanned. "That was fun."

"Yeah," said Kris in the same voice, "real fun, we should do it again." Karina's eyes almost fell out of her head "I'm kidding. It's late we need to get some sleep so we can start out early in the morning. We should get to Mississippi by lunch."

Kris looked at Karina. "We did it, we did it!"

Karina picked up the notebook on the desk in the room then she reached for the phone. "Room services anyone? Fear makes me hungry."

Kris laughed and went into the bathroom. When Karina picked up the phone to dial room service, she panicked. She had been in Memphis for more than a day and she hadn't thought once to call Lori. What was she going to say when she and Kris returned? She knew Lori was mad at her for leaving her at Teresa's house. Karina had left without even discussing it with Lori. Karina called room service but she was no longer hungry.

* * *

When Kris and Karina returned to Mississippi, they were greeted with cheers and pats on the back as did Kaitlin and Kaila who had flown in earlier from California. While Karina and Kris were still in Memphis, Katie and Kristin had returned the day before.

Lori watched as Kris and Karina came into the house. She watched as everyone greeted them like they had greeted the others. Lori had to admit that it had been pleasant at Kay's grandmother's house. Everybody had been nice to her. Kay had even told her some of the things that had transpired. She was surprised that Kay had been willing to tell these things to her. What a fantastic tale. Lori wasn't sure she believed all of it but if Karina was willing to come all this way, and leave her here, maybe it was real. She was still upset with Karina. Although she was just as happy to see them return especially Karina, she didn't say a word when Karina and Kay's sister came rushing through the door.

Karina was smiling at the reception she and Kris had gotten. She couldn't wait to tell Kay and the rest of the women what happened in Memphis that is until her eyes fell on Lori. What had she done? Correction, she knew what she had done. She looked away. She didn't want to explain why she left Lori with strangers to go off with Kris to Memphis but she knew she had to. She had seen it in Lori's eyes, first she seemed happy to see Karina, and then she saw something else, was it sadness or disappointment?

Lori stared back at Karina and wondered, not for the first time, if what they had was enough. Karina had left her with strangers for two days, well almost two days. It didn't matter how long and why hadn't Karina called her? She released Karina from her gaze and turned and went upstairs to the room where she had spent the night.

"Excuse me," Karina said to no one in particular, "Lori, wait!" The women watched as Karina hurried up the stairs behind Lori.

"What's that all about?" Kris said. "Never mind," said Kay. She went into the dining room and asked the rest of them to follow. "Come on guys." When they were all seated she turned to Kris, "Care to elaborate on what you and Karina found out at the MLK museum."

Chapter Forty Four

Lori closed the door and plopped on the bed. When would she learn not to be so trusting? Here she was in America for the first time in a strange house with a bunch of women. Lori couldn't remember all those names. She shook her head. Lori heard the knock on the door. She knew it was Karina. "Well she can just wait. She kept me waiting." She pretended like she hadn't heard Karina.

Karina stood on the other side of the door. Why was she knocking this wasn't Lori's house and besides she had every right to be in the room. Still she knocked again; *so much for courage* she wasn't this scared when she and Kris went into the MLK museum or when they met those mysterious women at the restaurant and at the museum. "Lori please let me talk to you. Please."

Lori cracked the door and whispered. She didn't want the rest of the house to hear her. "What do you want?"

"What do you mean what do I want? I want to come in. I need to explain."

"Why now? You weren't doing any explaining when you left me here with strangers."

Kay is my best friend! She wanted to scream but she said instead, "I knew Kay would make sure you were comfortable." *That was just how Kay was.* "I'm coming in now." Before she could take a step, Lori jerked the door open. Karina almost fell on her face. As she tumbled Lori reached out to keep her from falling, but she couldn't quite catch her so they both tumbled forward landing on the floor with a thud. Lori was pinned underneath Karina. When she tried to push Karina off of her she was only pinned harder.

Karina touched her cheek and tears formed in Lori's eyes. "Please, Karina let me up." Karina relented and stood up pulling Lori with her.

"I am so sorry *cara.*"

"Why are you sorry now?" Lori jerked her hand from Karina.

Karina reached again for Lori's hand. Lori didn't move she kept her hands at her side. She stared back at Karina like she was a stranger. Karina dropped her hand "Please listen to me *cara*. I . . .," she couldn't say it.

"Please what." Lori stood waiting for some answer, some explanation. They were having their first fight.

Karina looked down at the floor, she felt like she was 13. She was a doctor for God's sake and a damned good one. She worked miracles at the hospital. She had gone to that shop and had a strange encounter with the woman, had gone to Memphis and yet another encounter. She understood that Lori was angry. If it had been the other way around, Karina knew she would be too. Karina looked at Lori. What if Lori had changed her mind about them? She shook her head. She didn't want to even think about it.

"Why are you shaking your head?"

"What?" Karina was trying to think of how to explain to Lori how she felt, but that was all that came out of her mouth.

"Never mind," Lori turned and headed for the door. Right now she didn't know what to do, how to respond to Karina. She understood why Karina had gone to the museum and by rights Lori was not suppose to be there. But damn it, she was. Leaving her with Kay was only part of the reason she was angry at Karina. She was also angry, no not angry hurt because she wanted Karina to acknowledge what they had. She said none of this just reached pass Karina for the door knob.

Before she could leave, Karina grabbed Lori's arm. Karina had surgeon hands, quick and delicate at the same time. Lori knew of Karina's successes. She didn't have many failures and that was one of the reasons she had been attracted to Karina. Right now she just wanted to get as far away from Karina as she could. But when Karina touched her she couldn't move.

"Please Lori, wait." She looked at Lori and saw the tenderness and warmth she always found there. "I love you."

Again Lori stumbled. *My God she said it.* "Wow," was all she managed to say when she turned around to see the truth in Karina's eyes.

"Yes wow indeed," said Karina. She was as surprised as Lori. She cupped Lori's cheek and kissed her there. "Please Lori we are going to get through this. Right now, there is so much going on, but you have my word when all this is over and we return to Italy, we will sit down and see where we are going. I can only hope that wherever we are going it will be together." She grabbed on to Lori's hand. "I need to tell Kay what happened at the museum."

When Lori looked at Karina, she was smiling. "Okay." Did I just forgive her?

Lori sighed and both turn to go back down stairs.

* * *

When Karina and Lori returned to the living room, Kay asked "Is everything okay?" It will be Karina thought. "Yes, everything is fine."

Kris looked at the both of them. She had enjoyed Karina when they were in Memphis. Karina and Lori looked so close so connected she wondered why. It reminded her that she needed to talk to her mom. Where did that come from? She hadn't thought about her mother since she had arrived home, she knew her mom was aware that she had come, everyone in town for that matter. She hated small towns. But looking at Karina and Lori made her want to see her mom. It was time she made amends for not coming home often enough.

On the other side of the room Kristin was thinking the same thing. She wanted to go home. She was afraid. Afraid everything would still be the same, and that her mother would still be the same woman who disapproved of her friendship with Kay. She spoke before she lost her nerve. "Ah Kay, If you don't mind after Karina and Kris finish, I think I'll go see my mother."

"Me too," said Kris. "What she said, I don't mean I need to see her mother I mean I need to go see ours".

Well, well, well, I think things are looking up. Kay was pleased. They both needed to make peace. Kay really didn't know Kristin's mother. She had seen her lots of times. Kristin's mother was a realtor in Matlin as a matter of fact; she was one of the only two in town. A lot of the people in town acquired property through her. "Go on you two; I am sure they will both be happy to see you? If anything changes, I will bring you up to speed when you return." Kay looked over at Kaitlin. When would Kait find her peace? After Karina and Kris finished telling everyone what happened in Memphis, they left the house.

Chapter Forty Five

Kristin walked to her mother's office. She knew her mother, Marlene was in her office and that someone in town had already told her Kristin was here, what with the ruckus at the court house. She pushed the door open, she had hoped to enter quietly, but she forgot about the damn bell that hung over the door. When it sounded everyone in the office looked up. Kristin blushed. "Hi everybody," she said.

"Well as I live and breathe," the bubbly woman who was her mother's assistant said as she jumped up from her desk and gave Kristin a bone crushing hug. Kristin could barely breathe. "My God I haven't seen you for a long time. Your mother talks about her lawyer daughter all the time. By the way she talks I thought you would be a Supreme Court justice by now."

"Sorry no such luck, I'm still just a lawyer," Kristin replied. Her mother had been talking about her?

"That's nothing to sneeze about either. Go on in, your mother is in her office."

Kristin knocked on the door. Without looking up her mother said "Come in." People went in and out Marlene's office all the time. So she was never surprised by the knocking.

When she looked up, the face that was the mirror to her own was standing in her doorway. She couldn't say anything. She had never been lost for words. Marlene was a seller of property and good at it because she had a gift. She could sell anything. She just chose to sell property. She kept staring at her daughter, trying to make sure it was really her. She knew Kristin had been in town for a couple of days. It had hurt that Kristin hadn't bothered to see her until today but she really couldn't blame her. Now her daughter was standing on the other side of her desk looking like she wanted to run. Marlene wanted to grab Kristin and hug her and never let go, making that sadness she saw in Kristin face go away but she didn't know how Kristin would react. It had been so long.

"Hi Mom, I hope I'm not disturbing you . . ." Kristin didn't know what else to say, so she just stood there.

Marlene looked at her only child and tears formed in her eyes.

What's this Kristin thought her mother never cried. She started again. "Mom . . . I want . . ." Her mother didn't let her finish.

"Wait let me close the door. Adele is probably chopping at bit." Marlene smiled "small town." She turned and walked over to her daughter and touched Kristin cheeks.

Marlene had watched her daughter walk out of her life because of what she had been taught, racial prejudice. She knew she couldn't blame her parents completely, but back then, she was afraid, afraid to go against them, right now though she was just ashamed. She had changed but would Kristin believe her? "Oh mom," Kristin leaned into her mother's hand.

"I know honey. I know. I missed you too. I've missed what we had before and because of my cowardice, you felt you had to leave. I've changed. I know it will take some time before you will believe me but that's okay. I love you and I can wait."

Kristin didn't know what to say. She had missed her mother too. She didn't know how much until she walked into her mother's office. When her mother wrapped her arms around Kristin she fell into her mother's arms. Each one thinking about all the time wasted.

*   *   *

Now that Kris was committed she had to go. She had talked to her mom, but things were never settled between them. She almost turned around and walked back to Teresa's. Almost, this was the time. She couldn't back out now. She went to the house she grew up in and knocked on the door. When her mother opened the door she just stood there and looked at Kris. Then she smiled "Hi my precious daughter."

Kris wanted to be mad but all she felt was hurt. Her childhood flashed before her eyes all the times she felt alone. All the times she felt unloved.

Michaela watched the emotions that crossed her daughter, anger, sadness, and hurt. She reached out to Kris. She had to make things right somehow. "Come in Kris I know it is time for us to talk or for you to talk. I am here and I am ready to listen." Michaela was prepared to accept whatever Kris had to say. She would not discount Kris's feelings.

Kris walked into the house. The house looked the same. Her mother traveled a lot so she didn't spend a lot of time on buying things. This was okay with Kris. She didn't miss things she missed her mom.

"Let's go talk in the living room," her mother said. "I know you have a lot to say"

Where do I begin? Kris wondered as she followed her mother. She needed to do this and she hoped her mother would understand when she finished. They sat down and Kris propped her feet on the giant coffee table. At least when she was young it felt that way. Now it didn't really look that way. Kris was almost six inches taller than her mom so even when she was sitting she towered over Michaela. "Mom I want you to know that what I am about say is how I have felt all these years why I left home," she began. Could she say it, she needed to say it. "I always felt unloved. It seemed like granny and you were always talking about Kay. I was the baby, the only child, for five years and it may have been a part of the reason I felt this way when Kay came along. I know it sounds selfish but I felt ignored. You didn't seem to have time for me anymore. Being with Kay the last few days made me realize I was never mad at Kay. It was you and granny that I was mad at. I have made my peace with Kay. Now it is with you and granny that I must make peace."

Michaela didn't know how to respond. She always suspected how Kris felt. How could she let it go on so long? She loved both of her girls, hopefully, both the same. Maybe it was because Kay came back home when she finished college, and when Kay was younger, she never made a fuss. Maybe she did subconsciously favored Kay. She hadn't realized it until Kris said it out loud.

"I am so sorry Kris. If I have given you any reason to think this, then again I am sorry. I love you. I watched you grow into a wonderful woman. I know I traveled a lot and didn't get to come to your games often, but I was always rooting for you in my heart. When you went to the pros I followed your progress. You don't know how painful it was when I found out you had injured yourself. I wanted to come running but I knew you were in another kind of pain and I couldn't seem to reach you. Please forgive me my daughter, I love you with all my heart and your grandmother loves you too."

Kris was surprised she didn't know her mother had figured out that she felt that way about Granny. "Mom . . ."

"Don't say anything. I heard you and someday you will know that I love you as much as I love your sister. You two are my life, my light. Without you and your sister I wouldn't know what to do."

Kris started crying. She was doing that a lot lately. When had she gone soft? She laid her head in her mother's lap. It felt so good to be this close. She missed it. Michaela ran her fingers through her daughter's hair like she did when Kris was a child. Like always it seem to soothe Kris. Kris sighed, "I'm sorry too and I missed you like crazy."

Michaela laughed then. Kris had her eyes closed so she didn't see the tears in Michaela's eyes. "You know something my darling daughter? I missed you like crazy too."

* * *

When Kris and Kristen returned to the house, no one said a word. Everyone had a look of anticipation on their faces, albeit a cautious one. They were studying the pictures of the hands with the markings that had been on all of their discoveries. Kay had gone up stairs, she said, to get something.

When Kay came back she was carrying a small box. It looked like it was made of cherry wood. It looked old and worn, something sparkled on the top. They all watched as she held it like it was a delicate piece of art. It was now time for them to put it all together so they could hopefully, do what Teresa had asked them to do.

Chapter Forty Six

"Sorry," Kay said, as she walked down the stairs. "I am guilty of holding something back." Kay placed the box on the table. "This was something I asked Karina to bring with her." Before she opened it, she told them about the encounter she had had in the store when she had first seen the box and Karina went on to tell them what she had experienced when she had returned to the shop and her encounter with the woman she met as well.

You could hear a pin drop. "It's funny," said Kay after Karina finished her story. "From what you've all told me, and what happened to me and Karina, it seems like we've had a lot of help along the way, like some psychic underground railroad."

They all nodded silently, each with their own thoughts.

"As you can see . . .," Kay started to lift the lid. Before she could, Kaila put her hands on Kay's hands, keeping her from opening it.

"Kay, wait. You weren't the only one keeping secrets. I want to tell you, the reason I agreed to come. I . . . you're going to think I am as strange as what we are doing. But I need to tell you . . ." Kaila turned to the group . . ."all of you. I've been having dreams, dreams about you, Kay. It worried me because you and I hadn't talked for a long time. Then you called out of the blue, I didn't know what was going on but I knew, I felt that it whatever it was, was important."

Kay was stunned. "What about the dreams Kaila?"

Kaila let go of Kay's hands. "The dreams were just fragments. I couldn't really say for sure what they were, only that they involved you . . . us. Before I came here, no one could have told me that I would believe in something so impossible, but seeing this place, seeing your grandmother, it felt right."

Everyone around the table nodded. They didn't seem at all surprised by what Kaila said. "Does that lack of surprise I see on everybody's face mean that the rest of you have had similar dreams?" Kay asked. They all nodded again. "Why didn't any of you say anything?"

"What were we going to say?" said Kenya, "without sounding like we had lost our minds." After everything Kenya had heard maybe she had.

"Even when you heard the tape, you said nothing? Remember, we talked about it at dinner that first night, how we were connected, how our names began with the letter K, said Kay." They all nodded they had forgotten, but now it was beginning to make sense somehow.

"It was like I was told to come," said Kristin. She hadn't wanted to come, but something had pushed her and now that she had made peace with her mother she was doubly glad she came.

"Kay," said Kris. "I had no intentions of coming home, either. I wasn't even thinking about it until the dreams. First I thought it was my guilt. Then, I started feeling like someone was with me."

As each one recounted their dreams, Kay sat down, unmoving; she had lost touch with everyone but Kyla and Kaitlin. Kyla never left home. As for Kaitlin she knew why she kept in touch with her. Why was it they were all having dreams? Kaitlin hadn't said anything. She wondered if Kaitlin had had dreams, too. But before she could ask her, she watched as Kaila looked at Kaitlin as if she was asking permission to say something. "Tell her about the painting, Kaitlin." All eyes were on Kaitlin.

She cleared her throat. I guess it's time for confessions. "Since it appears that we have all neglected to mention something, I guess I'm next. As you know Kay I started back painting after . . ." Kay was surprised when she saw the look on Kaila face. She looked as if she understood Kaitlin's hesitation. She realized in that moment that Kait had shared her secret with Kaila. Kaitlin's broken heart was indeed healing.

Kaitlin swallowed the lump in her throat and continued. "Anyway, one day I was at the beach and suddenly the brush seemed to have a life of its own. I started painting, the brush commanding me to paint the picture. Like everyone else I had been having strange dreams and I thought maybe I was dreaming again. I know it was me painting but it was as though someone was guiding my hand. After a while I didn't feel it anymore and when I looked at what I had painted, I almost fainted. On the canvas was a picture of us. I don't mean just you and me. It was a picture of all of us. I didn't know what it meant at the time and sure didn't know who the other women were, until I arrive at Aunt Teresa's and met all of you." She looked around the room and spread her arms to encompass them. "Even you," she pointed at Lori.

Lori hadn't said much since she and Karina had talked. Now she sat there, eyes wide and unbelieving. "Karina . . . what's happening?" She whispered so only Karina could hear. Karina was sitting next to her. "I don't know *Cara*. How could this be? No one knows . . ." Karina clamped her mouth shut." Only Kay knew about their relationship.

"What is it Karina?" Kris asked.

"Nothing, go ahead Kaitlin, finish what you were saying, sorry I interrupted." This shocked everyone even Kaila and she had seen the picture. She didn't remember Lori. When she started to ask Kaitlin, Kaitlin answered. "Kaila saw the picture when we were back in San Francisco." She turned to Kaila. "Lori was in the picture but she was just a form. I think you may not have notice because you readily recognized the rest and because of the other picture." Kaila knew what picture she was talking about and nodded.

"Why didn't you bring the painting back with you?" Kay asked.

"I did."

"Where is it?"

"In my bag," Kaitlin held her hand up as if to quiet everyone. "I know I should have said something sooner. But so much had gone on. How could anyone keep up?"

"I think we need to go over everything right now," Katie said. It was truly confession time.

"You're right," said Kenya. Everyone else agreed while Kaitlin went to get the painting.

*   *   *

Kay waited until Kaitlin came back. She wanted to see the painting for herself. She knew everyone else wanted to, too. "Well Katie," Kay asked. "What do you have to say?"

"It was the same for me," Katie answered. "I had dreams too. About us, and like everyone else, I only saw fragments. Besides I teach little kids. I thought maybe I had told too many fairytales." They all laughed. Indeed what they were witnessing may as well be a fairytale but would it be a happily ever after one.

When Kaitlin returned she held up the painting for everyone to see. An aqua blue sea covered the background. The women in the picture were dressed in lavender clothing. They were all staring at something,

something there faces didn't give away. Light illuminated from a house in the distance. 'It's Windsor Castle!" said Kristin.

"Let me see," said Kyla. She looked closer. "I think it is, but how? The mansion was burned down."

"You're right," said Kay as she took a closer look. "I think this is a picture of it before it burned." Kay had seen a picture of the mansion in the archives at the paper.

"Kaitlin how could you know what the mansion looked like back then, none of us were even born. As a matter of fact none of our parents either." said Kyla.

"And how could you know about us," Kristin, Karina and Kaila said at the same time. "Not to mention Lori," said Karina.

"I don't know," said Kaitlin. "Like I said I just started painting." She looked over at Lori. "In my mind's eye I could almost see you, but I was only sure when you showed up with Karina."

Karina and Lori were stunned. Did Kaitlin somehow suspect? No she couldn't have, no one knew she had only told Kay a week ago. She looked at Lori, who looked just as shocked as she was. "This can't be real." Karina stared at the painting again. But if it was not Lori it might as well be her clone. The woman in the picture had the same dark brown eyes and Karina notice the birthmark on the woman that Kaitlin said was Lori. Kaitlin had painted it perfectly. It was just like Lori's. Karina didn't say anything. She couldn't take her eyes off the painting.

Lori was still shocked at what was happening. She wanted to go back to Italy and forget she ever asked Karina to come.

"What does it all mean?" Kristin asked.

"I don't know," said Kay. Everyone was staring at Kay as she tried to get a grip on her emotions. She was the leader of this group. She felt overwhelmed with what was happening.

Kay held her hand up. "Look everybody I am as shocked as all of you. When my grandmother first told me her story, I wanted to run. In fact I almost ran into the back of someone's car. I left the community center in a daze. I had no idea what would happen, but I knew in my heart I couldn't disappoint my grandmother. Somehow, I got up the courage to call all of you in spite of what it meant.

What we are doing and have done has made me realize how important it is to stay in touch with those people who have touched your lives in some way. I confess I have been hiding. I lost touch with most of you.

In a weird sort of way this has brought me back. And you know what? I am scared, too and I have doubts, a lot of them. But I know one thing for certain. I would never have gotten this far without any of you. Your presence here has given me courage and the strength to keep going. I can only hope that that courage will transform into action. And I hope you, all of you will be right there."

Kay turned to Lori. "I'm sorry that somehow you may be a part of this," she said, and then as if she had read Lori's mind, "I wouldn't blame you if you hopped on the next plane out of here. And that goes for the rest of you." Kay fell silent waiting for their verdict.

"That was a nice speech," said Katie, "but like I said before I'm in."

"That goes for me, too," said Kyla. Kyla laughed. "Besides, I live here."

"What about the rest of you?" Kay looked around the room at the women. She had been honest, she wouldn't hold anything against them and she meant it. She would be disappointed but she understood, too. She made a silent promise to herself as she waited for the rest of them to answer, that from now on she would keep in touch, even if they did decide to leave.

Kenya spoke first. "I can't speak for the rest of you, but I know ever since Kyla and I left the church with the hand, I've felt like what we were doing was right. Okay I will confess at first it felt like I was going to be dammed when Kyla and I went inside, but finding out how brave Kyla was." Kenya wouldn't mention why she thought Kyla was brave, Kyla would tell her own story. "I wanted to follow this through. So Kay if you still want me I will do whatever it takes to fulfill your grandmother's promise."

Everyone else basically said the same and they all agreed to keep going, even Lori. Her motive however was different she knew Karina would stay and although she was shocked and afraid, she was not about to leave her, so she would stay too.

*   *   *

With all the confession, Kay still hadn't opened the box. Her hands rested on the lid. "I guess that settles it then. It's time to find out what else is in store for us." Kay lifted the lid.

185

At first to everyone's disappointment, it looked empty but when Kay reached to feel around inside, she discovered there was a secret compartment in the side. She could fill it through the red silk lining that covered the inside. When she pulled it away at the cover, inside there was a piece of paper. The note said: "Within these walls lives the truth. You must journey here to the beginning." They all pondered this new revelation.

Katie picked up the copies of the pictures they had taken which had been scattered about on the table. At bottom of each picture the same symbol appeared on everything they had found so far.

*   *   *

While everyone was concentrating on the box, Katie was trying to remember what her Aunt Teresa had said about the place in the woods where she and the other midwives visited, a place where the guardian, she said lived. Teresa had talked about the pain she felt when she went into the woods that day to find everything gone, how her aunt had panicked when she couldn't find the house. The woman and the house had vanished. She remembered her saying how she had searched for the woman for hours. When Teresa couldn't find anything she had gone to the ruins, the very ruins that Kaitlin had drawn in the painting. Not the way it was now, but the way it was when it was called Windsor Castle.

When Katie thought about all the places they had gone. How they had found the same symbols on the hands, all in different languages but the meaning was the same "First Born." It was even on the last page of Anne Frank's diary. She had forgotten. Before she could voice the revelation Kaila spoke.

"I think," said Kaila. "The person who may or may not be in the woods is the key and the ruins have been mentioned several times. Everything seems to point to the woods and to the ruins." They all nodded in agreement. Everyone seemed to have come to the same conclusion.

"Yes," said Kay. Her grandmother had described the woods and had told them the approximate area. Kay had never been to that part of the woods. She had no reason to. She did wonder why no one ever tried to build anything there with the way progress was invading the south.

"Let's go over everything we have done so far." The women gathered at the table again trying to put together all the pieces. It was time to find some answers and it all pointed to the woods.

"Wait a minute Kay," Kenya said. "Are you sure? We don't know where this is. Your grandmother said it herself that the woman in the woods had disappeared. How are we going to find a woman or a house that is no longer there? Besides it's been a long time the woman couldn't possibly be alive. She would have to be over two hundred years old"

"I don't know," said Kay. "But I have a feeling we are about to find out. Tonight we're going to the woods." The women looked afraid but they all nodded. They knew Kay was right. If they were going to solve this, and fulfill Teresa's request, tonight they needed to go to the woods. In their hearts they knew there they would find the answer.

Chapter Forty Seven

It was after midnight when the two cars drove away from Teresa's house and soon stopped at the edge of the woods. Kay drove her car and with Kristin in the front seat and Karina, Lori and Kaila in the back. Kris drove the other car with Kyla up front and Kenya, Katie and Kaitlin in the back.

Kay knew her grandmother said the woods were sacred ground but what could they do? It was 2010. No horses and carriages. They would get as close as they could and then they would walk the rest of the way.

When they got out where they would start walking, they all looked around. Together, they drew courage from each other. Kenya nervously laughed and blew out a breath. "Kay are you sure we should have started so late," said Kaitlin.

"Yes I'm sure. Granny said they always went at midnight."

"I know but . . ." Kaitlin jumped when Kay touched her. "Look, we're all scared, but we've come this far," said Kay. Kenya who was usually the talkative one was quiet. They were all quiet. They were walking into destiny.

"Let's link hands," said Katie.

"What for," said Kris. But the bravado she tried to show wasn't working so she pretended. "Okay for you we'll do it."

Kay took the lead followed by Kyla, Lori, and Karina. Lori held tightly to Karina. She had been happy that Karina had come back to Italy to be with her and when she decided to come with Karina, at first, then mad because Karina had left her at Kay's grandmothers when she went Memphis. Now she wondered why hadn't she let it go and stayed in Italy.

Behind them Kris and Kristin, followed Katie and Kenya who brought up the rear.

They walked further and further into the woods into the unknown with only the silence for companionship. There wasn't any sounds; no rustling of trees no call of the night crawlers. They kept going however, neither wanted to chicken out on the other. When they got close to where Kay thought was the place where the house used to be, in the distance there was a light. It appeared to be some kind of illumination. Three trees stood, their limbs seem to stretch toward the midnight sun. Their footsteps slowed. There breathing hesitant but still they kept going.

When they passed the trees it was as if the woods opened up for them. In the clearing there stood the house. It looked like exactly how Teresa had described it. Like a rundown hut. Then it was as if someone reached out to them and they were captured by the light and it drew them in. Still they were silent. Teresa had said it was sacred ground. They approached the house. It didn't look like any house they had seen. It looked run down. The door to the house suddenly opened.

They were about run. Then "*She*" appeared. They were shaking as they stared at the woman. No one moved. It was if the women's appearance had them rooted to the ground. To their astonishment, the woman was also exactly how Teresa had described her. It was if time had stood still.

Not quite, something was very different, the woman was pregnant. This was something Teresa hadn't mention nor was it in anything they had seen and discovered so far. They all started to talk at once but the woman raised her hand and they fell silent.

Kris was transfixed. The woman looked like . . . her.

The woman smiled "I know you have come far to get here." The woman rubbed her belly and there was movement. How could this be?

She answered as if she could hear their thoughts. "All things will be revealed in the ruins. The clues you had been given were left a long time ago to people born before even Melana and Meira. They were ordained to follow the way of the first and now I must go to them so that the baby will live." She looked as if she was about to have the baby right there.

They were all standing there hands still linked. This frightened Kay. What if she did?

"I will tell you." The woman's eyes were like Karina's and Kenya's. They both looked at each other. What was happening? When the woman opened her hand, they saw it, the same symbol they had seen, "first born."

"Why . . . how can it be?" Katie stumbled over her words. "You look like . . ."

"Yes I know." Then she pointed at all of them. "If you look real close we are alike, all of us. Each pieces of each other, you were all brought here so that you may take me to the ruins."

"Why couldn't you go there yourself?" Kyla asked.

Kaila stood there shaking her head. It couldn't be. She was used to facts not this. Her way of thinking had been turned upside down.

Kris wanted to run. She had asked to be here but now she wondered if she had made a mistake. There was no mistake; however, the woman that stood before them was her mirror image.

The woman looked at all of them and answered Kyla. "I could not go to the ruins it was not my place then. It was not time. My place was here in the woods to watch over the midwives to help them to be centered in their work. They had to keep the promise your grandmother had to keep the promise until they were ready for me to come."

"When who was ready?" asked Katie.

"The women in the ruins of course," she said it like it was just stating the obvious.

"But why send us to all those places?" Kenya asked, "If the answer was in the ruins all the time."

"I can only say that it was necessary. I cannot give you any more than that."

"Well," said Karina "Why are you still here and why did you leave?"

"I did not leave. The women in the ruins created a shield to protect me and the unborn. Eras were changing. People stopped believing in the abilities of the midwives. Progress forced these women to stop practicing. Forced them to quit doing what had been done for centuries. We must go to the ruins." The woman seemed like she was in pain.

They looked at each other. Karina the doctor in the house stepped forward. The woman reminded Karina of the mothers she would see in nursery where she had spent a lot of her time when she wasn't in surgery. It was strange although she loved the babies she never thought to have any of her own. And when she thought about it, all the women here were well into their thirties and none of them had any children, except for Kay's cousin Kaitlin. Karina didn't know what had happen, but she knew the baby had died.

It was if Karina had spoken aloud, because when she reached for the woman, "*She*" shook her head and Karina stepped back. "I know all of you have questions but you must not despair none of you. It will be okay. Now again we must go to the ruins."

Chapter Forty Eight

They all got back in the cars. Kay didn't think the woman would make it. She looked as though she would have the baby right there in the car. The woman sat in the back between Karina and Lori. Everyone was quiet as they drove.

In the ruins nothing moved. "Are you sure this is where we should be," Katie said to the lady, when they all got out. "There is no one here." The guardian looked at Kay.

"This is the place," said Kay as she reached in her pocket. She held out her hands so that everyone could see what she was holding. "These were in the bank box along with the book." She opened her hand and there they were the hearts, one made of wood, one made of glass.

"Why didn't you tell us that you had the hearts?" Kyla asked.

"I don't know." Kay didn't know why.

"It was not time to reveal the hearts," said the guardian. "Until you found me the hearts would not have worked." She looked at Kay. "You know what to do." "Yes I do." As they all stood transfixed, they watched as Kay took the hearts and placed them the way Teresa, Melana, and Meira before her had done all those years ago. She placed the hearts in the columns of the ruins. At once the ruins came to life with light. The light almost blocked out the moon. Teresa had told them about the power of the hearts, but seeing it was awesome. Out of the light they came.

Out from the night they rose stretching out their hands Midwife hands, Granny's hands. Hands stirred into civilizations dipped into the nectar of life. They were young too young to be midwives but as they watch they seem to age. They looked at them all and smiled.

Fatshe leso lea halalela "The land of our ancestors is holy."
"Beso bo, my people, beso bo"

Automatically they knew they were in the presence of greatness so each of them lowered their gaze and bowed their heads. "Please you do not have to bow your heads."

The women in the ruins were beautiful. They really couldn't describe them with mere words, couldn't tell where they were from. Again as the woman in the woods had done, the eyes of the women drew them. They were topaz like the tiger's eye. Golden brown, there was also turquoise like the Cherokee necklaces around her irises, their pupils were like jade no they were purpled no they were black like pearls. They were much more as they stared. They didn't speak the air around them moved in slow motion. As if they were controlling it. Hair flowed black like the Nile, Golden like sunset. Light was glowing from the tips of their fingers.

Kay and her friends and cousins all stood there rooted to the spot. Then the women descended a heavenly stairway. The stairway was just like the one in the painting Kaitlin had created. Long flowing robes floated about them like clouds. Their eyes were all seeing. One of the women carried a book the other one a symbol or something. Both looked like each other, they could have been mother and daughter. One of the women started to speak.

"Mother and daughter, midwife and midwife, this was how the world started—bringing life out of the darkness.

Long ago before the son of man was born, Pharaoh reigned. He was a jealous man. He was upset that it was foretold that a prophet, a messiah would appear on the earth to forgive man but what he didn't know was there was another, born of Abraham. One whose power held a gift, a gift held only by midwives, this gift was passed down a millennium before the light of the land was covered with the animals and the plants of the world. Before Egypt and the pyramids before the African queens the Irish Queens and all the goddesses in the land of Greece, it was foretold but not written in the word.

These women would nurture and nourish the earth. Protecting them would be two who would be the keepers. The one was hidden so that none would know. The women or guardians lived in secret and every time a girl child was born of these women, these midwives, then the secret was passed on. There would be no male babies born to these women. They had been born to bare only females. The hands, the hearts were a symbol of life that had been touched by them. The babies born of these women passed it on;

they are part of it all. Melana and Meira were direct blood line, a part of one soul and two women. In order for the secret to be passed on, both women had to do it together. The women of this line aged slowly."

"Why Melana and Meira?" asked Kay. "There were plenty midwives. The practice has been around a long time."

"Yes this is so, but you see, Melana and Meira come from a line of midwives who carried the mark. Not all midwives carry the mark. Once they found each other, the guardian passed on the hearts. They carried the hearts which you now carry."

"Why was my grandmother alone, why didn't she have a twin?"

"Teresa's twin soul was lost. Sometimes the mark of time twist things and we are lost. Teresa is strong but we knew since she was alone, she could not complete her journey. We allowed Teresa to live longer then, made her forget. We wanted her to live a more normal life than the others. We made her forget so that the third generation, all of you, could help her. Through you, the cycle could be complete.

Man no longer wanted women to practice midwifery naturally. They wanted women to become educated smothering their gift. The soul never forgets and that is why you are here one of you will carry on the promise we made. We disobeyed Pharaoh and we allowed the gift to live. This was treason. We had to leave and start again. We had to find a way and we did."

"But who are you?" asked Kay.

"I am Shiphrah and this is my soul twin Puah, we were once Hebrew slaves of Pharaoh. Our words are in Exodus 15. From the beginning Pharaoh commanded that we destroy that which was promised to the world, he wanted us to destroy all first born of the Midwives. We disobeyed him because we knew what he asked of us would change the course of history, so we hid them. We passed this gift on to others so our gift would live forever.

Remember you have encountered many women on this journey. All of these women are guardians of the gift. They are all over the world.

Long ago we found the place in the woods. A place where the slaves of yesteryear's sprits gathered, a place seeped in shackles and chains. It is the one place where slavery still existed at the time. No one would think to look for her there. She was the last who would bear *"one* so we had to hide her in the house. Protect her from the descendants of the Pharaoh."

Kay and the others stood very still. They could hear the woman who was called Shiphrah clearly, but the sound did not seem to come from Shiphrah, but through her. The other one had not spoken.

As if Kay had said it out loud, Puah continued as if the voice of Shiphrah had somehow transcended to her. "They pursued her through time. Just as we were about to claim the gift again, the twin to Teresa was lost.

The one you bring here tonight, her womb holds the "Bekor," the one who transcended all others. She crossed the lands and brought fruit to the world. She is neither you, nor I, she is everyone. Her touch is the gift we pass on, the sprit, the soul. We placed the wooden heart and the glass heart in the hand of those who would keep the secret, the midwives. We all come for her. No matter if the seas part us or the mountains contain us we are all the same. When you look in the ruins you see all of us."

Before the woman could continue, Katie found the courage to ask. "Why did Teresa send us to those places when everything is here?"

Shiphrah answered. "Because each place held the keys to the ruins without it you would not be able to unlock the secret. Those women who you visited are women who have changed history. Rosa, Anne . . . Aine."

"What about the church with the hand? Why was the mark there?" Kenya asked.

Puah looked at Shiphrah. "That was me." Shiphrah spoke. "When I was looking after Teresa one day I saw her go into the church. She seemed lost so I put the symbol on the hand so when the time came," she looked at Kyla, "she would find her courage.

"We have always been in the ruins watching, helping, choosing the ones who would receive the hearts, calling them here. You do not all have the gift of life but you are all guardians."

*   *   *

Suddenly the woman they had taken to the ruins cried out. Hearing the cry, Puah pointed to the hearts and they floated to her. She held the hearts then she flung them and they were suspended.

Kay and the rest of them all stood rooted the spot when they heard the cry. Karina recognized the sound. The woman was in labor. Before Karina could go to the woman, she heard the rest of them gasped when Lori stepped forward. They all watched as she walked toward the woman.

"Lori!" Karina called but her voice faded into the light.

They all stood back in wonder as Lori touched the pregnant woman. "Karina," Lori said. "Help me." Karina found her voice then. "Lori what are you doing?"

"What we all have to do," said Lori. It was if someone else had spoken. When Lori turned, her eyes were dark. She walked as if she was in a trance.

Karina jumped when Kay touched her arm. "Karina," Kay whispered. "Go to her."

"All of you," Shiphrah commanded. "She needs all of you."

They all walked over to where the pregnant woman was. They laid her down on the floor of the ruins. Kristin covered her with a blanket from the car. Kristin didn't know how she knew a blanket would be in Kay's car but she didn't question it. "Lori," said Karina, "we are here with you." They formed a circle around Lori and the woman. As their hands touched each other, a light pierced the night forming a shield around the mother.

Karina kneeled along with Lori. The woman looked like she was in pain but instead of crying the woman was smiling. Karina was a surgeon she had never delivered a child, but Lori looked as though she had done it before. It was as if Lori was someone else.

Lori touched the woman's stomach. "The baby was coming." In silence the woman bore down. She grabbed Lori's hand as the baby slipped from the womb. Lori and Karina wrapped the baby in part of the blanket and laid the baby on the mother's breast.

When the baby appeared, the souls of the women who had descended the stairs cried out. "When we pursue our place in the universe we do not do it individually, we do it collectively. Voices heard in the background the past, and voices in the foreground the future." All eyes fell on the baby.

No one moved when Lori reached down again and held the baby. The light that had seemed to come from the six women as their hands had formed a ring around the woman had gone out. That's when they all moved at once.

Kay moved forward first. She looked at the baby. Something was familiar about her. While the rest of them hovered, Kay remembered. Kay cried, "Oh, my God! Kait!" She pulled Kaitlin forward so she could see. She pushed the rest of them out of the way. Kaitlin fell to her knees, "My God!, My God!"

"What is it?" Kris, Katie and Kyla dropped to their knees beside their cousin. "What is it Kaitlin?" They all said at once.

The rest of them didn't know what to do. Kristin and Kenya were about to kneel too. Kaitlin was shaking so hard. Kay was crying too. Lori knelt beside Kaitlin and passed the baby to her. Tears streamed down Kaitlin's face. "It's Alain."

"Who is Alain?" Kristin shook Kay. Kay couldn't say anything else. Kristin looked at the others but no one said anything.

"How could this be?" said Kay

They all looked at Lori. She looked as though she was waking up from a dream "What, why is everyone staring at me?" She asked. That's when she saw the baby. "What's going on?"

Chapter Forty Nine

All of them looked up when they heard singing. Shiphrah and Puah were chanting. The stairs once again appeared and other women could be seen. All of them were there. Karina and Kris recognized the women in Memphis. Katie and Kristen saw the woman at the Holocaust Museum. Kaila recognized the woman at the Mormon Church. Even the woman in the shop in Italy was descending the stairs. Last to come down was Melana and Meira.

Kaitlin turned to the stairs, her face wet with tears as she held tight to the baby, the rest of them crowded around Kaitlin as if to protect.

Shiphrah spoke. "Kaitlin you have suffered much lost. We could see your heart was torn. We knew the Bekor would return but we did not know what form she would take, whose soul she would reside in. Like a baby she is fragile and will need care until she takes her place. The world is a strange place; there is so much the world has made."

Kay remembered her grandmother's words "world made."

"You all must guard and keep her." Shiphrah addressed Kaitlin. "Like Teresa, you have lost one who was a part of you so; we give you the Bekor to raise as your own. She will be special. The world will know her as yours. Tell Teresa that her twin has been reborn. The rest of you are a part of the first born throughout time."

The woman called Puah reached out her hand. "She will grow up as a normal child, Kaitlin and when the time is right, she will take her place among the midwives. "The guardian," she pointed to the woman who now looked like she had never given birth, will now become a part of us. We reside in the ruins first to protect the gift, second to continue to watch over the union of midwives."

The other women who appeared in the ruins said nothing.

"Why Lori," Kay asked. "Lori wasn't supposed to be here?"

That's right," said Kenya. "Lori doesn't begin with the letter K." Katie watched Kaitlin with the baby.

Lori looked at them and said. "My middle name is Lori. I never liked my first name, so I never told anybody, but it is Keturah."

"Yes," said Puah, "the name given to Abraham's wife, the one hidden from Pharaoh."

"Midwives have always known this because of the hearts they received from us. Yes she is the one who houses the hearts. We sent you to those places because the people worthy of the hearts suffered and died for the goodness of man and we must continue to past the gift and it is only through us. Anne Frank, Rosa Parks, Athena, Nefertiti's all bare the mark, hands from the first midwives." The women who had descended the stairs looked out at the women and smiled. They then turned, along with the guardian from the woods; they walked slowly up the stairs and into the light. All that remained was Shiphrah and Puah.

"We must go now; the sun will soon fall over the ruins," said Shiphrah. "Take Bekor knowing we are always beside you. You have done well my daughters" Shiphrah and Puah ascended the stairs into forever.

*　　*　　*

They all sighed at the same time. Tears fell as they turned to leave the ruins. They knew they would always be connected to something far greater then themselves. They looked back. The ruins had returned once more to its place in the silence.

Kay was so glad her friends were a part of it. They were ready to help not knowing what would happen. She hoped it wouldn't take something like this for them to remain close. She realized then that she could no longer hide in her solitude. She needed the people that had been a part of her life. She would embrace and open her heart to whatever the future had in store for her. Kaitlin would need help in raising the baby. In a way the baby belonged to all of them. They were godmothers. She watched as they crowded around the baby. Kay had never felt so much love. Just then Kenya looked over and with a smile she started singing a lullaby and Kyla joined in soon the rest of them were singing.

*　　*　　*

Kyla had gotten over her fear and Karina and Kris had exorcised their demons. Kay and Kris were as close as ever, even Karina who was so afraid to tell Kay about Lori. And Lori who would have thought that she would be a part of this. Not even her grandmother knew. At least Kay didn't think so.

Kaila hadn't believed in miracles, or even unexplained phenomenon. She was a scientist. She dealt in facts. If she hadn't seen it happen she would have never believed it. How were they going to explain the presence of the baby? Kristin is a lawyer maybe she could tell everyone that Kaitlin was trying to adopt and it finally came through. But no one was thinking about what would happen when they returned to their daily lives. They were headed to the community center.

*   *   *

Teresa was waiting. It was early morning. She knew where the women would be so she waited for their return. She hadn't seen the girls since they met her at the Center. Kay had been keeping her abreast of everyone. She prayed that everyone would be safe. Teresa wanted to see it through before her time on earth was up.

Chapter Fifty

No one in the community center said a word as the women walked through the doors the next day as they headed to room 22. Why no one question this parade of women no one would ever know. They all crowded around Teresa's room. Each remembering the things they did and the fantastic things they had seen.

Teresa held her breath as Kaitlin carried the baby and place the little girl in her arms. "Aunt Teresa the woman in the ruins . . . it's . . ."

"I know child." Teresa wiped at the tears that were falling down her cheek. "I didn't get a chance to know her. She told me one day she would return. It's too late for me but, Kaitlin, you will get another chance. You know she's special right?" Kaitlin nodded.

Kay looked at all her friends and her family. She was so proud of them all. Her friends had become a part of her family. They finished what her grandmother started. They had done it without going to jail. "One day," said Kay "we will be able to say that we did something good not just for the good of midwives but for the good of the world. Too bad we won't be able to tell anybody and who would believe us anyway."

There could be something said about having a lot of women in the family and a few women friends. Although Kay was happy, her heart told her that it was not over. That maybe some time soon, it may happen again maybe in the next millennium but for now it's good.

Teresa smiled. *My time is done* "Now I can rest."

"What does that mean?" asked Kay. They all looked at Teresa, all waiting for an answer, but in their hearts they knew.

"We all must face the final chapter," said Teresa. "It is not in my power to take away." She looked at all of the women who had given her hope. Then she took Kay's hand in hers. "It's okay, I am not going anywhere today," *But soon, because they are all waiting, waiting at heaven's gate with a glass of Moonshine for me.*

The End